Charlottesville Fantastic

ARCANE ECHOES FROM VIRGINIA'S HEARTLAND

Edited by James Blakey & Catherine Simpson

Whitaker Lyon Press

Broadway, Virginia

Praise for CHARLOTTESVILLE FANTASTIC...

You know the places—the River, the University, the Orchard, the abandoned mountaintop Hotel. But... do you know the mystery? The humor? The magic? The TERROR? CHARLOTTESVILLE FANTASTIC's band of local authors has come together to proffer an intriguing question: what unsettling stories might hide among the shadows cast by brick buildings and rolling vineyards? Crack open this Old Dominion tome to find out... if you dare.
—**Chris Register, Author of *Conversations With US* and founder of the Charlottesville Writers Critique Circle**

By turns spooky, playful, and downright chilling, CHAR-LOTTESVILLE FANTASTIC laces its speculative stories with a touch of Southern charm. Whether you're in the mood for cursed books or deadly time loops, helpful ghosts or Bigfoot sightings, there's something for every fan of the supernatural in its pages.
—**Katharine Schellman, Author of *Last Call at the Nightingale***

Some funny, some serious, all just a little spooky, there really is something in this collection for everyone. Whether you are a born and bred Charlottesvillian or a visitor looking for a book to give you a feel for the local culture, CHARLOTTESVILLE FANTASTIC is bound to capture your attention and spark your imagination.
—**Samantha Koon Jones, Book Critic for *The (Charlottesville) Daily Progress***

Library of Congress Control Number: 2024913805

ISBN: 979-8-9909340-1-6 (Paperback)
ISBN: 979-8-9909340-2-3 (Hardback)

Whitaker Lyon Press
4464 North Pointe Drive
Broadway VA 22815

WhitakerLyon.com

Table of Contents

My House Mother is a Vampire

CAROLINE BORAS

THE GHOSTS OF RUGBY Road didn't mind their Greek housemates and neighbors. On the whole, the loud music and parties and group dinners and wristbands almost made them feel alive again. The old brick homes also helped to disguise the more obvious signs of haunting. Flickering lights were a side effect of old wiring, creaks were the house settling, hair ties went missing because of a kleptomaniac sister. All mild inconveniences, explained away by the over-caffeinated, over-stressed, and under-imaginative minds of the college students with whom they cohabitated.

Yes, the ghosts of Rugby Road were quite happy with their chosen haunt.

Until that ridiculous fourth year Ainsley Bell—President, Eta Mu, "Be the change you want to see in the world," per her email signature—invited a vampire into the house.

"Elsbeth Hayes?" Ainsley had asked, leaning against the door. The ghosts had seen her practice that move several times, propping herself against various surfaces in the president's suite. It was a game for them. They'd notice Ainsley leaning, then start scooting the dresser out from under her. They never let her fall. They were a benign bunch at this house, after all.

They just liked to see her trip a little.

That day, however, the ghosts were frantically waving at her, miming vampires. They quite enjoyed the version of *Dracula* that showed at the film festival back in the nineties and several of the ghosts were crawling down the side of the house, lizard fashion, as the Count was known to do. But for whatever reason, Ainsley was not taking the hint.

Probably because she couldn't see them, but that was beside the point.

"Oh, please, call me Betty," the vampire said. The creature barely opened her mouth when she spoke.

The ghosts resumed their pantomime, this time using their fingers to indicate fangs.

"Betty, sure." Ainsley pushed off the doorjamb and motioned for the vampire to follow her into the house. "Come on in."

If Ainsley had listened to the ghosts yelling at her to TURN AROUND, she would have seen the vampire smiling, showing off her fangs. As it was, Ainsley missed the predator sizing up its prey and within three days, the vampire was installed as Eta Mu's new house mother.

Untenable! A vampire trodding on ghost territory. It was impolite paranormal behavior, for one thing. Everyone knew that towns along the Blue Ridge Mountains belonged to Bigfoots and Wampus Beasts and, most importantly, *ghosts*. But it wasn't just the encroachment into the region that made the ghosts mad. No, it was simply bad manners to start terrorizing a home that was already haunted. The ghosts were there first and mostly harmless, clogging toilets and slamming doors. Only once had they burst a pipe, and that was more of an accident than a true act of malice—Ainsley, dressed in a sparkly crop top and reeking of tequila, stomped through the front door well after quiet hours on thirsty Thursday while the ghosts loosened a gasket under the kitchen sink. They refused to feel bad over the consequences of their justifiable shock.

Sharing a home with an army of second years was bad enough, never mind the Ainsley of it all. The girl kicked off her Reign of Terror by banning the burning of incense in the house, meaning that if the ghosts wanted to bask in the smoke, they had to loiter around the Episcopal church over by the hospital, and they agreed that haunting near a hospital was in poor taste. But now? Now, there was an actual blood-sucking monster in the house, causing real problems.

***

"Madam President, what is Regionals doing about the bedbug infestation?"

It was chapter, a month after Miss Betty moved in. If the girls had listened to the ghosts, they would have known that they weren't actually being snacked on by bedbugs and mosquitoes and spiders every night but were, in fact, the victims of a series of vicious vampire attacks. The ghosts said as much when the vampire insisted that the girls start taking iron supplements because the catering crew's macaroni and cheese "wasn't nutritious enough."

"She doesn't like the flavor of processed cheese in the bloodstream," one ghost tried to tell second year Britt Wallace as she choked on one of the iron capsules. "But you're probably anemic, too." The ghosts were loath to give the vampire any credit, but they all believed that no one should be eating food that matched the school's colors.

Ainsley scratched the bites on her neck. "I am in communication with Regionals about getting the emergency funds to fumigate the house."

A chorus of boos. The ghosts joined in, thrilled that the girls were *finally* speaking their language.

"Madam President, we have the funds—" the finance girl started.

Ainsley dropped her hand to the table. "Absolutely not. I am not dipping into the Founder's Day budget because you ladies can't handle a few bug bites!"

So, the girls of Eta Mu carried on, itching and eating their iron pills and complaining that Miss Betty banned Parmesan garlic fries from the fried-day menu, on account of carbohydrates not being good for one's health.

The ghosts did what they could to tell the girls that they were in mortal danger. While they enjoyed the revolving door of second years in their illustrious sorority haunt, the ghosts dreaded the thought of one of the sisters joining their ranks. What if something happened to Ainsley, and they had to suffer her to-do lists for eternity?

No. The ghosts could *not* risk that.

Their haunting efforts increased. They knocked down the extra thick blackout curtains the vampire hung up in her apartment in an attempt to burn her with the sun. They relocated the Catholic girl's rosary beads from around her headboard to the vampire's doorknob in an attempt to burn her hand off with the plastic holy object. One ghost wrote "Miss Betty is a vampire" in neon green on the white board mounted outside one of the bedrooms. Only the handwriting was very of its time–1762–and illegible.

The ghosts were out of haunts by Founder's Day Eve. The girls were lethargic, not bothering to wonder at how the third step from the top squeaked without anyone stepping on it as they languished on the sectional instead of trying to sneak into the bars at the Corner. They hadn't even hung this year's Founder's Day banner, if it had even been painted, which meant the ghosts couldn't indulge in their favorite Founder's Day Eve tradition of loosening the banner knots so it drooped. Nothing wound Ainsley up more than a droopy banner.

The ghosts who were fastest to despair threatened to join their friends at the fraternity house across the street. What was the point of haunting if the audience didn't care that their coat hangers were all hung the wrong direction?

They were fighting about which was worse: staying in the sorority house with a vampire, the Eta Mu's, and Ainsley, or moving in with boys, when Dana H. screamed.

The ghosts zoomed to her room, where the vampire was attacking Dana H.'s roommate, Corinne... something. Dana H. skipped her iron pill that night, heard the vampire come in, and saw the whole thing.

In a nefarious turn that even the ghosts didn't see coming, Miss Betty's pills were laced with a sedative.

Dana H. screamed and tried to attack the vampire with the only thing on hand, a calculus textbook. Her frantic thwacking did nothing to slow the vampire down as she escaped, turning into a bat and flying off. Dana H. ran to wake up the whole house, except Ainsley. Ainsley would *not* be helpful in this emergency. Besides, Miss Betty had convinced her to take two iron supplements with dinner that night since Founder's Day nerves were making her even more unpleasant to be around than usual.

Britt took charge when Dana H. roused her, thank goodness. Dana H. had one setting—shrill—and was in hysterics after having seen a vampire in her room. The ghosts feared what would happen when Dana H. realized that the vampire was still in residence.

Vampires were notoriously lazy. It was one of the reasons ghosts, as a whole, took umbrage with the species. Terrorizing a home such as this took decades of care and attention. Once Miss Betty got her fangs into the Eta Mu's with Ainsley's thoughtless invitation into the house, she had no reason to leave.

That, and no one else had been ridiculous enough to invite a vampire into their home. Typical Ainsley, making it easy for her sisters to be trapped in a building with a monster.

Luckily for the second years, Britt had a plan.

"We're safe here." She ushered the second years into the chapter room. "Only Eta Mu's are allowed in."

The ghosts, decidedly not Eta Mu's, watched as the girls set to work, barricading the doors and disassembling the wooden chairs to sand the legs into pointed stakes. Britt stood at the front of the room, making a list of the evidence that Miss Betty was a vampire.

"She sleeps in a coffin," Rebecca M. said. "Like a Chi O."

"The Chi O's don't sleep in coffins," Corinne said. Someone had produced an "Eta Mu Loves the Hoos" T-shirt from the storage closet, and she tied it around her neck like a cape. "They're just initiated in one."

"What, so our house mom is a Chi O?" someone asked.

"No, our house mother is a vampire. Please keep up!" Britt pointed to her list. "We have to get rid of her before the alumnae reception! How are the stakes coming?"

The ghosts couldn't bear witness to Britt turning into Ainsley 2.0, so they went to see how the real thing was doing.

She was passed out, fresh puncture marks on her neck. Apparently, the vampire hadn't drunk her fill from Corinne. Ainsley mumbled something about a banner, and the ghosts took that as a sign to leave, disturbed at the endless lists.

Re-entering the chapter-room-turned-armory left them equally disturbed. It wasn't just Britt's list, which expanded to include *"sparkles?"* The ghosts didn't really want to watch a room full of second year sorority girls make weapons to attack their house mother. The Eta Mu's were doing important work, the ghosts knew, so they didn't feel comfortable interrupting the work by jiggling the doorknob or pulling someone's hair.

A couple of the braver ghosts peeked into Miss Betty's room to confirm their suspicion that she remained in her nest. There she was, in her coffin, sleeping off the meal she made of Corinne and Ainsley. Gross.

The ghosts regrouped in the foyer, squabbling about whether it was too soon to try loosening the screws on all the furniture in the formal dining room, a cherished haunt from the late aughts. When that plan was deemed too recent, some ghosts floated to the game corner to swap around puzzle pieces.

This was the problem with haunting. Too much free time.

Finally, Ainsley rolled out of bed. Her alarm had been going off since five, so the ghosts kindly silenced it for her. She was groggy, then furious when she realized she'd overslept and that her army of second years hadn't hung the banner, baked the snickerdoodles, set up chairs in conversational groupings, or arranged the twelve pillar candles to commemorate the twelve founders.

The ghosts were equally disappointed by the lack of decor. They had their affinity for messing with the banner, yes, but they also loved the smell of cinnamon in the oven, and the candles were a reminder of the good old days when the girls weren't banned from burning incense. But, the ghosts thought, Ainsley would be so proud to see her sisters' handiwork. After all, the stakes were quite impressive.

Ainsley tapped out a series of angry messages in the sorority group chat. First text: FOUNDERS DAY IS FINEABLE. Next text: FOXFIELD IS NOT AN EXCUSE TO MISS. Then: WHERE'S BANNER?

The ghosts had been furious when Ainsley said the girls couldn't go to the horse races. They tampered with the heater so the water in her shower was a touch too cold for a week in protest. The rest of the house's water was also a touch too cold for a week, but the ghosts believed Ainsley understood the message.

As she typed, Ainsley stomped toward the chapter room. "I have to do everything myself," she grumbled. She was hitting send on a particularly nasty message—even for her—when she walked straight into the door. The ghosts *loved* doing this kind of thing as a haunting, bracing the door so a resident couldn't walk through it on their first try, and they wished that they were responsible, rather than the second years.

Ainsley banged on the door, demanding to be let in. After confirming that *yes*, Ainsley was alone and *no*, Miss Betty was not there—what does that have to do with anything—the girls opened the door enough to drag Ainsley into the room.

And, typical, Ainsley did not appreciate the ingenuity of her sisters. She raged at the broken chairs. She scoffed at Dana H.'s tale of Corinne's attack. "I am not even going to address *this*." She waved a dismissive hand at Britt's evidence board.

The ghosts were affronted on behalf of the second years. Hours of hard work met with Ainsley's scorn? They flickered the lights in solidarity.

"See, even the ghosts agree that something is going on here!" Britt snapped.

"Oh my god, Britt, there is no such thing as ghosts!" Ainsley snapped back. "Or vampires."

Britt refused to stand down. "When you eliminate the impossible, like, whatever remains is the truth, Ainsley."

Ainsley didn't take this well. "I don't have time for this," she said, in her *most* Ainsley voice. "If you're gonna be crafting in here, the least you can do is paint a banner." She stomped into the supply closet, which the ghosts rearranged quarterly, and came out a minute later with the box of pillar candles.

"The alumnae will be here in an hour. I expect your little *Supernatural* cosplay to be over by then, 'kay?" Ainsley motioned toward the barricaded door. The second years reluctantly let her out.

"Take this!" Dana H. shrilled, holding out a stake.

Ainsley made a sound of disgust and stomped out.

Britt took the stake. "I'll go with her. Buddy system, yeah?" She scanned the room. "Lexi P., I'm leaving you in charge." Then, she ran after their President.

The ghosts figured the girls in the chapter room had everything well in hand. Besides, they wanted to see what else Britt would do to defend their home if Ainsley refused to.

They weren't disappointed.

As Ainsley set to work arranging the candles on the table in the foyer, Britt sprinted to the kitchen.

"She didn't get rid of it!" she yelled, triumphant. Britt ran back into the foyer, holding an industrial-sized canister of garlic powder over her head.

Ainsley was too busy ignoring Britt to see that she'd upended the container and was sprinkling the garlic in a circle around them. "Perfect." Ainsley wiped her hands and stepped back to admire the candles. "Isn't it?" Britt agreed, finishing the circle.

Ainsley looked up at the click of the lid closing. "What is this?" she asked, pointing to the dusting of garlic on the hardwoods.

"We're safe!" Britt said, a huge smile on her face. "Miss Betty can't cross in here now!" She shook the container for emphasis.

"Brittany Marie Wallace!" Ainsley snapped. "You cannot dump garlic in the foyer!"

"I literally just created a circle of protection, a thank you would be nice."

"You created a mess, that's what you did!"

"I created a mess?" Britt asked. "You invited a vampire into our home, so, like, glass houses, Madam President." She sprinkled the garlic again, drawing a line between herself and Ainsley.

"Oh my god, she's not a vampire!" Ainsley stomped off to the kitchen. A couple of the ghosts followed, wondering if they would finally see Ainsley snap. The rest watched Britt, who had taken to drawing a pentagram within the circle.

One of the ghosts remembered that Britt took some sort of witch class in the fall. Another considered whether garlic powder was an adequate substitute for a garland of garlic, which was what the doctor used in that film festival movie.

"Good news," Ainsley called, returning to the foyer. The ghosts who monitored her trip to the walk-in freezer—without locking her in, as this was a time of crisis—came with her. "I found some frozen snickerdoodles. We won't have to hit up Kroger."

Britt, now finished with the pentagram, didn't reply, her focus solely on extending the line of garlic up the stairs.

"Can you bring me a lighter while you're up there? I'm worried the wicks on these candles are too short to light!" Ainsley called.

"We aren't allowed to have lit candles in the house!" Britt called back. Another victim of Ainsley's Reign of Terror, gone after someone lit a pumpkin spice marshmallow candle in August.

"We can for this! I'm sure one of the potheads in your pledge class has a Bic upstairs!" Ainsley looked at Britt's handiwork and made an unhappy noise. She stomped through the living room to the vampire's suite. She pounded on the door.

"Miss Betty! We need a broom, please!"

Content that her screeched request would be fulfilled, Ainsley returned to the foyer, where Britt almost knocked into her as she ran down the stairs. Ainsley stumbled and made a sound of disgust, which Britt ignored. She dropped a hot pink lighter into Ainsley's open palm.

"I will not reveal where I found this contraband, since I've decided to protest your dangerous leadership, FYI," Britt said.

"Be the president, Ainsley," Ainsley muttered to herself, attempting to light the candle. "It's super rewarding, Ainsley. You won't regret it—"

The candle lit.

Several ghosts were watching from within the garlic powder circle of protection slash pentagram.

Then the girls were screaming.

It was one thing, the ghosts figured, for the girls to joke that they lived in a haunted sorority house. It was probably a very different thing to see the spirits in residence within the pentagram.

One of the savvier ghosts moaned, "Ainsley!" drawing out the syllables of her name. "It is me, Prudence Brooks Kilgore!"

Ainsley gasped. "The first president of Eta Mu?!"

"Yes!" the ghost continued. It was thrilling, finally being able to talk to the girl they'd haunted for years. If only things weren't so dire, they could tell her to cut bangs or streak the Rotunda. "I've come to warn you, you're in grave danger! Your sisters are right, your house mother is a vampire!"

Miss Betty chose that time to appear, the noise from the ghosts finally rousing her from her daytime slumber.

"Get her!" a ghost, not the one impersonating an Eta Mu founder, yelled.

The ghosts charged the vampire, who, with nowhere else to run, was forced out the front door, into the late April sun. Ainsley didn't watch as their house mother turned into a pile of ash on the lawn. She was still fixated on the so-called Prudence Brooks Kilgore.

"It's a Founder's Day miracle!" Ainsley said, on the verge of tears.

"I'll say," Britt agreed, looking out at where Miss Betty used to be.

"Hang the banner, welcome the alumnae, tell no one what happened here today," Prudence Brooks Kilgore instructed. The other ghosts thought this was overkill, and also that Prudence's voice was distinctly that of a male streetcar driver from the late 1800s.

The candle extinguished—Ainsley was right, the wick wasn't long enough to burn—and the ghosts vanished from sight. Britt went to the chapter room to mobilize the girls again, this time to hang the freshly painted banner and sweep up the garlic. After all, the alumnae were coming.

"I totally think we have a carbon monoxide leak!" Britt said, when someone asked what was going on.

Founder's Day came together, against all odds. The worst Founder's Day the alumnae could recall, but, in the ghosts' opinion, every Founder's Day was the worst Founder's Day they could recall.

And that night, unable to sleep without Miss Betty's iron pill sedatives, Britt crept down to the chapter room. She snagged a pillar candle from the box in the storage closet, drew a pentagram on the floor, and lit the candle with her hot pink lighter.

"So, which one of you stole my Bodo's punch card?"

Clickbait

Deidra Whitt Lovegren

Part I: Storge (στοργή) - Familial Love

WHEN FELICITY SAW HER new classroom, her heart sank. The musty room was drab, smelled of rodent droppings, and felt colder than it should have. In all of her years of teaching, Felicity hadn't seen a more dispiriting place.

"Don't you love it?" Dr. Maycomb asked with a smile that didn't reach his eyes. "Generations of Virginia's finest young men have sat at these desks."

"I—"

"Dooms Academy was founded before the signing of the Declaration of Independence. The flooring is made from Carolingian Red Oak. The desks are mahogany. The window frames? From the black walnut groves near Grand Caverns." He stroked the wood as if admiring it for the first time, ignoring the scrawls of graffiti etched into the grain by bored students waiting for the bell to ring.

Felicity nodded politely. "It's all very historic."

"Like most places in Virginia, you can't turn over a rock without finding some remnant of bygone days. Dooms has always been at the crossroads. During the American Revolution, British soldiers marched through our town on their way to Winchester. General Jackson took a shortcut through Dooms to join Lee at Richmond."

Felicity took a step toward the door, but one of her heels wedged in the flooring. She struggled to wrench it free, succeeding in time to see Dr. Maycomb appraising her toned calves.

For a woman pushing forty, it thrilled her to catch a man's eye, even someone as persnickety as the headmaster. *What would he be like in bed?*

She dismissed the thought as quickly as it came.

***

When Felicity visited Dooms Academy, the all-boys' school tucked neatly into the Blue Ridge Mountains, she hadn't planned on signing anything. But Dr. Maycomb had been insistent on hiring her, turning her inquiry into an offer. Before his assistant could bring them a second cup of coffee, Felicity had signed the teaching contract, as her divorce cost more than she planned, as her ex-husband's debts were greater than she imagined.

"Is the salary correct? It's quite generous."

Dr. Maycomb sighed. "Colleges aren't graduating many education majors these days, so compensation has risen proportionately. Boarding schools require a greater commitment from their faculty."

She wondered if she had made a horrible mistake.

The tour of the campus did little to alleviate her concerns.

***

Dr. Maycomb walked behind the teacher's desk and pulled out a maple paddle. "A relic from the days of yore. Spare the rod, spoil the child—so the scriptures say."

"Samuel Butler."

"Hm?"

"Samuel Butler wrote the idiom about sparing the rod. The verse from Proverbs says—"

Click.

Felicity stopped mid-sentence. "Did you hear that?"

"Hear what?" Dr. Maycomb tilted his head.

"It sounded like a camera."

"There's no one here but us." Dr. Maycomb returned his attention to the paddle. "In the olden days, I earned a few whacks myself. Probably the only way I learned arithmetic." He chuckled to himself, putting the paddle back into the drawer. "Corporal punishment is out of fashion these days. Change is inevitable."

Felicity scanned the room before they left.

"Now, come with me and I'll show you the residence halls."

She walked in front of Dr. Maycomb on the narrow pathway leading to the center of campus, letting her hips sway a bit more than was necessary. "I believe you mentioned I could move in early August?"

Dr. Maycomb cleared his throat. "Early August, of course. Sooner if you wish."

Felicity calculated how many more nights on her friend's couch she could stand.

"The Women's Dormitory was recently renovated," he added. "I'm sure you will find it most suitable."

"I'm sure I will."

He removed his glasses. "We want you to be comfortable here, Felicity. At Dooms, we're family."

Part II: Philautia (φιλαυτία) - Self-Love

August carried over July's oppressive heat and humidity. Even the cool dales of the Blue Ridge remained steamy and fetid.

Sipping her Diet Coke, Felicity sat on the concrete stoop, her thin t-shirt dripping with perspiration. Hauling boxes from the parking lot to the top floor of the Women's Dormitory proved taxing. She hadn't seen one maintenance man to charm into service.

Other than her clothing and shoes, there wasn't much for Felicity to move. She had no family pictures, no heirlooms, no bric-à-brac, no mementos. Her parents were dead. She had a brother she hadn't talked to in years. Most of her friends evanesced during the divorce. She had no children. Her ex-husband decided there would be none, complaining bitterly whenever she broached the subject and confessing that he didn't want her to lose her figure.

Felicity threw her soda can into the trash and stood in front of the dormitory.

Home, sweet home.

She returned to her room, taking the stairs two at a time. Once inside, she tore off her sweaty clothes and prepared for a nice, cool shower.

Felicity caught her reflection in an antique mirror. Her naked body still looked good. She preened, lifted her breasts, frowned as they sagged lower than she liked when she released them. She turned sideways and viewed her buttocks, firm and round, courtesy of countless Pilates classes.

Click.

She whipped her head around. The door was closed, the curtains drawn. The dorm was hardly four hundred square feet, far too small for anyone to hide.

She saw no one.

Part III: Philia (φιλία) - Friendship

"Hi—!"

Outside her room, Felicity was startled by a young woman, easily a decade younger, her hair lustrous, thick, black as ebony. Felicity's hand absently crept toward her own thinning tresses.

"Hey! I'm Connie." The young woman put down an armful of shopping bags on the landing. "I didn't mean to scare you."

"You didn't," she lied. "I'm Felicity. I'll be teaching Humanities this year. What about you?"

"Biology. Gah, I hate ninth graders!" Connie rolled her eyes. "I asked Maycomb if I could board early."

Felicity fell silent, not prepared for sharing her innermost thoughts.

"My boyfriend—my *ex-boyfriend*—and I are no longer together. Our lease was up, so here I am!"

"Sorry about your ex. There's a lot of that going around."

"You too?"

"Yep."

"Bad breakup?"

"Bad divorce."

"Ooh, an *expensive* breakup. Maybe my generation got one thing right. We do relationships on the cheap." Connie laughed, struggling with her bags.

"Let me help you," Felicity said, taking Connie's key, wiggling it into the lock. "When you get settled, come over. I have a bottle of wine in the mini-fridge. You can tell me about your asshole ex-boyfriend."

"How'd you know he's an asshole?" Connie raised an eyebrow.

"They're all assholes in the end."

"I'm more worried there won't be another *beginning* for me. Maybe Matt was the last man to want me?" Connie asked in a sing-songy voice, flipping her hair, implying she didn't consider that a realistic possibility.

"You're worried Prince Charming won't show up?"

"I would settle for Prince Pays-Half-The-Bills."

"Ah, the secret of life: low expectations." Felicity smiled, pleased to have made a new friend. "So, see you later?"

"On one condition."

"What's that?"

"You spill the tea about your D."

Felicity smiled at Connie's bravado. "My divorce? I'll tell you what you need to know."

Connie pouted.

"Fine. I'll start by telling you how horrible my ex-husband is in bed."

"That's more like it!" They both dissolved into giggles like teenagers.

Click.

Felicity paused, her hand resting on the doorframe. She glanced at the ceiling, then down the hallway. "Connie, did you hear that?"

"Hear what?"

"A loud click."

"What?" Connie looked at her straight in the face. "I didn't hear a thing."

"It's strange." Felicity frowned. "I hear clicks everywhere on campus."

"Maybe it's the cicadas—they're all over Virginia this time of year."

Part IV: Pragma (πράγμα) - Enduring Love

"Autumn is my favorite time of year," Dr. Maycomb intoned, addressing the somber faculty and staff in the auditorium. "There is a coolness to the mornings. The leaves have begun to turn, greens giving way to reds and yellows. My friends, before the students return next week, I want to remind you of our duty. Almost three hundred years ago, Reverend Endings founded Dooms Academy. His vision was to preserve the love of man and ensure its transmission."

"Quite a charter," Felicity whispered to Connie.

Connie suppressed a laugh and swatted her arm. "Shh," she protested. "You're going to get me in trouble."

"Let us encourage our young men to continue what Reverend Endings started so very long ago." There was a smattering of applause.

An extraordinarily handsome man took a seat beside Felicity. Black hair, graying about the temples. Hazel eyes, flecks of gold. White teeth, framed by full red lips. His narrowly fitted Oxford shirt emphasized his muscular chest. He leaned in and whispered, "Am I late?"

"Almost." She offered her hand in greeting. "Love your tie."

"My mother would thank you. She taught me the meaning of *meandros*," he said, pointing to the red interlocking lines. "To us Greeks, they symbolize eternity and infinity."

"Which is about as long as Maycomb has been speaking." Felicity grinned.

"Would you like to sneak out and get lunch?" He loosened his tie.

"Are you buying?"

Part V: Ludus (ερωτοτροπία) - Flirting

Dmitri Papadopoulos taught Greek, World History, and Photography. His classroom was right next to Felicity's.

"Are you ready for Monday?" he asked, popping his head through her classroom door.

"Ready as I'll ever be."

He entered, proffering a large, colorful sign festooned with beautiful calligraphy. "I made this for you."

"Thanks, Dmitri. What does it say?"

"It's your name in Greek." He looked sheepish. "I thought you could put it on your door."

"It's lovely." Felicity took the sign from him and examined it closely. "I've never been to Greece. Did you spend your childhood there?"

"Yes, but there wasn't much to do when I was young. I usually explored the caves by the sea."

"You are very thoughtful. I'll hang this on my door right now." Felicity bumped into her desk, causing the tape dispenser to fall to the floor.

Slowly, she bent over to pick it up.

Dmitri didn't notice.

***

On the first day of class, Felicity was impressed by the dapper young men milling about campus in their blue blazers and maroon ties. Resolute and serious, they stared at their schedule cards in earnest.

She stood at her classroom door, hair up in a loose bun, over-sized glasses perched on her nose. She wore a white blouse, a gray pencil skirt, and ankle-strapped heels.

The sexy librarian.

Dmitri appeared in the doorway with an extra cup of coffee.

"Care for some liquid courage?" He handed her the cup.

Their eyes locked as the bell rang.

"Thanks." As she took it, he winked at her.

Sipping her coffee as the boys filed in, Felicity felt giddy with excitement. *The start of a new school year held infinite possibilities.*

"Good morning, gentlemen! Welcome to Humanities."

The students sat silently, pallid faces and stoic expressions.

She glanced at her attendance roster. "Hezekiah Amos Adams?"

"Present."

Felicity noted Hezekiah, a thin boy with pale, watery eyes. He wore his hair plaited down his back, tied at the end with a velvet ribbon.

"Theodore Albert Farmington III?"

A portly young man with hair greased into ringlets slowly raised his hand in acknowledgment.

"Raymond Archer McGillicuddy?"

A head full of pomade slicked back into a pompadour.

"Bobby Smith?"

Blond feathered hair, thickly hairsprayed from side to side.

The room was a goddamned parade of hairstyles. And their names! Felicity wondered if Connie's roster read like a genealogical pedigree chart, too.

***

After school, Felicity splayed out on the floor, attempting to make order out of chaos. Loose leaf paper, labels, worksheets, and manila folders lay in piles at her bare feet.

"Did you survive your first day?"

Felicity looked at Dmitri, sultry as a sunset.

"I did," she replied, holding out her hand for Dmitri to take. He clasped her by the wrist and pulled her to her feet, watching as she put on her high heels, one at a time.

"Felicity, I have two favors to ask you." He tipped her chin up with his cool fingers to peer into her eyes.

"Name 'em."

"First, I'm taking the Photography Club to the caverns in November. Any chance you'd like to come?"

"Of course." Felicity moved closer to him. "Anything else?"

"I'd like to see you after dinner." His hands snaked around her waist to the small of her back, thumbs tracing the curve of her hips. "Will you walk with me?"

She answered him with an open-mouthed kiss.

Part VI: Eros (ἔρως) - Erotic Love

The first few weeks were a blur.

Connie had asked to grab a cup of coffee with Felicity several times, but Felicity didn't have the time to spare. She spent her afternoons preparing for class and her evenings waiting for Dmitri.

When he finally texted her, she would scuttle across campus, entering the Men's Dorm through a back staircase that led directly to his room.

"Do you like it here?" Dmitri asked as they lay tangled in the sheets.

"I can't imagine being anywhere else," she replied truthfully, snuggling into his chest, breathing in his musky scent, relishing the weight of his arms holding her.

From their first night together, Felicity had felt at peace—one with the universe, senses heightened. Color appeared in new hues, sound resonated more euphoniously, taste amplified into orgiastic pleasures.

Dopamine is a helluva drug, she laughed to herself, trying to divine the mystery of it all.

There was no denying it. Since becoming intimate with Dmitri, she felt centered and whole.

She quit primping for hours in front of the mirror, lamenting the fine lines around her eyes and mouth. She stopped fretting over the folds in her neck. She luxuriated in her body instead of mourning how the years had pecked away at her beauty like a sharp-beaked vulture.

Dmitri made her feel cherished and adored as the months passed like whispers.

***

Felicity languidly ran her fingers along the books on his nightstand. "Tell me why you like history so much."

"Because mankind is fascinating. Take the Monacan Indians. They settled in Virginia far earlier than Reverend Endings." He turned on his side.

"Mm-hmm," she murmured, half-listening.

"Monacans mined copper, made jewelry, traded with the Powhatans. They buried their dead in mounds—a practice unheard of by other tribes."

"Cool."

"When newspaper photographers came in the mid-1800s, the Monacans refused to have their pictures taken. They called the white men's cameras *soul-takers.*"

"Is that why you teach photography? To snatch people's souls?" She abandoned the books and traced his earlobe instead.

"If I had that kind of power, I wouldn't take people's souls. I would take their love." His white teeth gleamed in the dark.

She slapped his chest. "You thief of hearts! Well, I won't give you mine."

He held her wrist before she could swat him again. "Contrary to what most people believe, there isn't an endless supply of love, Felicity. Love is elemental—as finite as water."

"Water is wet," she purred.

He held her at arm's length. "Love has to be retrieved at some point. You understand. Don't you, Felicity?"

"Sure, I do," she said, sliding off her pajama bottoms. "What do you say we retrieve it now before I have to leave?"

Part VII: Mania (μανία) - Obsessive Love

Felicity sat on the school bus with the silent boys from the Photography Club, waiting for Dmitri to arrive. She breathed in slowly and deeply, exhaling in an audible sigh.

"I'm sure he'll be here shortly," she said aloud, trying to convince herself.

As usual, the boys said little in reply.

Click.

She turned around to see one of the boys futzing with his camera. She began to say something, but seeing the blank look in the boy's eyes made her turn around and fold her hands in her lap.

She checked her watch. *Fifteen minutes late.* It was unlike him.

Felicity had been interested in visiting Grand Caverns in Grottoes, but Dmitri told her there were more interesting caves closer to the school. He assured her they would be less crowded and more photogenic.

She tapped her foot in frustration, then concern. *Had something happened to him?*

Looking over her right shoulder, she spotted Dmitri walking around the corner into the bus lot, talking animatedly, hands waving. Her smile froze into a grimace. Felicity saw whom he was with.

Connie.

Connie and Dmitri chatted and laughed while casually boarding the bus.

"Hey all!" She raised her arms. "Who's ready for some spelunking? Woo hoo!"

The boys' indistinct muttering didn't dampen Connie's enthusiasm for the outing one bit.

"Connie, I didn't know you were coming." Felicity slid over, making room for Dmitri to sit next to her.

"I thought we needed another chaperone," Dmitri said offhandedly, bypassing Felicity, sliding next to Connie instead.

"Dmitri said there's eight caverns to explore. *Eight* caverns!" Connie giggled. "How are we going to see them all? Maybe we can split into groups."

"Maybe we can," Felicity replied, eyes ablaze, teeth gritted.

***

The bus ride was torture.

The entire way, Dmitri and Connie teased each other like childhood friends.

Is he sleeping with her? Felicity watched their movements through her peripheral vision. She remembered what Dmitri had told her the last time they were in bed, his words burned into her skull.

Love is elemental—as finite as water.

She dug her nails into her palms to keep from screaming.

An hour later, the school bus turned off the main highway and onto a winding gravel road. Felicity watched through the windshield as a deep fissure in the mountainside loomed ahead. There were no other cars or people to be found—simply an abandoned ticket booth with a moldy sign that read "Do Not Enter."

"This is the maintenance entrance," Dmitri explained. "Tourists enter from the northern mouth of the cavern. They pay a fortune to see far less. We're going right into the pit room. Are you ready?"

The boys rose from their seats, picked up their camera gear, and filed out, one by one. Connie followed, jabbering about how exciting it all was.

Felicity reached out to touch Dmitri's shoulder.

He flinched.

"Dmitri, we need to talk," she said. "I don't understand why—"

"We need to get to the caverns. We'll talk later."

He exited the bus.

She had no choice but to follow him.

Part VIII: Agape (ἀγάπη) - Godly Love

Felicity's eyes adjusted to the inky black as they entered. Dim light from low wattage bulbs threaded into the gloom. Slowly, they made their way in single file, step by step, down the steep passage. Dmitri led, followed by the boys with cameras at the ready—and two women.

"With every footstep, you can sense the passage of time. Feel the coolness of the cave, boys. It's the breath of history. Here—in the heart of the world—past, present, and future are one." Dmitri's soothing voice reverberated off the walls.

"Keep your eyes open. You *stalag-might* see something!" Connie laughed at her own joke.

The boys didn't respond.

Connie tried again. "A cave's favorite music is rock and roll."

This time, even Connie didn't laugh.

Felicity grasped the slick pipe rail with both hands, feet skittering down the rocky trail, afraid to open her mouth. She wanted to scream at the boys for moving so slowly. She wanted to kick

Connie for making bad puns. She wanted to kill Dmitri for making her feel dirty and cheap—and ugly.

They trudged through passageways and tunnels until they entered a high-ceilinged chamber.

"Here we are." Dmitri sighed with pleasure. "It is time." The boys gathered around him like acolytes. As Felicity brought up the rear, she couldn't help but gawk at the beauty of the room. Lit just enough to show the glittering crystals and rich minerals lining the walls, the expanse was an underground cathedral.

"There *are* eight caverns!" Connie crowed.

Felicity turned to see the entrances clustered together like a honeycomb on the far wall. *They were enormous.* "What's written over each entrance?" Felicity asked, squinting through the murk. "It looks like the door sign you made for me." She turned to Dmitri.

"It's Greek." His white teeth glowed. "The etchings are from the 6th century BCE. The time of the Great Philosophers."

"Twenty-seven centuries ago? How did Native Americans learn Greek?" Felicity asked, more skeptical than she intended. "What's the translation?"

"They are the eight forms of love. I will explain everything to you later. For now? The boys have work to do. Felicity, stay here while I go with Connie. Do not leave. Stay here."

The tone in his voice shocked her into obedience.

Connie waggled her fingers at Felicity as they departed for the cavern marked *Philia.*

Confused, Felicity sat on a low stone pedestal, her arms folded across her chest. She watched the boys fan out, entering assorted caverns without trepidation, as if they'd been there many times before.

Her curiosity led her to follow a couple of the boys from a distance. Loaded like pack mules with photography bags and cameras, they filed into a cavern marked *Pragma.* As she crept toward the entrance, she smelled natural gas. A low, flickering flame illuminated the back of the cavity.

She entered, astonished at the heaps of mildewed wedding pictures and yellowed newspaper announcements and snapshots of elderly couples. Her fingers trailed over the piles until she spied an oil painting in an ornate frame. Dislodging it from the others, she saw the likenesses of herself and Dimitri, fifty years older, his arm tightly about her waist.

Stunned, she dropped the portrait and fell to her knees.

When she raised her head, the boys unzipped their photography bags, scooped out handfuls of memory cards, and tossed them into the fire, chanting something she could not understand.

The cards hissed and popped.

"In the olden days, I culled hearts by drawing the lovelorn's portrait on clay tablets with a reed stylus."

Felicity attempted to turn toward Dmitri's voice, but he held her firmly from behind.

"As an artist, rendering hearts is not difficult for me. However, it is time consuming. I prefer using twenty-first century technology. There are tens of thousands of digital pictures on each one of those cards. So much more efficient than hand drawings!"

"I—"

"Love wasn't held as dearly in the past as it is today. Life in the Bronze and Iron Age did not encourage many seekers. But if the Middle Ages brought mankind anything, it was the desire to love and be loved. Conquest and plague will do that, but it makes my collection so much harder."

"What are you saying—?"

His hands moved to embrace her.

"Felicity, I've recorded the remnants of love on limestone stela and oracle bones and papyrus scrolls. I've used quills and parchment and vellum to keep my tallies. From daguerreotypes to 35mm film to Kodachrome, each technological advancement makes my job easier. But I am alone in this." He nuzzled her neck.

"You're a monster," she whispered before his hands covered her mouth.

"I'm the monster? Mankind regenerates exponentially, straining the one resource the universe cannot produce anymore of—Love." He released her hands, turning her around to face him. He kissed her full on the mouth.

When he finally pulled away, there were tears in her eyes. As he wiped them away, her eyes paled, her heart sputtered, her breathing slowed. She grew cold.

As she gathered her senses, she saw the boys had silently surrounded them.

"Who—who are these children?" Her voice broke.

Dmitri ruffled the hair of the boy closest to him. "Who, these guys? They help me collect love," he said simply. "Think of my job as janitorial. It's quite simple. My brother is the reaper of souls. I am the gleaner of hearts. What's remarkable is how weak the body of clay is—how useless without heart or soul!"

"Your brother is *Death?*"

She collapsed into his arms. He held her until she stopped weeping.

"Y—you said love is finite as water."

"Yes, and like water, it takes many forms." Dmitri motioned to the secretions on the cave's floor. "And also, like water, love is recycled in much the same way: collection, evaporation, condensation, precipitation."

"I don't understand." Felicity wiped her eyes on the backs of her hands.

"I have an eternity to teach you. Just know the digital revolution has made it easier to track the vicissitudes of eight billion hearts, so many of them false. Ah, the poisoned fruit of the postmodern age. Still, it is quite a burden to reallocate a finite resource."

"Are you asking me to join you?"

"Of course. Dr. Maycomb said you would make an excellent addition."

"What about Connie? I thought that—"

Dmitri shrugged. "Unfortunately, the gods we serve require a sacrifice now and again. It's never my favorite part."

Felicity pushed him away. "How could you? Connie?! Connie!" Felicity's shrieks died in the dark. The boys with their pale eyes looked out from the caverns, heads cocked to the side in concern.

Dmitri motioned for them to continue their work.

"So Connie's really... dead?"

"Felicity, please," Dmitri replied in a sing-songy voice. "She'll be rejoining us in no time—like the boys over the centuries. And she'll have a job at Dooms Academy for eternity. It's not a bad death."

"She's gone."

"For now," he said, tucking a strand of Felicity's hair behind her ear. "By the time we finish our work, she'll be on the bus for the drive back."

Felicity and Dmitri stood in silence. The flames from the eight caverns emitted a warm glow as the stalactites dripped water into shimmering pools.

Time passed both quickly and slowly.

"So, will you walk with me—and help me with my work?" He kissed her neck.

Felicity put her hands on her hips. "You want me to collect love with you until death do us part?"

"I want to be with you." Dmitri smiled, his white teeth brighter than ever in the darkened cavern. "It's the only way for you to remain beautiful for eternity."

"For eternity?" She sounded intrigued. "I don't want to be sacrificed—like Connie. I don't want to die at all."

"Gods, Felicity."

"What?"

"You're already dead."

Save Our Cryptids - Volunteers Needed

J. THOMPSON

Feeling a vibration in his pocket, Zeke pulled out his phone: GETTING TOO CLOSE

Zeke looked up from his hiding place over the bank. Dillon was lying on the ground by the retention pond with a strange, gangly woman creeping toward him. Tattered, sodden clothes hung from the woman's thin frame, her face obscured by long dark hair soaked with pond water. While it looked more like a monster, the thing was supposedly some kind of water spirit. At least, that's what Dillon told him in the two-minute explanation he'd given on the walk here.

Ding! Another text. Zeke scrambled out of sight as the creature's head snapped toward him. Fumbling with his phone, he managed to get it silenced and read the text: WHERE'S MARI

Zeke had no idea how Dillon could type while playing dead. A loud, inhuman hiss from above made Zeke drop his phone. The creature crawled over the edge of the hill. Dirty water flew from its hair as it whipped its head, searching for the interloper.

As he crouched behind a small tree, clutching a shopping bag, Zeke cursed his own stupidity. Why didn't he do more research on things before he signed up? A lifetime of hasty decisions flashed before his eyes as the soggy slaps of the creature's footsteps approached. Zeke's lost phone dinged at the creature's feet. It leaped back, hissing and lashing out with clawed hands.

"Now!" yelled a woman running up the hill, clutching a bright pink travel tumbler. "Go! Just start throwing them!"

Zeke dashed from behind the tree, pulling a fistful of silica gel packets out of his bag. As the creature charged him, Zeke threw one at its feet. It recoiled, howling and sputtering as if shot.

The creature seemed to flow backward, not so much stepping as morphing to face the other way. It attempted to flee to the safety of the pond but was met with a barrage of desiccant packets from Dillon. Unable or unwilling to move past the little white sacks, the creature found itself penned in. Zeke and Dillon closed in, pelting the monster with their inedible ammunition as it shrank before their very eyes.

"Mari, get that thing!" Dillon shouted.

The dark-haired woman dashed forward, scooping the now doll-sized monster up in her oversized drink tumbler, and screwing on the lid. She slammed the cup into the ground in victory, and Zeke collapsed beside her.

"It's in there good, right?" Dillon picked up the Stanley tumbler and shook it, the sound of sloshing water emanating from within.

"Of course," said Mari. "We're lucky they still had one of these left, if they only had the off-brand ones, we'd have been screwed." She saw Zeke's confused look and elaborated, "Well, you really need one of the lead-lined ones if you want to trap a water spirit. Why'd they have to get so damn hard to find all of a sudden anyways?"

"Supply and demand, I reckon." Dillon helped Zeke to his feet. "Come on, the Chairman's down at the farmer's market, and he's got a mission for us."

"What? This wasn't the mission?" Zeke asked.

"I'm afraid not," Dillon said. "Let's go, there might be some of that fancy iced coffee left if we hustle."

After ten minutes of hiking across various parking lots, on the far side of Towncenter Drive, the trio arrived at the Albemarle Farmer's Market. Dillon split off to grab some coffee, while Mari and Zeke headed to a stall where a familiar face waited.

The Chairman sat in a cheap folding chair at an even cheaper table, stroking his long beard. He was so engrossed in whatever video he was watching on his beat-up phone that he didn't notice their approach. Mari slammed the tumbler on the table, scattering the small carvings he was failing to sell.

"Here's your damned water spirit, Boss."

"Oh, that was fast," he said, composing himself. "Zeke, good job on your first recovery. I knew as soon as I laid eyes on you that you were the right fit for this organization."

"Thanks."

"I did most of the legwork," Mari grumbled under her breath. "Even spent my own money on this."

"So, how's business been so far today?" Zeke scanned the table, looking at the strange array of wooden sculptures laid out before him.

"Slow, as usual." The Chairman sighed. "You'd think anyone would love to adorn their mantle with one of my hand-carvings of local animals, made from one hundred percent reclaimed wood, but no luck so far."

"So, woodcarving now?" Mari asked. "Was the door-to-door Feng Shui assessments not bringing in the cash anymore?"

"No, in the end, it wasn't any more profitable than the kombucha cart, nor the sourdough cookie sales. I know you liked them, but I think you were my only customer. Anyway, that's all behind us now. I've been working all month on perfecting my carving technique. Take a look, they're pretty detailed, aren't they?"

Zeke picked up an oddly proportioned statue that he could only narrow down to the category of "four-legged animals" and checked the price tag. A shocking number, not something he could afford on the salary of a community college adjunct professor. "Maybe this isn't the right venue." He returned the wooden beast to the only open space on the table.

"Hmm, perhaps you're right," the Chairman said. "I should set up at the Sunset Market too. An excellent idea from the new recruit. Ah, Dillon, can I interest you in a mountain lion? Or perhaps a cardinal?" he asked as Dillon arrived with an armload of coffees.

"Nah, spent all my pocket change on coffee." Dillon looked down at the vaguely bird shaped lump. "Now what's this about a new job?"

"I personally prefer the term mission, instead of job. Job sounds so corporate."

"Get to the point already," Mari groaned.

"Fine, Big Bill's been spotted in the Three Ridges Wilderness. I need you to go down there and tag him."

"Woah, woah, woah." Mari took a step back. "Isn't there somebody else who could take care of this? I've got stuff to do today."

"Yeah, I'd rather not, if it's all the same to you," Dillon said. "Why's he so far south, anyways?"

"Who's Big Bill?" Zeke asked.

"Well." The Chairman cleared his throat. "We keep tabs on several interesting denizens of our fair region through our extensive tagging program. Understanding the movements of our less-mundane neighbors is an essential part of our ongoing conservation efforts. I'm sure you've seen the process in nature documentaries before. Catch the creature, check for an existing tag, affix a new one, and set them free to roam the wilds once more."

"I'm not really sure that answered my original question."

Ignoring Zeke, the Chairman pointed at the other two. "Now as for you, I'm wise to your tricks. The two of you have been pushing missions off onto junior members for months. You may think they're all too nice to call you out on it, but we all need to do our fair share of work to protect this fine corner of our commonwealth. Plus, I was hoping you'd walk Zeke here through our tracking program."

"But, isn't there some other mission we could take?" Mari protested. "I had to chip Big Bill last time."

"You're right." The Chairman raised his hands in defeat. "I believe it's time to review your eligibility for our membership benefits. You know, the ones reserved for our more active participants? I'd hate to see your card lapse."

"You wouldn't!" Mari stepped back in surprise.

"I'm not gonna try him," Dillon said. "Count me in."

The Chairman looked at Zeke.

"I'm already here," Zeke said. "Might as well see this through."

Mari sighed, defeated. "Fine, I'll do it."

"Excellent." The Chairman leaned back in his chair. "Now you two run along and get your gear packed while I walk Zeke through the finer points of injecting a tracking chip."

***

Two hours later, Zeke stared out the window of Dillon's truck as the trio rode along a narrow path, winding its way up into the mountains. The little two-seater truck struck a pothole, eliciting an indignant cry from Mari, who got stuck sitting in the bed. Dillon apologized, and she resumed holding her phone in the air, trying in vain to get enough of a signal to doomscroll.

How did Zeke get himself into this situation? About the same way he always did: doing enough research to get himself into trouble, but not enough to avoid it. Convincing his mother to sign him up for a kids' martial arts class, right around the time karate stopped being cool. Choosing the closest college to home, settling on a history major, and then learning the job market had few choices for him, even taking into account his specialization in Appalachian folklore. Moving to Charlottesville to be near family, only to find out that the only way to keep up with the cost of rent was to either get roommates or win the lottery. Finally, on advice from his therapist, joining a club to give meaning to his otherwise aimless life.

If he had paid attention when he read that faded flyer pinned to a telephone pole, he might have realized that the meeting he was showing up for was the TJWSCD instead of the TJSWCD. It should have been obvious in retrospect. I mean, one of them was a legitimate organization. The Thomas Jefferson Soil and Water Conservation District had actual paid positions and the other, some kind of volunteer conservation club. However, the members of the Thomas Jefferson Weald and Sprite Conservation District were so impressed with Zeke's knowledge of local history that they placed him on the roster before he had even realized that "sprite" was referring to spirits and not soft drinks.

Now here he was, sitting in the passenger seat of a weird little Japanese truck, halfway up a mountain, clutching an oversized syringe. The truck rumbled over a rock, jostling Mari once more.

"Damn it," she grumbled, stuffing her receptionless phone into a pocket, and pulling out another small device. "Why does he get to sit in the cab?"

"Because," Dillon turned to speak through the back window. "Zeke is respectful of my vehicle, and he don't try and vape in the cab when I told him not to."

"What's the big deal, it's just water vapor?" Mari blew a cloud into the mountain air.

"It ain't, and you know it," said Dillon. "Now put that away before you lose your grip, and it flies out the truck."

Mari took one defiant puff from the vape, then stuffed it into her pocket with her useless phone. They hit another bump and something started tumbling around the truck bed before Mari grabbed it. "Here." She handed the metal tumbler through the window to Zeke. "Keep this up front. I don't want it rolling around and breaking open."

"Wait, isn't this the water spirit?" Zeke asked. "Why do we still have this? Shouldn't we have left it with the Chairman?"

"What's he going to do with it?" Mari replied. "We have to let it out in the wilderness. If we put it in a stream or something, it probably won't bother us."

"Probably?" Zeke looked at the tumbler dubiously. He could feel something moving inside, sloshing unnaturally. "So, Dillon," Zeke said, changing the subject. "What made you want to join the Tee-Jay-Double... the organization?"

"It's a real mouthful, right?" Mari chimed in.

"Well, as you might or might not be aware," he began, never taking his eyes off the road. "Us Shifletts have long been a family of monster hunters. They say back in the day, in Europe, we were hunting werewolves and stuff like that. My ancestors settled around these parts and kept up the family tradition. My grandpa told me he cornered the Snallygaster up near Harper's Ferry. Almost got the sucker too, but it's a slippery devil. Well, there's not too many monsters 'round here anymore. Figured if we didn't want to put ourselves out of business, maybe I should do something to make sure we didn't kill off every monster in the whole country."

"That makes sense," Zeke said. "What about you, Mari?"

"The membership card," she said without hesitation.

"Membership card?" Zeke pulled the plastic card he was given when he signed up out of his wallet.

"Flip it over," Mari said.

Zeke turned the card over to find a long list of local businesses running down the back of the card.

"Saving the monsters is nice, but what's really great is saving money," Mari said. "I don't know what kind of deal the Chairman's got going on, but you can get a nice discount at practically anywhere in town. I don't know how I'd survive here without it."

"I think Mari would burst into flames if she ever bought coffee at a shop with more than three locations," Dillon said.

"You say that as if you don't pick up bagels twice a week, every week," she said.

"Oh, you, uh, saw me?" Dillon said sheepishly.

"Of course, I'm only there five days a week. Our supply of 'holy water' has to get replenished somehow." She added air quotes for emphasis. "It's not like anyone else would haul this stuff around town."

"Holy water?" Zeke asked.

Mari held up a jug of murky-looking liquid in answer.

"We're here," Dillon said. "Well, this is where he was last seen anyways."

He brought the truck to a stop in a small clearing. This area was rocky and steep, surrounded by thick trees, and on the other side of the clearing, the remains of a campsite, along with trash left by hikers. The already narrow road turned into more of a trail past this point, impassable except on foot. Long shadows stretched across the small clearing as the early evening sun dipped below the ridgeline.

They piled out, and Dillon pulled down the truck gate. "Alright, gear check," he said, before listing off items. Knife, rope, jumbo syringe and microchip capsule, bug spray, sunblock, and finally a pair of water guns, not the cheap kind you'd find at a dollar store, but the big expensive ones that were more like kid-friendly pressure washers.

Mari grabbed the jug of "holy water" and a funnel and went to work. A mix of yeast and something caustic met Zeke's nose as she poured the murky liquid into the toy guns.

"What is that stuff?" he asked.

"Bagel water," Dillon said.

"But, why?" Zeke was confused.

"Who knows?" Mari said. "Might be the chemicals, or just some lucky coincidence, but the water that gets emptied out of bagel boilers doesn't agree with the supernatural. The real question is, who was the first one to think of trying it out? I guess they really were just out here throwing crap at the wall to see what stuck."

Dillon picked up a squirt gun, Mari the second, and Zeke grabbed the pack and their chipping kit. After Dillon triple-checked that the truck was locked, they headed down the path, deeper into the forest.

As they walked, each of them scanned the trees for anything out-of-the-ordinary, like signs of a roaming monster. Zeke wasn't exactly sure what he should be looking for. Tracks in the dirt, shredded trees, or trampled bushes? No, he saw nothing of note, a few birds and curious squirrels. A chill breeze blew down the slope, causing Zeke to shiver. His companions seemed to be as nervous as he was, if not more so.

"How are we going to find Big Bill?" Zeke asked quietly. Something stirred in the forest beside them. They turned, only to see a deer bounding away through the underbrush. "Surely he's not going to be sitting alongside the path."

"He'll probably find us," Dillon said. "Big Bill can be a bit on the territorial side."

"When we find him, we'll distract him," Mari said. "All you have to do is sneak up to him and stick him with the syringe, simple as that."

"Right, simple as that." Zeke furrowed his brow. If it were anywhere near that easy, they wouldn't have been trying so hard to get out of this.

"Let's head that way." Dillon pointed to a rocky outcropping off the path. "The notes the Chairman gave me say Bill's fond of places with rocks to hide behind."

Zeke didn't feel great about leaving the relative safety of the path, but he was trusting in his new teammates' expertise. He followed as they stepped off the path, into the wilderness proper. Strange sounds echoed through the trees as they approached the secluded area. Large branches snapping in succession, a hissing sound carried on the wind, but Zeke couldn't see any source. The birdsong became quieter as they stepped past the boulders to an area where the trees were forced apart by the rocky ground. Soon it faded away entirely, leaving only the sounds of leaves rustling as the wind blew through the branches.

"It's too quiet," Mari said, but Dillon shushed her.

Zeke knew it was never good news when you couldn't hear any animals in the forest. He searched for any sign of movement, trying to keep his steps as silent as possible. He couldn't see anyone, but couldn't shake the feeling of being watched.

A cloud rolled in from behind the mountains, blocking what little light was left from the setting sun. Footsteps thundered around the rocks, and something leapt atop the stone, a huge creature silhouetted against the clouds. Scaly yellow-green skin covered a body twice as tall as a man, with long, muscular legs. Red eyes glared at the trio from beneath a crested head. The creature hissed and leapt ten feet into the air and landed in front of them. It raised its arms, displaying wickedly sharp claws as it hissed at the intruders.

"It's okay, Bill," Dillon said, his voice low. "We're not here to hurt you."

Bill replied with another hiss and stepped forward.

"Oh, he's mad," Mari said. "Don't try to reason with him, just shoot!" She pumped her spray gun, sending a stream of tan water at the creature.

Big Bill leaped aside and then forward. Mari stumbled as he knocked the gun out of her hands. Dillon fired a stream of water at the scaly monster, but he raked his claws along the ground, showering his attacker with dirt and rocks. Dillon rubbed his eyes as Big Bill rushed him, but Zeke pulled Dillon out of the way.

"Run!" Mari yelled.

They scrambled back toward the path, with heavy footsteps close behind. Zeke ran and ran, his heart pounding in his head and his lungs burning. When they reached the truck, he turned to look. The creature had vanished.

"What the hell... was that thing?" Zeke asked between breaths.

"That was Big Bill," Mari said. "I knew I shouldn't have come here. It's not worth doing all this for fifteen percent off at Shenandoah Joe's."

"Yeah, but what is he?"

"Ever heard of the Cumberland Dragon?" Dillon said. "It's some kind of lizard thing they found in Kentucky way back when. As far as we can tell, he migrated up this way after the Civil War. Mostly hangs around in the national park, up near Greene County."

"Might be why their team is called the dragons." Mari peered into the forest, searching for any sign of the beast.

"I wonder if he's movin' around on account of the wildfires?" Dillon asked.

"How would I know?" Mari said.

A rush of air and the tearing of leaves as Big Bill crashed through the canopy heralded his arrival at the campsite. He hissed and advanced on the truck while Mari pulled on the door handle in vain. "Open it up, open it up!" she yelled.

"I'm goin' as quick as I can!" Dillon fumbled with his keys on the other side of the truck. He yanked open the door and hit the unlock switch. Mari scrambled in as Bill's claws raked the side of the truck, screeching like nails on a chalkboard. "Aw, I just painted that door!" Dillon griped.

"Start the truck, Dillon!" Zeke yelled as he scrambled around the clearing, avoiding the monster as he chased the only easy target left. The little truck roared to life. Both Zeke and the creature turned toward it. Zeke ran straight for the vehicle, aiming for the open tailgate, but Bill was faster. The creature got out in front of Zeke, but he juked under his deadly claws. Zeke dove into the mini-truck's bed as Dillon hit the gas.

Despite his painful dive into a metal bed, Zeke breathed a sigh of relief as the little truck rumbled onto the road and left the hissing beast in the dust. The relief was short-lived. Bill, apparently still feeling slighted, gave chase, quickly gaining on the slow-moving vehicle.

"Hurry it up," Zeke said. "This is no time to drive careful."

"I'm goin' as fast as I can," Dillon said. "This thing's only got a top speed of thirty miles."

"What? I thought you were driving that slow to keep the ride smooth."

Mari leaned out the window and checked behind them. "We've gotta shake him!" she shouted. "He'll catch us in no time."

"What do you expect me to do about it?" Dillon held the wheel with a white-knuckled grip.

As the truck swerved around a switchback, the creature held back. When they passed beneath Big Bill, he crouched low, then leapt down the hill. Mari yelled as the dragon landed directly in front of them. Dillon spun the steering, running his wheels into the ditch to avoid the creature. Bill swung at the truck as it passed. Zeke ducked, shielded from the creature's claws by the side of the bed.

"He's tearin' up the paint!" Dillon squeezed the steering wheel like he was wringing out a towel.

Zeke poked his head up to find the raging dragon vomiting forth blood-red fluid at the truck. Dillon jerked the wheel back toward the road, the truck nearly rolling over as the sizzling spray of liquid flew into the ditch beside them. They landed back on the trail with a crash. Zeke could hear everything in the cab that wasn't nailed down, scattering around the interior.

"It spits too?" Zeke looked back in disbelief as the monster resumed its pursuit.

"Yeah, it's poison," Dillon said.

"And it'll stain your clothes forever," Mari added.

"That dang tumbler is rolling around in here," Dillon yelled. "It's gonna get under the pedals."

"We have to do something," Zeke said. "Give me something!"

"What?" Mari yelled back. "Give you what?"

"Anything," Zeke said as Big Bill reached for the rear bumper. "Something I can throw!"

"This?" Mari fished a heavy toolbox out from between the seats.

"No!" Dillon yelled. "Anything but that! Do you know how much those cost?"

"What else is even in here? Can't throw the syringe!" Mari frantically rummaged on the floor.

Big Bill reared back to spit again.

"Come on, hurry!" Zeke yelled and held up his hand. A pink tumbler was passed out the back window, and he chucked it without thinking.

Bill swatted the airborne cup out of the air. In the next instant, the water spirit burst forth from the cracked vessel and attacked. As the two supernatural creatures tussled, Mari cheered and Dillon sighed in relief.

"Bring us back around," Zeke said.

"What? Are you crazy?" Mari shouted. "We're not going back in there."

"We have to finish the job." Zeke steadied himself and got to his feet. "Trust me, I have a plan."

"If you say so," Dillon said, spinning the wheel.

"Drive right past them!" Zeke held his hands up to maintain his balance as he braced himself against the cab of the truck. He hadn't done this in years, and certainly not from the back of a moving vehicle, but he hoped his muscle memory still held. The truck barreled toward the fight, Dillon screaming a battle cry while Mari frantically tried to reason with him.

Big Bill gained the upper hand, throwing the howling spirit to the ground. It writhed and howled as it lost its shape, becoming nothing more than a muddy patch on the ground. Big Bill hissed in triumph as Dillon's truck drove past without Zeke.

Zeke was in the air. To his surprise, his body still remembered the form. Honed by years of practice in after-school martial arts classes, his tournament-winning flying sidekick slammed into the side of the creature's head as he sailed past. Big Bill shook his head, turned toward the truck, hunched down as if to leap, then fell face-first to the ground.

Dillon walked over to the dragon while Mari ran over to check on Zeke.

"I got you." Mari reached down to help Zeke out of the bush he had landed in.

"Ah!" Zeke stumbled as he tried to put weight on his foot. "I think it might be broken."

"Not many people can say they broke their foot on a dragon's face." Dillon carefully stepped over the puddle of red spittle drooling from Big Bill's mouth.

"Nice work, rookie." Mari slapped him on the back. "I was worried we'd have to have to explain to the Chairman why somebody else has to come chip him."

"Speaking of chips," Dillon said as he inspected the dragon's neck with a gizmo attached to his phone. "Bill over here doesn't seem to have one."

"He lost it?" Mari asked.

"Dragons can't just take out their chip," Dillon said as he wiped off the syringe. "Near as I can tell, he never had one before today."

"Does that mean there's two of these things out there?" Zeke asked.

"Somebody else is going to have to get the next one." Mari climbed into the passenger seat. "We did our part."

"I'd reckon Zeke did your part, if you want to get specific," Dillon said. "So why don't you get in the back?"

Mari glared at him, but jumped out anyways.

"Well, it's still early." Dillon grabbed Zeke's hand to help him into the truck. "How about we grab something to eat on the way back into town? Or do you need to go to the hospital first?"

Thinking of the inevitable medical bills made Zeke's head hurt more than his foot. "How about we get some food? I'll go to the doctor if it still hurts tomorrow."

"Sounds like a plan," Mari said. "I'm okay with anything but bagels."

"We're not far from 151," Dillon said. "We'd have our pick of breweries, if we hurry."

The three of them headed down the mountain in search of food and beer. They'd had enough of the supernatural for one day. The wild and weird places of the world would still be there tomorrow.

A Hard Bargain

CATHERINE SIMPSON

THE POPCORN STAND WAS closed.

Of course it was closed, it was ten past seven on a Tuesday evening.

Brynn's smile grew hard as Luke tapped on the finger-smudged window, rattling the hanging bags of kettle corn. "Crazy. I've never seen this place empty like this. Never."

Brynn had never seen it open. "Let's keep going," she said lightly, trying to ignore the bone-deep frustration settling in. "We can eat the stuff we brought."

She'd packed a couple of things—a plastic-wrapped wedge of cheddar, a Ziploc full of broken water crackers, a bunch of grapes that had seen better days—but she hadn't exactly prepared a full spread. Hard to do when you don't know where you're going or what you're going to do there.

"Come on." She pulled her dark hair over her shoulder. "We don't want to miss the sunset."

Luke kicked at the popcorn stand's metal siding. A dull thump. Another, as he kicked again.

"Luke," Brynn said, sharper than she meant to. "Seriously. I don't want to miss it."

Another kick, another thump.

"Not after you put so much thought into this," Brynn added, trying not to sound sarcastic. He had, after all, remembered their anniversary without any prodding. "Come on, babe. Let's go find a good spot."

Luke allowed Brynn to grab his hand, leading him away from the empty popcorn stand.

"Now you're going to be mad at me," he said. Golden hour sunshine lit the hollows of his face, highlighting his cheekbones and petulant expression.

God, that face. He got away with a lot, with that face.

"I won't be," Brynn said. Luke's hand was hot in hers as he twirled her in closer.

"Good," he said. "I'd hate if you were mad at me."

She had to hand it to him—it was hard to stay mad at Luke for long. Some of her earlier frustration melted as he tucked a wayward strand of hair behind her ear.

"I need you, you know that?" he whispered. "One year down, forever to go. Never going to leave you."

Brynn murmured in agreement. He'd sat her down that morning, serious as anything, and she'd been sure that he was breaking up with her.

In that tangible moment before his words left his mouth—before she'd realized he wanted to surprise her for their anniversary—there'd been a glimmer of relief. Maybe it'd be nice, not having to wonder where Luke was all the time. Not having to get up before the crack of dawn to tame her hair and put on a full face, not having to change her everything to suit him.

Of course, breaking up would also mean that she'd wasted an entire year, and the thought of that was borderline untenable. Especially when he was making an effort—all those half-hearted promises of change were finally coming to fruition.

So here they were, on a sunset date.

"Hey, is that Tobin?" Luke broke away from Brynn to jog toward an approaching figure. Brynn, abruptly bereft, tried not to think about all those what-ifs that her brain had so easily concocted that morning.

"Tobin! Over here, man." Luke pulled Tobin into a complicated sort of handshake-hug, complete with hearty back-slapping and ruffling of Tobin's copper-colored hair. He ducked before Tobin could return the favor. Not that he needed it—Luke's hair was perpetually ruffled.

"Brynn," Tobin said genially. "I'd say it's a surprise, finding you here, but I can't. Luke's always got a girl glued to him."

Tobin's words were joking, but his tone wasn't. Brynn forced a laugh. "You here for the sunset?"

He was, obviously. As if there was anything else he'd be doing on the Blue Ridge Parkway just before dusk. Upon hearing his affirmative reply, Brynn's gaze shot to Luke. *Don't do it. Don't ask him.*

Luke asked him, benevolent smile plastered across his face. "Come sit with us, T. We've got crackers and cheese and everything."

Brynn's responding smile was undeniably brittle. So much for promises of change. "Yes. Join us."

A June bug buzzed past them, landing on Tobin's sleeve. He flicked it back into the air. "I'm intruding."

"No such thing." Luke looked meaningfully at Brynn. Her mind-reading skills were better than his; she knew exactly what he wanted.

Brynn unclenched her jaw. "You wouldn't be intruding at all."

"There you go. The lady said it herself." Luke beamed at Brynn—he liked it when she was flexible. Low maintenance, he called it. "No escaping us."

No escaping, indeed. Luke pulled Brynn close, squeezing her tight against his chest. "We'll celebrate later," he whispered. She relaxed against his warm body. "When that stupid popcorn place is actually open," he added.

His armpit smothered Brynn's responding groan. She freed herself, taking a deep breath of air that smelled overwhelmingly of Old Spice and whatever was blooming in the ravine to the side of the road.

"I know a good spot, a mile or so up the parkway," Brynn said, stepping toward the car.

Tobin stopped her. "I've got a better idea."

Of course he did. She refreshed her smile. "Where are you thinking?"

Tobin grinned widely. He had strange teeth. Small, and pointier than you would expect. Distracted by his teeth, she missed his answer and had to ask him to repeat himself.

"That motel? The abandoned one?"

Surely not. Nestled in greenery on the side of the mountain, the motel in question had long since been left to nature's mercy.

Rust trailed down the sides, and spray-painted plywood blocked broken windows. It looked at best, haunted and at worst, criminal.

Yes. That was the motel Tobin was referring to.

"Trust me, it's the best. Around back, there's this veranda... it's hard to explain, but it's perfect. Exactly what we're looking for."

Luke agreed with him almost immediately, gifting Brynn with another expectant look.

"If you say so..."

It was easier to get in than Brynn expected—a matter of a twist and a kick, or something like that. She couldn't really see what Tobin was doing, but whatever it was, they were inside before anyone had time to think twice.

Brynn eyed the leaf and plaster-caked carpeting with trepidation. "Is this safe?"

Tobin grinned and led them through the mildew-scented interior to the veranda he'd mentioned. Less of a veranda and more of a Juliet-style balcony, but he'd been right about one thing: the view was stunning.

"Oh, wow," Brynn said, momentarily taken aback by the ribbon of soft blue mountains stretching across the horizon. "I have to hand it to you, this is actually—"

Brynn stopped speaking. There was nobody around her.

"Luke?" Her voice sounded small. Insubstantial.

Hot wind whispered against her shins, and Brynn pushed aside her unease in favor of irritation. He was always doing this, getting her into things and then ditching her.

She yelped as a pair of hands landed on her hips.

"Sorry, babe. We almost forgot the food."

She forced herself to relax, letting go of the iron railing and leaning back into Luke's solid chest. "I thought you left me behind." She hadn't, but now that the thought had occurred to her... Brynn laughed uncomfortably. "Where's Tobin?"

"Right here!" Tobin emerged onto the balcony, bottle of wine in one hand and a plastic container of grocery store fruit salad in the other.

He caught Brynn eyeing his contribution. "Essential to the evening's festivities," he said, holding the container up like an offering.

He was *so* strange.

Brynn arranged everything on the threadbare towel she'd found in the back of Luke's car, letting her cracker shards crowd Tobin's fruit. He'd gotten the fancy mix, the kind where blackberries and raspberries and slices of kiwi joined the typical honeydew and cantaloupe. Even pomegranate, for God's sake.

"That looks great, babe." Luke handed her a Solo Cup with a healthy pour of wine, and Tobin sat on the edge of the towel.

Brynn sipped slowly, halfway listening to Luke and Tobin's never-ending game of would-you-rathers. The wine was sweeter than the bottom-shelf Barefoot she usually drank, but Brynn wasn't one to fuss about wine. Free booze was free booze.

"Brynn, what about you?" Tobin asked, jolting her from her reverie.

"Would you rather spend the night in that popcorn stand with both of us or spend the night here, all by yourself?" Tobin repeated.

"Uh, both of you, I guess. I wouldn't want to be left alone, and this place is creepy, and... yeah. Here. If I had to choose."

"Interesting," Tobin said in a reflective way that made Brynn wonder how deeply he was reading into her off-the-cuff answer. He snatched the bowl of fruit salad from Luke and offered it to her. "You haven't had any."

"I'm good," she said.

Tobin placed the bowl in front of her. Around them, the sun was still holding out, hanging low in the sky without dropping below the horizon. What time was it, anyways? Brynn felt around for her phone, but she couldn't find it. Must have left it in the car.

She reached for her wine. "I've got one. Would you rather always have to tell the truth or never be able to tell the truth?"

Tobin's smile grew. "A good one. Luke?"

"Always," Luke said decisively. "If people don't like what I have to say, they can suck it."

"Brynn?" Tobin asked. It wasn't just his teeth—his eyes were weird, too. Cat-like.

"Always." Her voice wasn't as certain as Luke's, though.

Thunder boomed in the distance, though the sky was perfectly clear.

"What about you?" Brynn asked.

"A good question," he repeated. "I'd have to go with never."

That struck Brynn as a rather honest answer. She glanced out at the sky, avoiding Tobin's feline eyes. "It feels like the sun should have set by now."

"I'm sure it does," Tobin said. "You've got to try the pomegranate."

Brynn's gaze fell uneasily on Luke, who was shoveling food into his mouth. "I'm not a huge pomegranate fan."

"All the same." Tobin scooped up a smattering of pomegranate seeds using a silver spoon that he'd seemingly produced from thin air.

Luke grabbed the spoon from Tobin and stuck it into his mouth. "Delicious." He caught a rogue bead of juice with his tongue and refilled the spoon. Double-dipping, Brynn's brain supplied.

She relented, though, taking a single seed and placing it on her tongue. An aril, she thought it was called. "Good," she told Tobin and Luke. "Better than I thought."

Both men smiled and fell back into easy conversation, Brynn half-listening again as she monitored the sky for pink and purple.

"What time is it?" she asked. The sky remained stubbornly bright in a way that was starting to feel artificial, like a midnight gas station aisle. Unclean, almost.

Tobin studied her, eyes unblinking. "Does it matter?"

Of course it mattered. "Just, you know." Brynn gestured at the surrounding mountains. "Wondering when the sun's actually going down."

"It'll go down when it goes down," Tobin said, his tone infused with something halfway between amusement and condescension.

Brynn forced a smile. "If you say so."

"I do," Tobin said, eyes locked onto hers. Brynn, the first to break eye contact, reached awkwardly for the fruit in front of her, picking up an unripe blackberry and setting it back down.

Luke stood without warning, nearly knocking the empty wine bottle to the ground. "Gotta pee."

Alone with Tobin on the balcony, Brynn felt even more awkward. Humid air stirred fitfully, curling around their bodies like breath—warm and moist and contained.

"So," Brynn ventured, "where are you from, again?"

Tobin ignored that. "I've got a would-you-rather. A good one."

"Oh?" Brynn wished she'd swallowed her pride and asked Luke to grab her phone from the car. Something wasn't right.

Tobin leaned in. Up close, his hair was wrong, too. Shinier than it should be. Glittery, almost. Glimmering. "Would you rather be with Luke all day, every day, for the rest of your life or never see him again?

Brynn let out a breath that was supposed to be a laugh. "That's kind of a rough would-you-rather."

"Is it? I'll give you another. If you had to pick, who would it be: you or Luke?"

Brynn shook her head, resisting the urge to turn tail and search for her boyfriend in the cluttered expanse of the motel lobby behind them. There was no use asking for clarification with a would-you-rather—she'd learned that lesson long ago.

Her non-response only drew Tobin closer, though. The individual freckles across his nose seemed to blink in the too-light sunlight.

"Answer," he said, not unkindly.

"No thanks."

Tobin's eyes lit up. "What would it take to get you to answer?"

Brynn pursed her lips. What did he mean, what would it take?

"I'll make a deal with you," Tobin said. "You answer my question, and I'll give it to you. Whatever you want."

Brynn scooted backward, her shorts snagging on the rough iron of the balcony as she left the towel. Tobin remained in place.

"You can't give me whatever I want," Brynn said, "and I'm not answering that question. You obviously know what I'd pick."

Brynn was pretty sure that most people would choose themselves over another person, unless the other person was their kid or something. *Maybe* their life partner, if it were a soulmate sort of situation. Regardless, she wasn't going to waste time feeling guilty—she knew who Luke would choose.

"Fine," Tobin said. "Another question." He inched forward, bringing the towel with him.

Brynn wondered how she'd missed the careful way he held his body, making sure not to touch the balcony with his bare skin.

"What do you want?" Tobin asked.

"The sun to go down already," Brynn mumbled.

A slow grin curled onto Tobin's face. "Easy. If you answer my question, that is."

Brynn edged away, trying and failing to be subtle. She craned her head over her shoulder. "Luke? Where are you?"

"He'll be back when it's time. Look at me."

Brynn looked.

"Keep looking," Tobin said.

Brynn kept looking. Had she thought that Tobin's eyes were feline? That wasn't quite right. They were something different now. Reptilian.

Brynn blinked. The sun had gone down, leaving nothing but the faintest wisp of salmon pink in its wake.

She inhaled sharply. "Did you do that?" That wasn't the right question. "How did you do that?"

Tobin smiled. "Now you've got to answer my question. What would you give if I promised to grant you the thing you want most in this world?"

Such strange phrasing. Brynn tried to parse his words apart, looking for a trick within them. "Nothing," she said. "I don't want anything from you."

"Oh, but that isn't true."

This time, when Brynn backed up, she slammed into the iron railing. Cornered. "What's that supposed to mean?"

Tobin tilted his head. His pointed ears matched his teeth. Somehow, they were easier to see under the cover of darkness. "You want Luke to come back, right?"

"What?" Brynn shrieked, her heart threatening to beat its way out of her chest. "You can't—you wouldn't—"

"Of course not," Tobin said, as if she were crazy for even suggesting it. "My point is merely that you *do* want something. Everyone does."

"You're scaring me," Brynn said. What she hoped to accomplish with that statement, she wasn't sure, but it didn't seem to do much.

"You want..." Tobin trailed off, but Brynn didn't fill in the blank. "Something to do with Luke, I think."

"Nothing to do with Luke. Leave Luke alone."

Tobin brightened. "Leave Luke alone? That's your desire?"

"No," Brynn said quickly, imagining all the ways a request to leave Luke alone could be misinterpreted. Then, imagining all the ways her *no* could be misinterpreted. "I mean, maybe. I don't know."

Amused, Tobin took a sip of wine from the bottle that Brynn had thought was empty. He held it by the neck, an idle reveler at a party that had dwindled down to two.

"How about this?" he said. "I'll guess what you want, and if I'm right... well, we can take it from there. Deal?"

"I suppose," Brynn said uneasily. She still wasn't sure what was going on, but Tobin—he wasn't *normal*. That much, she knew.

"Just three, though," she added. "Three guesses."

A fairytale number for a fairytale bargain.

"If you insist. More wine?" He offered Brynn the bottle, and she took it.

Tobin studied her while she drank, the wind whipping around them. Brynn wondered if this was how baby birds felt in their nest, right before they got pushed out.

"Money," he said. "Humans always want money."

Brynn shrugged. The wine rushed through her veins, molten honey, imbuing a sense of confidence she hadn't felt in quite a while. "I mean, I'd take it. Who wouldn't? But no."

"Fine." He thought for another second, eyes wide in the face of the wind.

"Beauty." Tobin's crooked grin skewed apologetic in a deliberate, disingenuous sort of way that Brynn didn't buy, not one bit. "More beauty," he amended.

"Rude," Brynn said. "And no." How shallow did he think she was, that her deepest desire was being *pretty*?

Another moment of silence, Tobin's gaze locked on her. Brynn tried not to squirm as his grin turned knowing.

"Ah," he said softly. "If it isn't money, and it isn't beauty, it's got to be love. How... sweet." He said the word *sweet* like it meant *trite* or *pathetic*. Or *stupid*.

Brynn's eyes moved toward the darkness where Luke had disappeared. She was quick, but Tobin was quicker.

"You know," he said, his voice silky-sweet, "I could make you irresistible. He wouldn't be able to take his eyes off you. His world would revolve around you."

"That's not exactly what I want," she said, because it wasn't.

"Isn't it?"

Brynn made an exasperated noise, forgetting her trepidation for a second. "I don't want it to be a waste. This whole year, I mean."

"I'm not sure that directly translates into a wish," Tobin said. "That being said, I'd hazard a guess that being with someone who finds you irresistible won't feel like wasted time."

Brynn narrowed her eyes, recalling the thoughts running through her head that morning. Weighing the possibility of Luke's utter devotion against, well, anything else. "Maybe I don't want him anymore. Maybe you were wrong, and I don't want love at all."

Tobin's eyebrows raised, nearly disappearing into his hairline. "I'm trying to help you out," he said, voice all innocence. "You were the one who said you didn't want it to be a waste."

He was right about that. Brynn rubbed her temples, cold iron digging into her spine. "I just want him to change. To do all the things he said he would."

Tobin steepled his fingers. "Okay, okay. Less about love, more about... keeping promises. Meaning what he says, saying what he means. I could make that happen."

"How do I know I can trust you?"

"I made the sun set for you, didn't I?"

Brynn conceded that he had.

"There. That's your proof."

Around them, the wind built. There still weren't any clouds, and the moon had disappeared as well. "You make him change his ways, stick to the straight and narrow, and then what?" Brynn asked. "What's in it for you?"

"What's in it for me?" Again, a look of delight cartwheeled across his face. "Why, who says that there needs to be something in it for me? For all you know, I'm an incredibly altruistic wish-granter, out to make the world a better place."

"Me," Brynn said. "I say that. Because you aren't."

"Fair enough. I'll make sure that he keeps his promises, every last one, and... how about this: this time, next year, you bring me someone else to, ah, befriend. Deal?"

Something in the back of her mind, buried within her lizard brain, was sounding an alarm bell. "Exactly one year from now?"

"Yes. Now decide, and quick. Luke's coming back, and I doubt you want him to hear this."

"Fine! Fine."

"Do we have a deal?" Tobin stuck out his hand. His fingers appeared to have several more joints than the typical person. Footsteps sounded behind them.

"Deal."

They shook on it. Brynn expected to feel different, to feel something washing over her or zapping her or pulsing through her body, but she felt nothing.

"In that case, let it be done," Tobin said.

Luke emerged from the darkness, empty-handed and smiling. "Sweet. It's done?"

Brynn blinked at him.

"If you're done with her, I'm ready to go. Beyond ready, actually. It's been a long year."

Tobin let his head loll to the side, and he leaned back on his elbows. Indolent prince once more, lounging on a towel. "It's done."

"Wait, what?" Something was washing over Brynn, more akin to dread than to magic.

"It's time to go," Luke said. "As in, it's time for me to leave."

"I don't..." Brynn looked to Tobin, hoping for a lifeline that didn't come. "You mean us, right? Time for us to leave?"

Luke laughed, a full-bodied cousin to the laugh that Brynn typically heard from him. "Sure. If he lets you. Lord knows what kind of bargain you struck with him."

Brynn's lizard brain piped back up. A year. Their anniversary. It'd been a year since she'd met Luke, one year to the day. She looked from Tobin to Luke, fears growing by the second.

"Luke," she said, her voice low. "What do you mean, what kind of bargain?"

"Babe," Luke said, using the tone of voice he favored whenever Brynn was being particularly unreasonable. "It's a little too late for me to tell you not to make deals with fairies."

Brynn tried to speak, but nothing came out of her mouth.

"Besides, I'm on the way out. I held up my end of the bargain. Didn't I, Tobin?"

"You did," Tobin confirmed. "One human person and one year's commitment in return for a lifetime of irresistibility."

"Are you *kidding?*" Brynn's voice had returned, though the pitch was closer to that of a chihuahua than a human woman. "He's like that because you made him that way? With *magic?*"

Tobin shrugged. "More or less. If he could prove that he was irresistible enough to keep someone for a year, I said I'd make him irresistible forevermore. Let it be done."

Luke held out both hands, waving them in an ambiguous gesture that seemed to be a combination of *see?* and *I'm out.* Without further ado, he turned to leave.

Tried to turn. Before he made any headway, Brynn grabbed his shirt in a clawlike vise, hauling him back toward her. She flung him against the iron railing behind her, letting momentum take the lead. "Absolutely not."

Tobin cawed with delight, hands rising to his cheeks as he watched the proceedings.

"Let me go!" Luke cried.

Brynn's eyes narrowed to slits. "Not a chance."

"What'd she ask for, bro?" Luke sent Tobin a desperate glance. "Super strength?"

"Not exactly," Tobin said.

"Whatever it is, take it away. I don't deserve this, not after everything I did for you."

Brynn, seeing a familiar look of calculation dawning on Tobin's face, spoke before either man could say anything else. "What I want to know," she said, "is why you granted his wish, but you didn't grant mine." She jostled Luke's shirt for emphasis, but her eyes remained on Tobin.

"Ah, but I granted both of your wishes."

"You did not. Clearly, he hasn't changed for the better."

"That's what you asked for?" Luke broke in. "Lame."

"Shut up." Brynn dug the ball of her foot into his toe. "You didn't," she repeated, speaking between gritted teeth.

"I would argue that he's certainly making changes," Tobin said mildly. "But regardless, the deal was for him to keep his promises. No more, no less."

"You heard me say what I wanted, and you said you could do it!"

That slow, horrible, hateful grin spread across Tobin's face. "I said I could, not that I would."

Brynn let out a squeak.

"Technically speaking, he is keeping his promises," Tobin said. "Why do you think he's still standing there?"

Brynn turned to Luke. Without realizing, she'd dropped her grip on his shirt. He still stood there, though, a look of panic on his face. Just that day, he'd promised that he'd never leave her.

Suddenly, things didn't seem so bad. In fact...

A smile, the twin to Tobin's, crossed Brynn's face before she was able to school her features into a mask of neutral gratitude. "On second thought, you did give me what I wanted."

She grabbed a handful of pomegranate seeds from Tobin's forgotten fruit bowl and squeezed them hard, letting the juice run between her fingers and drip down to the iron beneath their feet. She thought about all the promises he'd made her over the past year, all the things he'd said he'd start doing. She could make this work.

She wiped her palm on Luke's shirt, leaving a blood-red smear. "Same time, next year?"

Where Do the Old Things Go?

CAITLIN WOODFORD

WHEN THE DEAD CAME to the house, the first thing to go was the rug. Nana June hadn't embroidered it with her own two hands for it to become a floor protector, shoved under the bookshelf so you could hardly see it. Why did this floor even need protecting? It was practically plastic, expensive enough to mimic wood while hiding the original hand-wrought floorboards, deemed too worn out to be presentable. This man threw his money around—all that money!—on useless things like this floor, just to cram a handmade rug below new furniture with no sentimental value. And the dead could not believe that Madison let it happen. What husband was this, who treated a family house like a paper doll to be played with, folded up, and torn?

I blame those parents of hers, barked Aunt Pat. *There was no need for them to up and move to Charlottesville proper. What do they have against the country?*

Not all their fault. There ain't no money to be made out here. Gotta do what you must, said Uncle Harold.

The dead got the rug out in time, bickering and tugging at the corners to maneuver it through the door. In the morning, Madison and her new husband Steven were perplexed by the missing rug and the scratches on the floor. What kind of thief dragged out a solid wood bookshelf only to steal the rug underneath? Steven's father stayed with them while they finished up the renovations—did he play some kind of bizarre prank before he left? Madison spent the entire morning looking for the rug until Steven convinced her that they could buy a new one. A nicer one, at that.

***

I just don't understand what he does, said Nana June.

He's a teacher. A professor down at the old school, said Papa Ken.

What school?

You know the school—Jefferson's college. University of Virginia.

Can you two give us a hand here? asked Aunt Emma.

The dead returned for their silverware. To keep it somewhere safe, of course. They didn't trust those metal inserts in the drawers. For "organizing," Steven told Madison, unknowingly in the company of the discerning dead. But you can't ever tell with these new things—the silverware had lived fifty years wrapped in the old towel just fine, and the dead wrung their hands over the possibility of rust in these new conditions. Aunt Pat gathered her wedding silverware and tucked it jealously in her apron. The others split the rest, pushing forks into the ripped cavities of sleeves and tucking spoons into socks. Only so many places for the dead to store their things.

But what does he teach? asked Nana June.

Some kinda philosophy, said Papa Ken.

Ohh, I just don't know about all that.

The next morning, Madison and Steven ate their cereal with plastic spoons. Steven would never say that he suspected their less-than-wealthy neighbors, which he would not admit to himself and couldn't prove, anyway. But deep down he was certain it was one of them, with their trucks and their front yards full of machinery and loose garbage. He made Madison drive down the mountain to Charlottesville to pick up a handful of security cameras, and he murmured obscenities against the "hicks" as he hammered nails into the wall.

***

The dead decided they would help their young relative with the decorating. No sense in covering up that gorgeous old fireplace with this plaster, or whatever in God's name it was. That silly husband had gotten rid of the mantle! Where was she meant to set out the picture frames? The dead brought sticks and hammers and they banged away at the wall, softer than a whisper in the moonlight. Soon the maw of the fireplace burst open and a cloud of dust enveloped the dead and set them coughing.

Who the hell was the last to use this thing? Don't you know you gotta clean it sometime? asked Uncle Harold.

Lord, I haven't seen this much smoke since they blasted cannons at me in Normandy, said Uncle Rags.

You been dead too long, Rags, there weren't no cannons in Normandy.

There were too, Harold. You weren't there, so how would you know?

"Must have been a freak gust of wind or something," said Madison. The security footage showed nothing but the whoosh of cinders blasting through the living room. She kicked at the footprints in the dust before Steven saw them. The neighbors disliked them enough as it was without him accusing anyone of theft. She felt that warm thread of shame slither down her gut as she remembered the looks they got driving around in his father's Lexus. The neighbors had all seen the lavish country homes sprinkling out from the city like spilled salt, and they all feared the swell of money-heavy pockets eyeing the hills.

***

The dead debated at length and decided Madison looked just like her great-nana Opal, and now they desperately needed to find a way to convey this information. Can't go around not knowing your own history, they affirmed to each other. What kind of person didn't like to know about their old relatives? Madison had Opal's eyes, that sweet little nose! Spitting image of old Opal, down to the unfortunate stubby fingers—but nothing to be done about that now. Surely someone had taken a photo of Opal back in the day? They tore through the attic, unearthing photo albums and journals from boxes in neat rows. Papers fluttered around the room.

You know, I had some knockout legs back in my day, said Aunt Emma.

Emma, I swear to the Good Lord if I hear about your legs again you'll wish you never had them, said Aunt Pat.

Enough of the bickering, both of you. Everyone's got perfectly fine legs and you ain't gotta use them any longer anyway, said Nana June.

Oh come on, Mama, she's been making fun of me since we were girls! said Aunt Pat.

And how old are you now that you still can't get over it?

"They're taunting us," said Steven. First, they found the photo on the table, then the paper carnage in the attic. Madison didn't bother to ask who he meant by "they." She was looking at the photo, the stunning resemblance between herself and this woman she didn't recognize. "Opal, 1930," it said on the back. She knew the name at least—her great-grandmother. Not for the first time since Steven had proposed the renovation, her childhood memories of the house flared hot like a deep hangnail. At least someone is using it, she told herself. At least it isn't completely falling apart. But still something flickered in her gut as she looked around at the geometric modernist furniture, the chandelier her in-laws and Steven had chosen, the soft green paint—the color of well-worn money. The strange wave of his family's wealth sometimes overwhelmed her.

***

Uncle Rags convinced the other dead to help him get his old tools from the hiding place in the walls. None of them were sure it was necessary, but he insisted they would be useful for Madison. They found a large stone and used it to crash through the snot-green paint, then pulled up the boards. Rags' box was within—stuffed with some standard tools, and others he had obviously fashioned himself, complete with hollowed handles. For stashing some cash, he explained. He pulled out bills: ones and fives and twenties. The dead chattered—could they help Madison escape with this? Would $204 be enough to get her through six months or so? Surely, she didn't want to stay with this man. None of the dead could quite manage the conversion to the current prices. They weren't out buying things, how were they supposed to know?

Rags, are you sure there's no more of this? asked Nana Opal.

Hell if I know. I stashed so much in this old house I couldn't keep track of it all, said Rags.

They settled on the cash from the toolbox, plus one of Nana Opal's rings that had fallen in the kitchen sink when she was washing dishes—the old girl was pleased to find that she could finally unstick it from down in the drain, now that they were dead. They cracked open the pipe like a fresh oyster, and out tumbled the diamond-flanked pearl set in a silver band.

That'll get her out to California or some other place sunny for sure, said Nana Opal.

Madison woke to find a wad of cash and a ring stuffed in her pillowcase. The dead groaned when she put it on.

No, Madison, you're supposed to sell it! they cried.

***

When the dead decided to tidy up and take down a few of Steven's questionable art choices, the plastic floorboards rattled with his rage.

There's no need for him to scream like that, said Papa Ken. *I was coming around to the idea of the old boy sticking around, but this is just ugly.*

He's gonna wake up the whole damned mountain with that throat, said Aunt Pat.

Against Madison's protests, Steven called the police.

"Really fixed the place up, haven't you?" they said when they arrived, scratching their bellies. They watched the security camera tape of the paintings popping off the wall, but they weren't sure what Steven expected them to do. It looked like doctored footage, it was inexplicable otherwise. "Are you sure you haven't

just misplaced the paintings?" they asked. While they encour-
aged Steven to file a report, Madison saw a few neighbors peering through curtains, others slowing down as they drove past the
house to stare at the cotton-candy police lights splattering the
siding. "Those paintings were commissioned," groaned Steven.
"I'll have to see if my abstractionist can squeeze in a rush job."

***

The dead talked among themselves and decided they had
not done enough for Madison. The situation was untenable.
Who would help her if not her relatives? Clean slate, they
agreed—never even had a chance to live in the house as it
once was. It would be a grand surprise! They got to work as
soon as the couple fell asleep. They pulled out their whole
collection—the rug, all the old cabinets, the photos that had
once hung on the wall, the little oak table. They could feel
the bones of the old house murmuring beneath their feet, and
they chased the vibrations. Layer by layer, they peeled back the
years. Paint seared off the wall, the floor splintered and disin-
tegrated; curtains withered, shadows lurched, a spark sputtered
into life in the fireplace. The dead poured their love into every
inch of the house and it buckled under the weight.

Madison woke early. Outside, the mountain range stretched
out in both directions, the two tallest peaks shifted in the quickly rising dawn, curling up like twin blue cats against the grainy
expanse of sky. She walked down the stairs, turned toward the
kitchen to make some coffee.

Sitting at the old table was her red-cheeked grandmother,
furiously crocheting a scarf. Uncle Harold and Uncle Rags were
laughing, sprawled across the worn couch as Rags read from the
newspaper. At the stove, Aunt Pat poked at some eggs in a pan,
sloshed the gurgling coffee pot. The rest milled about, chatting
and bickering. The first flickers of early morning light filtered
through the warped-glass windows, softening the corners of the
cabinets and shining across their faces, all of them a little blurry
in the voice-clattered room. Madison's own hands and feet felt
blurred, too, but she didn't have long to think on it.

"Good morning, sweetheart," someone said to her, and the dead began to turn their heads.

Biodynamic Aeroconducive Gels

TIM FREER

THE MAN ATE HIS bagel like a lovesick fetishist.

His lips pursed in ecstasy as, with slight caresses, his right hand guided the swollen ring of bread around his upheld left forefinger. Raised high, jabbing the air like an assertion—an exclamation of obscene, unabashed absurdity. Hunched over the back table, he examined the glossy topography through wide-framed sunglasses, seeking the ideal real estate, the fallow turf in which to plant his next disgusting bite.

Who orders a peanut butter and lox bagel?

"What the hell is wrong with that guy?" a low, deep voice muttered into Minerva's right ear.

Minerva jerked her head to the side. Her coworker, Alex, craned forward, leaning against the broom with his hands clasping the handle, pimply chin perched on his knuckles, eyebrows arching up into his waves of sandy blond hair. He seemed equally grateful to have a counter and three rows of tables separating them from the odd man.

"Not so loud!" Minerva hissed. "I don't know what his deal is, but he's only taken three bites in ten minutes. And we're closing soon."

"Are you going to kick him out?"

"Me?"

Alex's steel-gray eyes lazily met Minerva's. Already distancing himself from a potential confrontation, despite his basketball player's height and build.

Minerva, with her squat stature, cherubic face, and bouncy raven-colored curls, was unlikely to scare off the timidest teddy bear salesman.

It was just her luck that the shift manager, Dimitri, had been summoned by the missus an hour ago to deal with a clogged bathroom drain. *Go on home,* Minerva assured Dimitri. *No one is here tonight, anyway.* Of course, the only customer to appear since had to be a freakin' nut job.

"God, I don't know," Minerva said, to ward off Alex's placid stare. "I'd rather not have my eyes scooped out with a plastic spoon."

Alex snickered, shrugged his broad shoulders. "I'm sure he's harmless."

"Why don't you go take care of him, then?"

Alex rocked his chin back and forth on the broom handle, as if in thought. "I dunno. You've worked here longer than I have. You're, like, a manager, almost."

"In that case"—Minerva tried to stand a little taller—"I order you to go take care of him."

In the distance, the pervert launched his next attack, face lunging into the glutinous sinew with savage gusto. Unable to use his other hand to stabilize the bite, he ripped the flesh away, like a stray dog at an unattended shawarma stand. The bruised bagel barely held together in the wake of this devastation.

Alex scrunched up his face. "I said—almost like a manager."

"Damn you," Minerva said. "You good-for-nothing college kids. Always passing the buck. No initiative."

Alex shrugged again, lolling his head to the side to face the window. Preston Avenue blushed a burnt orange, tinged by the modest glimmer of scattered streetlamps. Occasionally, a black hulk of oblong metal with searing headlights hurtled past.

"It's getting dark," he observed.

"No kidding!"

"Do you think we should, like, call the cops?"

"And tell them what?" Minerva frowned. "That there's a guy here who eats his bagel weird?"

"Oh, man. He looked at us. I think he wants something."

The man, with rather quaint properness, dabbed the last bits of peanut butter and salmon from his lips and scooted out from his booth seat. Leaving the debris from his bagel to languish amid a graveyard of used napkins, he marched toward the cash register, the bottoms of his blue herringbone trousers tucked into polished, clunking army boots. His overlarge gray blazer fanned out behind him, exposing a black Led Zeppelin T-shirt depicting a winged, naked man.

Minerva stood in a wide stance, knees slightly bent, a ready position. Alex uncurled his spine, climbing to his full height, gray eyes peering down from his canopy of hair. Then he hastened past the prep counters, sauntering back toward the kitchen as quickly as the sticky tiles would allow, scuffing the floor along his route perfunctorily with the broom.

"Coward," Minerva muttered at his back.

A pair of hands slapped the counter, and Minerva found herself face to face with the man, now standing at the register with his sunglasses perched on his forehead. A twinkle of genuine cleverness lurked Santa-like in his eyes, so rich a blue they seemed almost purple. He scoured the overhead menu, bouncing on his heels, stupid smirk wrinkling his waxy skin. Perhaps in his fifties, beard and mustache mottled black and gray. More hermitic professor than wandering wastrel.

"Can I help you?" Minerva made sure to edge her question with impatience.

The man blinked several times rapidly, seeming not to understand.

"Yase," he said at last in a buggy drawl. **"I re-quoh-ire more flae-vohrs."**

Minerva could not identify his vaguely European lilt. Was he Russian or Estonian or something?

"We're closing soon," she said, flattening her voice. "Fifteen minutes."

The man's eyes widened. **"Five-ten men-eats?"** he said, as if this arrangement of words helped to clarify anything.

"We are closing," Minerva said slowly, pointing her finger at the flat-faced clock on the wall. "Eight o'clock."

"Ohhhh, clock," said the man with a wink. **"Will eat close. More flae-vohrs quick. Please po-ta-eyto salad."**

It took Minerva a couple of breaths to conjure words. Best not to ask too many questions with this kind of freak.

"Uhhmm. Kay." She jabbed the appropriate buttons on the register. "That'll be $2.03."

The man wriggled his bristly wrist from his sleeve, exposing a small tattoo—a crescent moon interlocked with a five-pointed star.

"Cash or card?" By sheer force of will, Minerva prevented her eyes from rolling. The man tried this same stunt when ordering his first bagel.

"Ah." He smiled through pursed lips, lending his face a mischievous tint. **"Soary, soary. I have soar-prise you donoat scan."**

He rummaged around in his trouser pockets and withdrew a smooth brown leather container which, to Minerva, seemed the right size to house his sunglasses, or perhaps an unnecessarily fancy pen. Instead, it popped open to reveal a frayed stack of bills and a separate compartment for coins.

The man snatched a wad of paper and held it close to his face, scrutinizing the markings on each slice of currency while muttering to himself. After selecting a few, seemingly at random, he slapped them onto the counter—a pristine $5 bill, a desiccated €20 note, and a purple-tinged slip depicting a peacock inscribed in a language Minerva didn't recognize.

The man rustled through his coin collection, cobbling together a pile on the countertop. Quarters, pennies, and nickels were equally interspersed with foreign currency of astounding variety, size, and color—from metallic green to ruby red to shimmery opal.

Once finished, he stepped back, lower lip protruding, and gestured open-palmed toward the offering. As if to say he'd provided all the ingredients to make an especially complicated meal.

Minerva's wits flew back to her. She plucked the five and a nickel from the collage and jammed them in the register, thrusting the appropriate change into the man's outstretched hand.

"Alex!" she cried.

Her hesitant coworker's head, bent upward at the Adam's apple, emerged through the gap between the prep counter and the overhead menu.

"Minerva, what. I'm busy, like, cleaning."

"Don't sass me," Minerva spat. "Get this guy some potato salad from the fridge, now."

Alex's neck retracted from view like a turtle in slow motion. Minerva fake-smiled across the counter but only held the expression for a moment, the corners of her mouth not structurally sound enough to maintain their upward arch.

"Here you go, sir." Alex shuffled up front and slid the plastic potato salad cup across the counter. His eyes flickered upward. "Nice shades, by the way."

The man chuckled. **"It hay-elps with radi-ah-tion."**

"Radiation?" Alex raised an eyebrow, catching Minerva's eye but seemingly oblivious to her frantic finger-to-lips gesture, which she'd thought was universally understood to mean '*shut the hell up.*'

"Yase." The man nodded. **"You know. Hay-pens. When blow up meteors."** His hands mimicked an explosion, and he made a whooshing noise with his mouth.

"Uhh, meteors?" Alex said. "Why would you need to do that?"

Was that genuine curiosity in his voice?

"You know. For gov-air-ment. I—"

"My apologies, sir," Minerva cut in. "You'll have to excuse my coworker and me for just a moment. Alex, may I speak with you in the back, please?"

She yanked her colleague's collar, dragging him behind the bagel boiling kettle.

"Why exactly are you encouraging this guy?" she said.

Alex shrugged, tugging his shirt collar back into place. "It seems like he needs help."

"Um, yeah! He needs to be institutionalized."

"I dunno, Minerva," Alex said. "He's clearly not from around here, but he doesn't seem dangerous. Just confused. Haven't you heard that it's good for Alzheimer's patients if you, like, play along with their delusions or whatever?"

From the counter they heard the sound of delighted, manic, and slightly off-key humming.

"Oh my god, what is he doing now?" Minerva moaned, peeking around the side of the bagel kettle.

The man, holding the potato salad cup aloft like a holy relic, swooped to the opposite end of the counter, where customers picked up condiments and napkins. Eager to sample it all, he plucked several packets of ketchup and mayonnaise and mustard and grape jelly and coffee creamer.

"Sir," Minerva warned, "if you would wait a second—"

The man, still humming, popped off the cap of his potato salad and crushed the condiment packets into the plastic tub with one clench of his fist. Before Minerva could even cry out, he dug his hands into the lumpy depths. He stirred for several seconds, squinting in concentration, apparently seeking morsels of a certain size or texture. At last, he extracted a palmful of dripping potatoes.

"Sir," Minerva pleaded, aghast. "Don't—"

The man slapped the glob of mixed paste into his mouth, multicolored goop splattering his cheeks and running down his chin. He closed his eyes as if seeking nirvana, loudly sucking the starch from the potatoes, jaw popping from the effort. His arms fell to his sides, and he lifted his nose skyward as he swallowed. Nostrils gaping, he took two deep, wheezy breaths.

Then his eyes flashed open, and he clicked his tongue.

"Still not ee-nowf," he called to Minerva and Alex, peering over the prep counter as he cleared the carnage from his face with additional napkins. **"More flae-vohrs."**

"Why do you need more flavors?" Alex asked.

"Alex, stop it!" Minerva breathed through her teeth.

"I do noat know, exact." The man scratched the back of his head like a dog at a flea. **"With-oat more gel, I can-noat mind-meld with ship. I can-noat leave."**

"Gel?" Alex squinted. "What kind of gel are you talking about?"

"Yase, you know," the man said, a bit of wind returning to his sails. He pointed up at the *Bodo's Bagels* logo on the menu display. **"You sell here. BODO's B. A. GELS. Is make your own?"**

"Just one moment, sir," Minerva chirped to the front. She hissed into Alex's ear, "That's it, I'm calling the cops. Now. You keep the freak distracted."

"Minerva, I think you're overreacting."

"Alex, are you even hearing yourself?" Minerva said. "The man just made barf paste and smeared it across his face!"

"Do you want him to leave or not?"

"God." Minerva dragged a hand down her face. "I want to finish cleaning and go home and forget this ever happened."

"I re-quoh-ire more flae-vohrs," the man's voice echoed toward them.

"I'll take care of it." Alex nodded stoically.

Minerva tried to grab his arm as he marched to the front. "Alex, no, damn it—"

"What flavors do you require, sir?"

"This is bullshit," Minerva grumbled, kicking open the door to Bodo's small back patio, extracting her phone from her pocket. She dialed the infamous three digits with trembling hands and planted herself in a wobbly plastic chair.

Two minutes later, she burst inside, storming up to the counter to find that Alex and the crazy man had gotten side-tracked from the whole "eat-and-leave-in-ten-minutes" thread, instead falling into a deeper exploration of the merry delusions of insanity.

On a tray between them, they had constructed a veritable tower—a cinnamon raisin bagel stacked with a scrambled egg, breaded eggplant, shrimp salad, tomato, sour pickles, and tabouli.

"Are you guys five?" Minerva resisted the temptation to jar the tray, upending their game of edible Jenga. "Building gross bagel castles like kids at the beach? What is this?"

"I'm still fuzzy on the specifics." Alex scratched his temple. "But the gist is, Uurb here inhaled some toxic gas from a comet. He, like, lost his mind-meld."

"Mind-meld?" Minerva growled.

"Yase." The man nodded. **"I steel taste the irony."**

"It's sad," Alex said. "He, like, needs our help finding the right flavors, or else he can't connect with his ship."

Better hurry, Minerva thought with a tingle of dark satisfaction. "What did you say his name was? Herb?"

"No, Uu-rb," Alex clarified.

"Great, thanks."

"I soary, rude." The man extended a still-greasy hand. **"I am Uurbitrapholesio Bolearistasis. Uurb for sho-art."**

Minerva kept her arms crossed but yielded an abbreviated salute. "Minerva."

"Okay Uurb, ready?" Alex asked.

Uurb gave a thumbs up, clamped his hands around the Frankenstein bagel, then stuffed his face with it. Spurred by Minerva's ultimatum, he devoured it with bone-chilling haste. A thirty-second David Lynchian horror film of gnashing teeth and fleshy flotsam and oozing orifices—a truly gruesome sight to behold.

After this latest feeding frenzy, Uurb conducted the same ritual as before, swallowing his last disgusting swallow, closing his eyes, and inhaling deeply of the temperature-controlled air—once, twice. Re-grounding himself in the real world, he shook his head vehemently, bits of tabouli bouncing from his cheeks.

"No mind-meld," he said after a swallow. **"I can-noat understand what wrong."**

"I'm getting dizzy from all the possibilities," Minerva grunted.

"Don't listen to her, Uurb," said Alex. "We'll get you out of here."

"At least the police will," said Minerva.

"Po-leez?" Uurb blinked, not understanding.

"Minerva," Alex groaned, rolling his eyes. "Did you, like, actually call the cops?"

"Like, yes!" Minerva spat, unable to keep the acid from her tone. "They should be here any minute to put a stop to this madness. Thank God. I need to get up early tomorrow."

"But what if he's not lying?" Alex looked into Minerva's eyes with puppy-like naivete. "If he can't do his job—if he can't stop meteors from striking the Earth, then—"

"Cut the crap, Alex," Minerva said. "I haven't heard about any meteors hurtling toward Earth lately, have you?"

"Well, why do you think that is?" Alex blinked.

"I can't even!" Minerva threw her hands into the air.

Uurb grabbed a newspaper folded up on the counter and scrutinized it. Face twisting into even greater confusion, he pointed to the date in alarm. **"Meese-print?"**

Minerva rolled her eyes. "That's from yesterday. It's October 15, 2024."

"Not Twenty-Four Oh-Two?" The man clapped a hand to his forehead. **"Oh, how fool am I! Soary, such many soary. How you say, I have butter on the finch-hairs. BA Gel not exist in toa-day. Flae-vohrs far less poh-tent in your time."**

"Are you actually trying to say you traveled here from the future?" Minerva said.

The man frowned. **"Yase. Noa. Between different time cur-tains. Or else meteor hit Earth and why-pa out."**

"So what happened with the dinosaurs, then?" Minerva arched an eyebrow. "I guess you really dropped the ball there."

Uurb's eyes bulged. **"I did woander why—not see more dino-sowers."**

"No way!" Alex gasped.

"A likely story." Minerva drummed her forearms with her fingertips.

"I have such soary," Uurb rushed to assure her. **"Will correct err-aur. Somehour. I have a loat on my play-et to catch up."**

"Come on, Minerva," Alex implored. "The police will be here before long. We're Uurb's only chance."

"Oh my god, fine!" Minerva bellowed. "I'll chip in for one last attempt to get this man the hell out of here. If he's completely insane, which seems the most likely scenario, the boys in blue will take care of the rest."

"That's the spirit, Minerva!" Alex smiled.

"Shut up." Minerva looked Uurb dead in the eye. "Okay, freak. You need the most potent flavor possible, and we haven't finagled that for you yet. What else can we try?"

After a moment of blank glances, each of the three searching the walls for inspiration, Minerva met Alex's eye. The two said at the same time: "Horseradish."

Within minutes, Alex and Minerva had scoured the refrigerator shelves and the back pantry, gathering all the ingredients they could muster. Minerva slathered an entire bottle of horseradish on both halves of an everything bagel, so much that the paste was a half-inch thick. Layer by layer, they built the bagel's interior with liverwurst, roast beef, sausage, maple-glazed ham, tofu, hummus, Neufchatel cream cheese, bean sprouts, jalapenos, bacon bits,

spinach, and red onions. They crowned their multifarious creation with a literal cherry on top.

"God, that looks disgusting," Minerva said, beholding the mon-
strosity with a curled lip.

"It's perfect," gasped Alex. "Uurb, let's get you home."

Uurb flashed a solemn thumbs-up, flexing his fingers in antic-
ipation.

"Three—two—one—EAT!" Minerva and Alex chanted.

On cue, Uurb smashed the bagel halves together and brought
the leviathan to his lips, vacuuming it up from the inside out,
shredding its innards as shamelessly and barbarically as every
course that came before.

In spite of herself, Minerva half-expected Uurb to disappear,
or at least keel over from a heart attack. But when it was all over,
he still stood at the counter, blinking in glaze-eyed bliss.

"Almost they-err—I feel deep, on ton-guay," he gurgled as
if half-asleep.

A wail of police sirens yipped in the distance like a pack of
coyotes.

"Quick!" Minerva sprinted to the soda fountain and filled an
extra-large foam cup with splashes of Sprite, Coke, coffee, Pibb
Xtra, root beer, and orange juice. She thrust it into Uurb's hands.
The man brought the chalice two-handed to his lips and chugged
it down like a parched man at an oasis.

"Yase," Uurb cried out, chest lifting, eyes crossing. **"YASE!"**

The clock on the wall read 7:59, and the little red ticker was
ascending fast toward the stroke of eight. Flashing blue lights
blasted through the bagel shop's windows as a trio of police cars
jumped the curb into Bodo's parking lot, screeching to a stop.

"The ship calls at me," Uurb said. **"I re-tourn now. Many a
thanks for you."**

He crossed his arms and gave a quick salute, replicating Minerva's earlier gesture. Then he sprinted for the door.

"Hey, wait," Minerva screamed. "You have to pay for all this
food!"

"Hold on!" called Alex. "Do you, like, have an Insta account?"

Minerva and Alex chased Uurb toward the entrance as he
leaped through the door shoulder-first like an ornery cornerback,
barreling out blind into the night. But as they followed him out

into the crisp autumn air, there was no Uurb in sight—only a disheveled policeman shuffling his butt cheeks one at a time out of his sleek blue and white vehicle, tucking in his uniform.

"Oh my god, look." Minerva gasped and pointed.

High in the night sky, a sleek, silver, bagel-shaped object streaked toward the moon.

The Book Came Back

GENEVIEVE LYONS

MARIN DIDN'T THINK THE apartment was haunted when she moved in on a sweaty October day, summer's last gasp. (Or maybe second-to-last). She didn't believe in ghosts, and besides, the house had been built in 1962. Hardly old enough to harbor ghosts. The stove was avocado green, and the realtor had assured her that this was a good thing. Well, not the color specifically, but the fact that it was green, that it had been there so long. They don't make 'em like they used to.

Marin's new job didn't start for a few more days, and the cable guy hadn't been out yet to connect the Wi-Fi, so she needed to find a way to amuse herself. She texted Josh, but when he was out at sea, he wouldn't respond for ages. She already picked up groceries, oat milk and tofu and kale, at her doctor's recommendation, instead of the butter and eggs and pasta that her tastebuds suggested. But she heard the local farmers' markets (both of them! In a town this size!) were good and a place to meet people. And she sensed she might want to meet some people for the letdown she was certain Josh was going to deposit on her. So, she put on her Vans, grabbed an empty canvas tote bag, and walked a mile over several types of brick, to one of the downtown markets, a temporary tent village outside a mural-ed warehouse. Even the pavement was painted.

On the way, she passed bookstores, used and new. Outside the most enticing hung a worn painted sign that read *Daedalus Books.* The sign promised it opened at eleven. By the looks of the smudgy windows and peeling paint, it wouldn't open until the owner felt like opening.

At eleven oh seven, tote bag full of locally made tempeh and decorative gourds, Marin pushed the bookstore door and it creaked open. She glanced around for the proprietor, conditioned as she was after years of living in Paris to greet everyone with a "bonjour" and say goodbye with a "bonsoir." But there was no one in sight except a tuxedo cat.

Marin was visited with the thought, the certainty, that the cat's name was Thomas.

"Bonjour, Thomas," she murmured before her frontal lobe could activate to intervene.

The bookstore was narrow and dusty and disorganized. And empty. But it smelled comfortingly of stale coffee and paper and glue. Thomas followed her as she browsed. Judging her, no doubt. Giving her a look of disdain as she regarded the single bookcase that contained colorful paperbacks, probably the only books in the store published since 1990. Thomas swished his tail as he padded past on socked paws, glancing back at her, seeming to gesture: come this way. To the horror section.

Marin bought one book, an old gothic novel with a worn black canvas cover. A post-it inside the cover indicated, presumably, the price. The author's name rang a bell, and she wanted something that would hold her attention while she waited. Waited for the cable guy, her job to start, her first paycheck to be deposited. For her yachtie boyfriend to respond to her texts or break up. She paid by leaving a ten-dollar bill next to the cash register.

A cool breeze from the north ruffled the leaves of the white oak trees lining Locust Avenue. Fall arrived at that exact moment, it seemed. An acorn dropped, tapping Marin on the shoulder, star-tling her. She turned and noticed Thomas padding along several steps behind. She wondered if she should take him back to the store, but when he followed her into her apartment, she went to the cupboard and gave him a bowl of water. "Sorry, you won't like my oat milk."

She left the door ajar so Thomas could leave at his leisure.

But he didn't.

She settled in her secondhand loveseat and opened her book.

***

The cable guy came, but none of his tools worked, the cords didn't match, something was wrong with the electrical current. "I'll be back tomorrow," he said, "with a different modem. Sorry, ma'am."

After he left, the air smelled of something singed. The autumn chill in the air seeped inside and pooled like cold spots in a lake. Marin tried to make tea, but the gas stove kept going out. Shapes of light flashed in the mirror above the fireplace. Reflections of headlights, perhaps.

At midnight, Marin awoke to a creak and a thump. She propped herself up on her elbows, shaking sleep off her brain like cobwebs. Two yellow-green eyes flashed on the thrifted dresser across from her bed.

Thomas.

She turned on the bedside lamp, thinking *this is why Josh doesn't like cats*. The creature glared at her as if it had read her mind and scampered away.

The next morning, there was no sign of Thomas. She started the coffee maker and sat at her small kitchen table, reading, while she waited. The coffee pot sputtered and gasped and coffee ran down the sides of the carafe onto the floor.

"Damn it!" Marin snatched a dishtowel to clean up the mess.

Thomas stalked into the room and jumped on the table. Brazen as a peacock.

"Thomas!" she said, shocked, trying not to think of where his paws had been.

He stared at her for a long moment before batting her book off the table with one paw. Marin glared back at the cat as she reached to retrieve the book. She placed it on the table, cover closed, and turned to the coffee pot.

The stream of coffee diverted itself into the carafe.

"Stupid cheap coffee maker," Marin muttered. Josh took the French press when they moved out, though she pointed out the yachts he'd be working on would have top-of-the-line espresso machines. It made less sense, he said, for her to fly across the ocean with it.

Thomas gave a disdainful sigh that sounded exactly like he was disagreeing with her. He gazed at Marin's book.

"You don't like the book?" Marin asked. Feeling ridiculous for talking to the animal.

Thomas, of course, said nothing.

"Let's get rid of it, then."

It's not that she believed the book was cursed, it was more that she didn't have anything better to do with her time (yet) and besides, the plot hadn't sucked her in the way she hoped.

Thomas followed her to the bookstore, which pleased Marin. Her lease forbade pets, and she didn't want to break the rules. Not that he was a pet.

"Sorry, no returns," the proprietor said without making eye contact. He wore a blue apron over a white button down, yellowed with age. His horn-rimmed glasses appeared to have been designed and manufactured in the same era as Marin's avocado appliances.

"What do you mean?" she asked. "It's a used bookstore." He could sell the same book over and over.

He pointed to the handwritten sign, an index card with black sharpie faded to purple, edges curled with age, taped to the cluttered oak desk that served as the checkstand.

"Okay, then. I'll keep it. And you may have your cat back." Thomas padded toward the back of the store, aiming for a sunbeam swimming with dust particles. He gave a delicate sneeze and settled onto a braided rug.

"My cat?"

Marin looked up at the proprietor's face and raised an eyebrow. He realized Thomas' absence, right? Saw Thomas follow her back in? So it was true, this town was filled with characters. Already annoyed by the no-returns policy and in no mood to be kidded with or teased, she gave him a close-lipped smile, took her book, and stepped out the door.

The historic neighborhoods were dotted with free libraries, into which passersby could leave or take a book. Marin would simply trade one for another. After a few blocks, she found a red-painted library in front of a matching red-painted farmhouse with a gracious porch. She reached to unlatch the hook-and-eye. But it was fused, or rusted, or stuck. People reported that the mid-Atlantic region was hard on material objects, with the constantly fluctuating temperatures and humidity. Terrible, also, for allergies. In the final round of her interview, when it was clear she stood a real chance of getting the job, Marin asked what it was like to live in central Virginia. She expected to hear praise for the mountains, the southern small-town charm. But the curator and lead archivist exchanged glances, and the archivist said, "Virginia is the first place I've lived where it feels like nature might win."

Marin pressed upward on the hook-and-eye with her thumb, stopping before it punctured her skin.

Well, she'd find another little free library. Many tiny book outposts sat like literary oases among the anti-hate, pro-science yard signs and pollinator gardens. A half-mile later, she located one whose latch was a wooden bar on a rotating screw. But the door was so warped that it stuck shut. (Thanks, humidity). She tried and tried to pry it open.

"Ow!" A sliver wedged itself under her nail. Blood outlined the nail bed of her middle finger. She brought the fingertip to her mouth and removed the sliver by pinching it between her teeth. This wouldn't do—she'd need to wear gloves all week at work. Archivists were fussy about their hands, taking care of their skin and nails, the better to manipulate delicate old pages without damaging them. She didn't even like to wear lotion or skincare products.

She trudged toward home, holding the book under one arm, massaging her wound, a tingle in her hands and wrists signaling a flare-up of carpal tunnel.

A bus lumbered by, decorated to look like an old-fashioned trolley. On the next block, a chime jangled as the doors opened to emit a group of pedestrians. Marin approached the bus stop and stepped into the shelter, ostensibly to inspect the route map.

After the pedestrians crossed Water Street and strolled out of sight, no doubt heading for the sidewalk dining and art galleries of the pedestrian mall, Marin casually let the book slide out of her grip, down the side of her body and onto the bench in the bus shelter.

There. Done.

Safely home in her apartment, Marin set herself to the task of unpacking her sparse possessions. Besides, she needed something to read. She unwove the flaps of a box of books and slid them into one of the built-in cases in the living room, on the side of the boarded-up fireplace. Several more boxes followed. An archivist's one indulgence was old books. She arranged them like friends on the shelves while the cable guy tried again—and this time, succeeded.

At last Marin went to the kitchen to reheat leftovers from last night's tofu peanut stir fry. Outside, a gentle mist fell. She tried to eat mindfully, savoring what flavor could be coaxed out of the ingredients without the assistance of animal fat, imagining the polyphenols and vitamins and antioxidants calming the inflammation in her body. Sigh. She would've loved a creamy tikka masala, lush with ghee.

Tap-tap-tap. A knock at the door. Marin peered through the peephole, thinking maybe the cable guy forgot something. But a nondescript woman in jeans and a faded jacket stood a few feet from the door, eyes cast down. Marin could never have guessed her age; it could be between twenty-five and fifty. Marin eased the door open, an expectant look on her face.

"You dropped this at the bus stop." The woman thrust the book into Marin's hands. "I thought you'd want it back."

"I–" before Marin could finish, the woman turned and disappeared down the steps into the rising tide of twilight.

Goosebumps prickled down Marin's spine and through her arms to her fingertips. The book felt warm, almost electric. Persistent. Thoughts flashed through her mind like a slideshow. Someone at the bus stop watching her, undetected. Following her a half-mile home. Hours later. These facts alone felt vaguely creepy, before considering the fact of the book.

She closed the door and locked the deadbolt, gleaning comfort from the sturdy thunk of brass and steel sliding into its home. She leaned against the heavy oak, pressed a palm to her face and breathed deeply.

At this point, it was almost a curiosity. Could she rid herself of the book? Marin was one to persist. She slipped her feet into sneakers and snatched her keys. Out the door she went. The woman was nowhere in sight. Marin walked purposefully downtown to the public library, a large brick rectangle, Jeffersonian in architecture, white pillars and marble signaling its institution-ness. Around the side was the after-hours book slot.

Marin's fingers wrapped around the cool metal handle, half-wondering if the book deposit door would stick closed, or maybe it would be so full that her book wouldn't fit. But no: the offending book slid down the chute like a child on a water slide at Six Flags on summer solstice.

There. Done.

She felt lighter, unburdened. She was a problem-solver. The misty rain seemed to lift as she walked home.

***

Later, a midnight noise in the living room drew her out of sleep. It sounded like a clatter, and then the patter of raindrops. Or maybe cat paws? A shard of icy panic sliced through her chest as she imagined water slipping through the open window, damaging her books. She scrambled out of bed and clicked on the lamp.

Above the fireplace, something flashed in the mirror, sparking a cascade of anxious thoughts. No car on the road outside, no cat lurking around. She was alone. Alone as a person could be.

Marin had been around enough old objects to know that there was sometimes an... energy field, a vibe. Things happened.

Lightning crackled through the dark sky. A gust of wind laced with drops of cool rain blasted the window open on its side hinges. She crossed the room and battled it closed, pounded the frame into its home, wood swollen with humidity. She looked for something heavy, to hold it in place.

Then she saw it.

The book.

The book was back. On her shelf, between *The Canterbury Tales* and *Rebecca*.

Marin snatched it and flipped it open to make sure. Her own bookmark—the cable guy's business card—was still in place on the page where she'd given up.

A prickle of fear shot down her spine. Marin made three attempts to get rid of the book already, more if you counted the free libraries whose doors wouldn't admit it. But the book came back. Definitely bad juju. In the past she might've tried to dig into its history, figure out its story. But not tonight.

Marin stepped into yesterday's jeans, slid her feet into her hiking boots. She pulled on a hoodie and grabbed her keys and the book. Unsure where she was going.

Two hours later she returned, in the middle of the night, dripping wet and exhausted but satisfied. She'd dropped the book off a bridge, into the Rivanna. The bridge was outside an old textile factory on the edge of town that had been converted to a brewery, restaurant, and event space. Abandoned, on a rainy night after midnight. No one saw her. The river thrummed with rapids, swollen from the rain.

She stood under a scalding shower, letting the drops warm her muscles, then lit the stove for tea. The flame flicked on obediently. Curious. She tried the Wi-Fi. Her laptop connected and chimed with the orderly arrival of an email from Josh. It was morning in Monaco, the yacht docked in port, picking up charter guests. The rain had stopped. The window latch appeared to function properly. The mirror reflected only Marin's face, eyes shadowed with fatigue and cheeks rosy. She checked the bookshelf: only her own volumes, lined up like guards.

With the Wi-Fi working, Marin navigated to the public library website. She still needed something good to read. She placed holds on a few titles, finished her tea, and closed the laptop.

Finally, Marin settled into sleep, relishing the sense of calm. Cautiously optimistic.

In the morning, after a slice of whole-grain toast spread begrudgingly with Earth Balance, she searched her apartment and found only her own belongings. No mysterious books, no tuxedo cats. Maybe things really had settled down. In the afternoon, she went to the library to pick up her holds. She passed her card across the desk and smiled at the librarian, a jolly-looking woman with blue hair and trendy reading glasses. The librarian scanned the card and retrieved a set of books rubber-banded together. Two contemporary hardcovers with candy-colored dust jackets. And an old, old book with a black cover. Noticeably warped from water damage.

"Here you go. Enjoy." The librarian smiled over the rim of her readers.

Adrenaline gushed through Marin's veins. She felt cold all over. Her mouth went dry. "I... this one isn't mine," she managed to gasp. How was this possible?

"Really? No, it says right here," the librarian replied, pointing to the title on the computer screen.

"I'm actually... not sure I can finish all these," Marin said, scrambling for a way to leave the cursed book behind.

"Oh, in that case, skip this one." The librarian took one of the contemporary novels from the stack and placed it on a to-shelve cart. The old black book now on top. "Definitely don't leave this one, it's really something else. I literally could not put it down!" The librarian tapped the gothic novel's cover.

Marin flipped the cover open. A shiver slid down her spine. Stuck brazenly to the endpaper: the small sticky note with the price, same as before.

A fire. Marin needed a fire. She'd tried leaving the book behind, dropping it in the river. Time to pull out the big guns.

That evening, Marin dressed in black leggings, a dark gray sweatshirt from library school, and a baseball cap. She wandered the sidewalks of her new town. She'd seen fire pits in backyards. Surely someone was toasting marshmallows with their kids, would step inside for bedtime long enough that Marin could toss the book into the flames. Or better yet, someone would be irresponsible enough to leave the embers behind after a party. Maybe she should go to the blocks where undergraduates rented dilapidated old houses and littered the yards with red plastic cups.

She'd prowl all the neighborhoods until she succeeded.

Her knees ached, her carpal tunnel throbbed. All caused by the book, she knew. Finally, a stroke of luck. Marin discovered a pizzeria, Neapolitan-style, with a huge wood-fired oven, near the railroad tracks on the edge of downtown. Lampo. The logo was a bolt of lightning. It seemed apt, poetic.

For at least an hour, Marin lurked outside, watching the baker slide pie after pie into the oven using a peel with a four-foot handle. An expediter ran back and forth from the baker to the back door of the restaurant. Occasionally, he added wood to the fire. The smell of wood smoke mixed with olive oil, baking bread, and pork fat. Her mouth watered.

Marin's patience paid off. After a while, both the baker and the expediter carried a stack of fresh pizzas through the kitchen door, leaving the oven unattended.

She seized her moment.

She flung the book into the belly of the oven among the white-hot embers. The book flexed open in the sudden heat. Then, Marin turned and ran, sneakers slapping on the pavement, not stopping until she was at least a quarter mile away, heart pounding in her ears.

There. Done.

Marin turned her face toward the almost-full moon, breathed in chilly air, felt her heart rate slow. She closed her eyes, and when she opened them, a huge cloud blocked the moon.

The rest of the evening passed uneventfully. Marin made herself a healthy dinner, used her new Wi-Fi connection to watch two episodes of a 90s sitcom, and read a chapter from the contemporary fiction bestseller that the librarian permitted her to borrow. She awoke a few minutes before her alarm, dressed in professional clothing, and commuted to her new job in the special collections.

Everything will be fine, she thought as the elevator descended into the cool, dim basement of the university library.

"Welcome, Marin." The curator greeted her with a smile on the other side of the elevator doors. "Let me give you a tour of the space." The curator badged into the special collections and led her through. "This is our main meeting room, where—"

Marin froze.

A tuxedo cat sat at the head of the conference table.

The Copper Plates

JULIAN CLOSE

"I'M NOT SURE WE need to do this," I said to Jen. "Jason always acts like he knows everything about everything. How do you know this isn't just more of the same?"

We were in the den of her split-level house on Angus Road, just two doors down from my own house, where we usually spent what little free time we had together in the summer.

"He was there when it happened. It was his team that had to switch fields. He *must* know something."

I wasn't eager to confront Jason, but she made a good point. "Let's do it," I said. Jen Marco was my best friend. She excelled at chemistry and physics; I liked computers. I wore khaki pants and button-down shirts; she wore jeans and a T-shirt. That's all meaningless, though. Our minds worked the same way—*fast*—and most people couldn't keep up, but we understood each other, sometimes without even speaking.

Jason's door was open, and we could hear him on his computer, probably working on his early decision college admissions essays. Of course, that meant he could hear us. Jen stopped outside the invisible line marking his territory, and I stopped right beside her as Jason spun his chair around. His expression darkened when he saw me.

"Oh, come on, Jenny. You brought Nosepick home again?" He walked over to us, pressed his index finger against the inside of his thumb, and flicked me on my nose, hard enough to hurt. "You got any good boogies in there?" he asked, "or are they already on your khakis?"

Fighting back wasn't an option. Jason was a rising senior, a big seventeen—one of those tall, hyper-athletic, dirt-bike daredevil, mountain-climbing Apollos with muscular arms, broad shoulders, big *teeth*, even. I was a small fifteen, the same age as Jen.

"Quit being a jerk, Jason!" she said. "We need you to tell us what happened that day four years ago with the construction crew."

"Nothing."

"It *wasn't* nothing," Jen insisted. "They moved your team to behind Jouette, when Reitmann was a *way* better field." Reitmann was the Fortune 500 military research company that owned the most and best open spaces in Charlottesville until they went bankrupt back in 2007.

"That was four years ago," said Jason. "Why are you asking?"

Four years ago, 2007, had been a dreamtime for us. Back then, the best teams in town were sponsored by the Marco family businesses, Marco Construction and Marco Security. Jen didn't like to talk about it, but everyone knew the downturn hit her family hard. Some German firm bought Reitmann's assets and immediately began selling off the land. They must have made a fortune.

"They ran into something when they were putting in the parking lot," said Jen, "and whatever it is, it's a big deal, because the theater was supposed to open in two weeks. But now everything is delayed, and nobody seems to know anything. Nobody can even see what they're doing there. They put up a tarp, three stories high. They're hiding something!"

"It's not the same thing," said Jason. "It's not even in the same place."

Jen crossed her arms and cocked an eyebrow in a way that said she'd figured something out. It made her small face, wrapped in curly black hair, look electric. "*What's* not in the same place?" said Jen. "I thought you said it was nothing!"

"It *is* nothing," said Jason, gazing fixedly at his hands.

I'd always thought of him as a together guy, if a somewhat malevolent one, so seeing him out of sorts was a little creepy.

At last, he snapped out of it. "Sit down," he said.

There was only one place for us to sit in Jason's room, and that was on the edge of his bed. Jen sat first and gestured for me to join her, which I did, carefully.

"Thursday practice. They're working with an excavator, about halfway between our field and Hydraulic Road, where the Nokia Pavilion is now. Suddenly, the excavator stops. The guy gets out and looks at what he's digging, and he starts shouting and swearing. I can't tell if he's afraid, or excited, or what. So, the guy goes and gets his supervisor, and the supervisor starts yelling at everybody to get back."

I was more than half expecting Jason's explanation to turn into some kind of joke at my expense, but he was serious. The spacey look was back.

"Coach Burroughs isn't there—just Carter—and he doesn't want to stop practice, but more and more people start showing up and looking in the hole with flashlights. A couple of people look like they're getting sick, and we hear the sirens. A firetruck pulls up, an ambulance, and a couple of cops. So, Carter tells us all to stay where we are, and he goes over to talk to them. The supervisor guy runs up to Carter, waving his arms, trying to get him to stop, but Carter doesn't stop. He goes right over and looks in the hole. Then he runs back and tells us all to go sit in the dugout and call our parents."

"What did you do?" asked Jen.

"What do you think?" said Jason, back to normal again. "We did what he said."

"You didn't look in the hole?" asked Jen.

"If you'd seen the look on Carter's face and heard the tone of his voice, you would have done what he said, too. And you wouldn't keep asking about it!"

"That's all?" demanded Jen.

"That's all. Get out."

I glanced at Jen: *Can we get out of here now?* She glanced back: *Sit tight for a second.* I did. For five or six interminable seconds, I watched as Jen fixed Jason with a withering stare, and Jason stared back almost but not quite as intensely.

Finally, Jason threw his head back in resignation. "Fine," he said. "Last year, I ran into Carter at Arthur Needham's big summer party. There were people there who'd graduated years earlier, and Carter was one of them. He was alone by the pool, and I'd seen him drink about nine beers, so I figured it was time to ask him what was in the hole. He said it was... a *disk*, like a big copper Frisbee. It wasn't very far down, just four or five feet. Said it was covered with wavy, irregular patterns, like the patterns worms make in wood."

I knew what he was talking about. You can see them if you rip the bark off any tree or fallen branch.

Jason continued, "The excavator broke through the dirt around the side of the copper plate, and from the right angle, they could see what was beneath it..."

I don't know if Jason noticed Jen putting her hand on my arm and gripping me as he spoke. I'm not even sure *she* noticed, but I did.

"Which was nothing," he said. "Like I told you."

For a moment, I thought Jen was going to hit him. "What? You..."

"*Absolutely* nothing!" said Jason, cutting her off. "It was a hole that went straight down. Nothing holding up the plate, nothing at the bottom. No bottom. Even with the most powerful flashlight. The sides of the hole were smooth, and it went down forever. Bottomless pit."

"Anything else?" asked Jen.

"A bottomless pit isn't enough for you?" asked Jason. "I told you what you wanted to know. Say thank you and leave."

Jen didn't say thank you, but she did stand and head for the door. I got up to follow, but not fast enough.

"Wait," said Jason, grabbing me by the arm as I walked past. "You guys aren't going to do anything, are you?"

"Like what?" I asked, trying to sound dumb.

Jason grinned, but he didn't let go. "Never mind. Listen, Shawn, you know I'm just fooling around with you, right? The truth is, I'm glad to have you around. I'm glad you spend so much time with my sister. I mean that."

"Well, I... thank you," I finally said, smiling.

"Seriously, it's like my sister has this permanent safe date, you know? I'm saying I don't have to worry about my sister getting it on with you—or getting it on with anyone—*because* of you. You're geeking her up too bad for the other guys. Do you understand?"

"Yeah," I said, smile gone. "I got it."

"Good," he said. "Get lost."

With that, the grab turned into a shove, and I was out the door.

***

I found Jen in the living room.

"Sorry," she said. "I just couldn't be in that room with Jason anymore, even if he was being helpful for once." She scanned my face. "Did he say something to you?"

"Hold on a second!" I said. "Did you learn anything from that?"

"Yes. That 'copper plate' sounds like what I'm looking for."

"You still want to do this, don't you?"

"I have to do it, Shawn!"

"Can you tell me why you're doing this?" I pleaded.

"I think I know what's behind that tarp," she said. "Just trust me."

A wise, strong, confident young man would have refused, objected, or at least demanded an explanation, but I was none of those things. "Okay," I said. "Tell me why I'm coming with you, again."

"Because," she said, turning her eyes down for an instant, "you want to protect me, and you aren't going to make me do it alone. They aren't going to catch us. It's just a parking lot, and they weren't even finished building it. When would they have had a chance to put up security cameras? There might be some cops watching at night, yes, but they go by once every fifteen minutes. We just need to walk like we're headed to the 7-11 until we see one pass, then double back."

"Jen," I said. "Carter killed himself about two weeks after Arthur's party."

Jen frowned. "He was going to get married, then his girlfriend, Gina, got killed by a drunk driver on 21 Curves. She was already pregnant."

"That's the story *you* heard?" I asked.

"That's *not* about this. Let's get some supplies from your house before your mother gets home."

"There's no hurry. My mother won't be back from New Jersey until tomorrow, so no one will bother us." I knew immediately I'd said the wrong thing. It sounded like I was inviting her to spend the night.

"Uh, well, listen," she said. "I should apologize to Jason, and my dad will be home soon." With that, I knew it was time for me to go. I'd always found Ivan Marco intimidating, and the 2008 crash had changed him for the worse. "Get whatever you think we'll need, and I'll meet you by the creek on Cedar Hill at midnight."

***

Midnight came, and I was there. I had some supplies in my backpack—a compass, a rope, and a flashlight. At 400 lumens, it was a good one, but certainly not industrial or military grade. It was hazy that night, with just a sliver of a waning moon, and I was nervous, as you can imagine. I'd seen one other person out—some creepy guy who was wearing a hoodie despite the heat.

After a few minutes, I saw Jen's silhouette coming down the hill. She was wearing a backpack too, and there was no mistaking her. I knew that little toe-push that lifted her head with every other step. I knew everything. In another minute, she reached me and gave me a half-hug, which is the only practical kind between people wearing backpacks.

"Were you followed?" she whispered.

I was about to tell her about the creepy guy I'd seen, but then I realized she was making a joke. "Let's go," I said.

When we got to Hydraulic, we turned right, heading toward Emmet Street. We walked slowly, waiting for a police car to pass as it made its inspection. In that, we were lucky, for we hadn't gone a block when a car came rolling toward us. It was a busy street during the day but not at night, and the police car was one of the first cars we had seen. After it passed us, it turned into the development, drove slowly by the site, then continued on its way.

The moment it was gone from view, we ran across the road and followed its path into the development. Straight ahead, about a quarter mile, was the roundabout with the Nokia Pavilion at its center. Barely a year old, the wooden structure was already rotten, sour smelling, and weak. Its heart had been eaten out by worms, leaving it as hollow and ready to collapse as its eponymous corporation.

To our right loomed the tarp, blocking out what little of the moon we had. To see, we had only the dim light from the houses on the other side of Hydraulic and the dimmer light from the more distant unopened theater.

We had been excited to hear there would be a new movie theater so close to us—with IMAX, even—but as the months wore on and the arcadian playground of our childhood was bulldozed under, we began to worry. When the rich soil by the creek, where we had dug up big, wriggly earthworms for science class, was paved over, and we had to hold cloth over our noses to keep from choking on the gravelly dust, the real dread set in. And when we saw what they were building—the witless crisscross of roads leading nowhere, the redundant coffee shops, the affected boutiques, the chain outlet stores and fast-food restaurants, covering almost a square mile—we knew our childhoods were over. The Reitmann development was like a strip mall, except that strip malls have the decency to only occupy a strip.

Our first real obstacle of the night was getting past the tarp. If it had any seams to exploit, we couldn't see them, so we would have to go under. The tarp was weighted at the bottom with cinderblocks in some places and secured with stakes in others.

"We can wriggle under there," said Jen, pointing to a spot between these two defenses.

I was going to object. This had gone far enough, and it was time to stand up to Jen and make her see that. Just then, behind us in the darkness cast by the tarp, something shifted, a shadow within the shadow.

Jen looked at me accusingly. "Wait? *Were* you followed?"

I stared into the blackness. Whatever had moved wasn't moving anymore. It was no longer visible at all, really, but I could feel it. "There's nothing there," I lied. At that moment, I was more afraid of that shadow than I was of the tarp. Turning toward the tarp, I said, "Follow me!"

I jumped the small curb onto the muddy field and closed the short distance to the tarp with Jen close on my heels. At the tarp, we got to our knees and removed our backpacks. After a minute of clearing mud with our hands, we had made a decent-sized entry point.

"Backpack!" said Jen. I handed mine to her, and she shoved it under, followed by her own.

"You first," I said. "I'll watch!" I meant I would stand guard as she crawled, monitoring behind us to protect her from whatever was following us, but I immediately heard how it sounded and hated myself.

"My hero," she said. Not cruelly, but still...

As Jen wriggled under, I made a point of scanning the darkness, not her, and I wasn't reassured by what I saw. Something man-shaped was out there. It had made its way to the spot where we left the road, but that's all I could tell. It was too dark.

"Okay," came her voice, "I'm through!"

Swallowing my own stomach, I turned from the road and dove face first into the mud, wriggling like a worm. Blind and without an inch to spare, I pushed forward. Finally, I felt Jen's hands on mine, guiding me through the warm squishiness all around me. I lifted my head and pulled myself up, practically yanking my legs through.

I stood, nearly choking on a sour, dank stench. If the night outside had been dark as the tomb, inside was dark as the very sarcophagus. A sudden warm hug from Jen let me know she was as scared as me, which was reassuring, in its way.

"Ready?" she asked.

"Go ahead," I said, and with that, she turned on her flashlight.

It was not immediately clear just what was inside the tarp with us, but a single feature dominated. A few feet away from where we stood, the ground gave way to a round hole, big as a house, a hole that went down only about five feet before ending in a huge, frisbee-shaped copper disk.

The top of the disk was shiny enough that the beam from the flashlight bounced off without noticeable dimming, and it was carved or etched with an irregular and incomprehensibly complicated maze-like pattern—a *worm* pattern.

"My *God*!" I said.

"My God," Jen agreed. "It's real."

After a moment, Jen lifted the flashlight from the plate to scan the perimeter of the hole. It didn't take her long to find what she was looking for. By the back of the lot, closest to the theater, there was a ramp.

"There," she said. "That's where we need to go." Jen picked up her backpack and put it on before advancing.

I got out my flashlight. I thought about putting my pack on, but instead, I shoved it into the gap below the tarp and threw as much mud around it as I could. I caught up to Jen as she reached the ramp leading downward, adjacent to the hole. Up ahead and lower down, I could see some sort of scaffolding.

"This is it!" said Jen.

I followed her, stepping on a series of sloping wooden boards. Eventually, my head was below ground level, and I hugged the wall to my left as closely as I could. When my head dipped below the plate, I felt an emptiness open to my right. Instinctively, I turned my flashlight toward that emptiness. A reflex, I now realize, born of my need to dispel it, but dispelled it would not be.

My flashlight's beam illuminated the far wall, a few rows of descending scaffolding, and, about one hundred feet down, a walkway that spanned the chasm, ending on one side in what looked like a control room of sorts. Below that, there was only blackness, and my flashlight was just powerful enough to reveal that it really was bottomless, or it might as well have been from any human perspective.

"Jen," I said, "this is *way* more than I signed on for. We should get out of here."

"Not quite yet," she said. "We're in the right place. That pattern—the one that looks like it was made by worms—isn't random. This is all theoretical, but I think the plate above us and the one Carter saw are devices for channeling gravity waves. Or, I guess, antigravity waves."

I looked into her eyes. "Antigravity is science fiction!"

"All science was once science fiction."

There was a noise, like an animal in a burrow, from the level above. Something was coming under the tarp.

"That could be... a fox?" I said it without much hope—and less conviction. I could feel my hands beginning to go shaky in the dark and was relieved that my voice wasn't doing the same.

"Let's just hope it's not a skunk." Jen didn't seem to be as scared as she should have been. Pointing downward with her light, she said, "That's where we need to get. That control room."

"What for?" I asked, but she was already heading down the first ladder, and I had to follow. Back and forth we went on creaking boards that seemed already to be rotting and sour, though they couldn't have been in place for more than a few days. With every level we descended, the smell grew stronger and worse.

When Jen reached the final ladder, I'd had enough. "Stop!" I yelled. "Whatever you're trying to do, it's not worth it. We need to get out of here!"

But she didn't stop or even slow. By the time I was climbing down the ladder, Jen was stepping off the lowest rung onto the walkway. As I descended, the loose ladder was clanging fiercely, and my mind was dwelling masochistically on what it would be like to fall into darkness forever.

Finally, I reached the walkway, which, unlike the scaffolding, at least had guard rails. I caught up with Jen by the control room's powerful steel door, a door that appeared to have recently withstood a sustained attack by axe and flame.

"Good!" said Jen. "They haven't made it through yet. One more day and we'd have been too late."

She swung her backpack off, unzipped it, felt around inside, and came out holding a modern key, such as you might use to start a flashy car.

I was dumbfounded. "How?"

"Who do you think designed the security system for Reitmann?"

You may think I'm a fool. Who could blame you? But in that moment, I had the first inkling that the story I now tell you was not truly my own. How much had her father, so silent and reclusive to most, confided in Jen?

Jen put her key in the lock and turned. The steel door clicked and swung outward. She entered, and I followed. The front half of the room looked like an abandoned air traffic control center. There were chairs, ordinary looking computers, and panels containing displays and controls the purpose of which I could not imagine. The back half of the room was unlike anything I had ever seen. In the light from our flashlights, I could see what appeared to be a library of metal cards protruding from a sheet of white marble that I swear was glowing softly. Jen grabbed at the metal cards, one after another, tugging with all her might, but they wouldn't budge.

She turned to me. "I'm going to have to override the controls to get one of these. This metal, when it is energized, has incredible properties. I only need one, and we'll be able to show the world what they did here, what they *can* do, before it's too late."

Moving to the left side of the panel, she put her hand on a small lever and pulled. "I need you to pull the one on the other side," she said. "I can't reach it."

"So that's why I'm here?" I said, "to help you bypass a Reitmann failsafe and steal some dangerous tech? No!"

"Just do it!" she pleaded. "You don't know what they did. It's too much power for anyone to have, and they've used it, Shawn! They used it in Afghanistan, in Northern Iran, in Southern Russia."

"Do you mean *seismic warfare?*"

"Not just that! Something worse. They stirred something up, deep, deep down. Help me, please!"

There is no real excuse for what I then did. Though you already know, I dare not face the just consequences of my actions, and it is for this reason that the names and details of this story have been changed.

Walking to the other side of the panel and finding the lever with my flashlight, I pulled it. At first, nothing happened. Then Jen grabbed a metal card from the panel and pulled it free. In the next moment, all changed.

Lights came on above—not all at once, but flickering randomly, illuminating this, then that, creating darkness one moment, then clarity, then blindness. A hum erupted all around me, and a vibration.

"Let's go!" I shouted, and Jen nodded.

She put the metal card in her backpack, threw the pack onto her shoulder, and the two of us ran toward the ladder. It must have been to let her climb the ladder more easily that she put both arms through the straps—it's more common to use only one. As we ran, the hum rose to a roar, and the vibration to a shaking. The shaking was too much for the ladder, which broke loose and fell.

The ladder thudded against the walkway and began to tilt. Tall as it was, it would have flipped right over that rail and disappeared into the darkness below. Realizing we were about to be trapped, I grabbed at it madly. Though I got a grip on it, its momentum gave it more pull than I could carry, yanking me into the guardrail, which, though sturdy in appearance, immediately buckled, leaving me with nothing else to grab. I was falling.

Jen grabbed me from behind, but she was so slight, she was pulled along with me. We both teetered toward an unspeakable doom, but just then, Jen's body suddenly became weightless—no, lighter than that—for she began to rise straight up into the air behind me. With her anchoring me, I was able to drag the ladder back onto the walkway. It was then I saw what was really happening. Jen was being pulled into the air by her backpack.

"The pack, Jen!" I shouted. "Let it go!"

To my relief, she did, wriggling out to fall back onto the walkway, landing right on top of me and pulling us both down. The pack flew upward, smacking against the plate far above us.

"I need another one!" she said.

"No time!" I warned her, and I was right. The shaking abated, replaced by something else, a sort of pressure, and the smell, the *stink*, rose to an impossible level. Every breath made me gag.

I managed to get to my feet, but when I did, I felt a presence below us. At first, I saw nothing, but then a flickering searchlight from above lit the depths, and I could see that something was rising.

It was a mass of slimy, bulging, glistening flesh—a boil of worms, one hundred feet across.

"Dear God," I shouted. "This hole. It's a *worm* hole!"

"Quick," shouted Jen, "the ladder!"

I lifted the ladder, somehow got it upright, and tried to reach the scaffolding with it, but it was about a foot too short. There was nothing to brace it against and no way to hook it onto the scaffolding above.

The worms closed the distance, and the sound they made was like a thousand disgusting fleshy noises. Each distinct, but all jumbled together and impossibly loud. All I could think to do was drop the ladder, embrace Jen, and shield her with my body as we braced ourselves for the agony of our fate.

But before I could do that, I heard a cry. "Shawn! Up here! The ladder! Hand me the ladder!"

Above me, just reaching the lowest level of the scaffolding, was Jason, who had clearly been following us. In his muddy hoodie, he had dressed more appropriately than we for crawling around in the mud, and he was carrying rope. Hope! But there didn't seem to be time.

Jason ran as I heaved the ladder up. He dove, hit the rotting boards of the scaffolding, and thrust out a hand, just in time to grab the top rung. With his other hand, he began wrapping the rope around it. "Now!" he cried, as soon as it was secure, "Come now!"

I practically dragged Jen to her feet and pushed her toward the ladder. As she began to climb, the noise around us grew louder, a churning of wet flesh that I shall never forget as long as I live. Jen climbed, and the ladder, secured only at the top, began to swing. I caught and steadied it.

"Go! Go!" I screamed.

I watched her place each hand, terrified that she would miss a rung and all would be lost. At last, Jason was pulling her up, and the two began the twisty back-and-forth climb up the scaffolding.

My turn. I hoisted myself up, putting my feet on the ladder, but there was no one to steady it for me, and it immediately began to swing wildly. It carried me back and forth over the walkway, out over the abyss, and then again side to side. As my foot reached the second rung, swinging so far that I felt almost upside down, I chanced a look down and beheld, fully illuminated from above, the sight that now haunts my dreams.

From the center of that mass of worms, something larger emerged. A single blob of wet, pink, gelatinous flesh, so large as to push all others to the sides of the hole. This hole may have been home to a million billion worms, but it was made by *one*—one single, ancient creature that man was never meant to discover—one hundred feet across, and how long? A mile?

Finally, I reached the scaffolding, and I heard a horrific smack as the monster struck the walkway beneath me with unimaginable force. Around me, horrible worm flesh rose as if to swallow me, but the walkway held. A moment later, it was receding, only to gather strength and surge up again, harder. With each assault, the walkway and control room shook more distressingly, but I dared not watch, only climb and run, climb and run.

I do not know how, deprived of oxygen and sanity, I managed to climb all the way up that scaffolding and run up the ramp, but once I was at the top, I saw Jason and Jen, who had lifted the tarp high enough for me to run underneath.

"It's trying to break the walkway!" I shouted.

"And it will!" Jen shouted back. "But not the plate. The plate will hold it. That's what it's there for!"

"Run!" cried Jason. "We can't be here."

"No, we can't," answered Jen, who, by then, looked and sounded appropriately terrified. "There's no way of knowing when that control room will fall, or what might happen when it does."

Upon those questions, our minds lingered as we ran. They lingered all through that sleepless night, throughout which I was, mercifully, not alone, and they lingered as we tried, like zombies, to go through the same motions we had once before in our ordinary lives.

We got our answer at 1:51 p.m., for that day was August 23rd, 2011, the day when all the state of Virginia shook, sending tremors up and down the entire east coast of America.

Any hope that someone might aid us in exposing what we discovered died last year with Ivan Marco, leaving the sad trio of Jen, Jason, and me to bear the burden alone. From our shared horror, a closeness arose between me and Jen, but it didn't last. She is gone, now, out west. Jason traveled even farther, to continue his studies in Australia, from where he never returned.

Only I remain here in Charlottesville to walk this ground, praying daily—though to whom or what I don't know—that I will never feel it shake again.

Warriors of Kroas

GINGER GROUSE

Noem sen Yanet ufDir shivered as the early evening breeze blew up from the desert, cooling his sweaty skin as it wafted over the summit of Bronaan Pass. He stood at the crest of the ridge, gazing down the V-shaped valley, splashed red and gold with the turning maples and oaks and walnuts near its heights. Farther down, where the hopper opened into the valley beyond, exposed talus sloped down to the golden sands of the Shendoa Desert. The early setting sun played over the dunes and rocks, turning them to a kaleidoscope of color and shadow that matched the forest above.

"Wake up, daydreamer!"

Noem startled and turned. Delilah stood with a hand on her hip, smiling, holding the halter of the donkey hitched to a cart laden with the day's harvest of acorns. She had already wrapped her body against the chill, and the hood of her cloak revealed only her copper-colored face, black eyes, and the first few inches of the glistening black hair tied back for the day's work.

Noem smiled back and looked down and away from her eyes. Their fire stirred a warmth in his chest whenever he found himself caught in their glow. He swung his cloak over his shoulders.

"Let's go!" Delilah chided. "It is going to be dark before we reach camp. We can unload in the morning." She clicked her tongue, and the donkey leaned into his load, jolting the cart and sending acorns tumbling to the path.

"Looks like you two hardly got into the race this time!" their kinsman, Jahani, ribbed them with a good-natured smirk. He swung in behind Noem and Delilah's cart, leading two more fully loaded carts.

"You cheated, Jahani." Noem grinned back, nodding at the passel of little children who had hung around with Jahani all day, eagerly scooping up the fallen nuts gathered on the tarps spread under the canopy. "What promise did you make to get them away from their hunting games?"

"Nothing! It's not my fault I am their favorite *sastaa* and not dour and serious like you all the time!"

Noem replied with a quiet grin and shook his head. "You're too young to be anyone's *sastaa*, Jahani."

"Why not? Everyone treats you like one, even people ten years older than us," Jahani teased, a tinge of bitterness in his voice.

"Not true," Noem replied, sighing. *Here we go again...*

"Noem sen Yanet," Jahani mocked, "the youngest elder in Donland!"

Delilah gently touched Noem on the arm. The rise in Noem's belly settled, the tension released.

"Whatever you say, Jahani," Noem said, tucking his arms into his cloak, shivering. Delilah nodded at the pouch secreted under Noem's cloak, silently changing the subject.

"Right, almost forgot." He smiled back at her. "Gather around!" he called to the children.

Jahani rolled his eyes as Noem rooted in the pouch and produced a pinch of dried tobacco.

"Just like his giver taught him," Jahani muttered as the three took a knee, the children prancing restlessly.

Delilah skewered Jahani with her eyes as she placed her palms to the soil. Jahani grudgingly followed suit.

"We give you thanks, spirits of the mountains and forest, for the gift of harvest," Noem whispered, scattering the tobacco with a slow sweep of his arm. He stood and nodded, his companions rising with him. The carts lurched forward again, down the eastern slope where the aroma of cook fires awaited them in their autumn camp five miles below. Ten miles beyond, their village of Kroas lay nestled among the hills of the bright Donlandan savannah.

The children raced down the mountain, their energy unabated even after the day's labor. The other villagers descended an hour before, but Noem had a stubborn mind to finish this grove before nightfall. He stayed because providing for the village was a sacred duty of care that he learned from his parents, especially his giver, venerated elder Milles. The work stilled his mind and occupied his restless, uncertain hands. Jahani had no love for the hard labor of husbandry, much preferring to use his strength training in the martial arts that made Donlandans renowned warriors, but he would not be outdone by Noem in anything. And Delilah was there, as always, to keep the peace between them, with words if she could, or a hard beatdown if she had to. For among a people of renowned fighters, Delilah had no rival. In the village of Kroas, only Jahani dared challenge her, always with the same painful result from which he never seemed to learn.

***

The air warmed as they descended into the hollow. Two rushing streams tumbled over waterfalls and converged in orchards of apple, pear, and peach, planted on the slopes of this mountain over five centuries ago. Spread out along the understory were perennials and vines—medicine and cordage and building materials. They walked in silence, and Noem let the calming sound of the rushing water fill his body.

Why does Jahani get to me? Thank the spirits for her... I don't know how I would cope.

He glanced toward Delilah and his eyes darted away again. Her eyes watched him in turn. He forgot about his irritation as her gravity drew his mind toward her. He sensed her strong, compact body's motion, concealed under the flowing cloak along with the secret gentleness that she saved only for him. He let his arm brush hers and their fingers clasped. At eighteen, they had passed through adulthood rites two years before. They were at the age when many started or joined households. They had played together as children, worked together in the fields and forests from the moment they could wield a hoe or swing an axe, and trained together to be warriors in the Old Ways.

The kind eyes of Noem's giver met his from the entrance of the family tent as they entered the camp, and Milles winked when he saw Delilah's hand in Noem's. Noem felt himself blush. As far as his giver and bearer were concerned, Noem and Delilah had been matched by the spirits themselves from birth. As was expected among Donlandan youth, they'd had their casual flings, but they always gravitated back to each other. The flush of Noem's face was a confession: *yes, Giver, I love her—you were right all along!*

The children were already bent over carved wooden bowls full of venison stew, sopping up the thick gravy with sweet slices of chestnut bread. The trio unhitched the carts and covered their cargo under canvas tarps for the night then joined in the meal.

Later that night, the villagers gathered around the fire and sang and danced as the autumn chill descended from the slopes above. One of the elders began to sing stories, singing them with such art and animation that the children begged for more.

"Very well," they said, "one more!"

They launched into the epic of Aphara Wari, the Spirit Warrior, a story of the rebirth of the climate-ravaged world eight hundred years ago. According to the legend, Aphara Wari was given dreams by the spirits of the Earth as a child, teaching them how to lead their people in the restoration of the land's fecundity. Deserted wastes became living forests and meadows and deserts, and once again the land gave people food and water and medicine. But there were others who saw the wealth in the land and sought to take it and return to the violent ways of old. A tyrannical warlord invaded the place Aphara called home. But Aphara called the people together, and when they joined hands, they found that they were one with the spirits, partners with all the creatures of the land who were their kin. So Aphara prayed and the land and water and air themselves rose up against the warlord and drove him away. Aphara, being the conduit for the spirits' collective power, fell into a deep sleep when the battle was over. It is said that Aphara still sleeps, and that the spirits awaken them whenever the land is in peril and its defenders need their help.

As a child, Noem had loved this story, but he never considered it as anything more than that: a story. There had not been war with the Alganians, their ancient foes, for a generation, so he had never known crisis. War was always a possibility. They all trained for it. But peace was agreeable to Noem and Delilah. For Jahani, the absence of war was an injustice against which he chafed more with every new day. Should war come one day, Noem almost feared the inevitable clash with Jahani more than the Alganians, who he had never met.

Storytime over, the elder sent the children to their beds. Delilah curled up against Noem by the central fire, a wool blanket draped around their shoulders, and he listened drowsily while others gossiped and chatted away. A cry from the darkness beyond the camp jolted Noem from his reverie.

"Raiders!" a man shouted. "Alganians, half day's run to the south!"

The people rose to their feet. Noem looked at his giver's face, which had gone pale.

"Are you sure?" Milles asked the breathless messenger as he walked into the fireglow. "There was no call on the radio."

The runner was not wrapped in the loose robes of a Donlandan savannah dweller. Instead, he was dressed for battle, clad in fitted tanned hides with a 9mm pistol and war club strapped to his hip. He carried a light pack on his back, which he swung to the ground.

Someone handed the runner a cup of ale, and he gulped it down thirstily. "I am sure," he said, wiping his mouth. "They found a way to jam our comms, so we're running tonight. I am the second leg. The first came from the ashes of N'tabia," he said, indicating that he'd just run at least thirty miles from where he'd received the first runner's missive. "There were two dozen killed, another two dozen taken captive," he continued. The villagers stirred and gasped in alarm, eyes darting from face to face. "The raiders burned half the village and got clean away. The village was totally unprepared."

"Is there any word from other village councils? Are we mobilizing fighters?" Milles asked.

"Nothing yet, other than the general alarm," the man replied. "Are your defense plans still in place?"

Milles nodded gravely. "We never stopped drilling, though we hoped it would never be needed again."

"Then it is time to muster and choose your captains," the messenger concluded.

By this time, the rest of the camp had gathered around the central fire. Milles placed his hand on the shoulder of the runner, who was already making as though to continue his journey to the next hollow.

"Stay. Rest. Eat," Milles said. "We will send a fresh runner to the other autumn camps, and we will muster in the village by nightfall tomorrow."

Noem clutched Delilah's hand as the gravity of the news sunk in, and he trembled. But she was calm, steady, at the prospect of war, seeming neither eager nor afraid. He looked across the campfire at Jahani, arms crossed on his chest, excitement and hunger radiating from his blue eyes, energy coursing through taut muscles.

Anticipating sleepless nights ahead, the people turned to their tents. But Noem knew he would not be able to sleep. A foreboding feeling of cataclysm and death settled over him.

"How are you so calm?" he whispered to Delilah as the rest of the camp filed away.

"What makes you think I am?" she asked, crossing her arms.

Noem arched his brows skeptically.

"I have confidence in my training," Delilah answered finally. "You should, too. You are a skilled fighter, and you have more courage than you think."

"How do you know?"

"You have integrity, and you know your own weaknesses, so you won't be overconfident. Not like Dumbass over there," she said, nodding in Jahani's direction. "But if you dwell on it too much, you'll get mind-tied." She reached up and placed a hand on his cheek. "Just remember who you're fighting for, and you won't flinch."

Sighing, Noem took her hand from his cheek and pressed it between his hands. "I better see to my parents," he said, looking in her eyes.

"Don't worry about them," she whispered, pulling him by the hand toward the darkness beyond the camp. Her own parents and sister were back in the village proper. She had come here to be with Noem.

Noem looked guiltily over his shoulder toward his tent.

"I said not to worry!" Delilah insisted, gently leading him away. "This might be our last night for a while..."

***

The next morning, the warriors of Kroas chose Milles, their most experienced fighter, to command them. To Noem's relief, the vote was unanimous on the first round. Even Jahani knew to defer to the elders in the matter. There were few decisions to make in the first few days—they had drilled for this scenario, month in and month out—for a generation. Once the alarm came, the next steps unfolded automatically. They had ready-made go bags stowed at forest rally points where they hid caches of arms and supplies, and by noon they'd arrived at Bronaan Pass, where they peacefully gathered acorns the previous day.

Their collective defense agreement with the surrounding villages assigned them to patrol a stretch of the Lauba Mountains between Bronaan Pass—known as Brown's Gap one thousand years ago—and Pannaan Pass, less than four miles south. In the middle, where they put their command post, was a massive boulder scree called Blackrock, or *Blagstaan* in the Donlandan language. Their tiny, stretched force of three hundred was to observe, track, report, and harass any Alganian raiders they found. Milles stressed that they would engage in direct confrontation only as a last resort.

The warriors followed the Old Ways, shunning industrialized warfare, so they were lightly armed with hand-to-hand weapons and crossbows, supplemented by a few rifles, shotguns, and handguns. Guns were a matter of intermittent debate in the village, but the long peace that had held until this moment had not incentivized a strengthening of the village arsenal. Even so, Noem, along with everyone else, breathed a little easier when the crates of rifles and ammunition from the village arsenal caught up to them on the mountain near sunset.

But Noem, Delilah, and Jahani had no use for guns on their first mission. To their exasperation, Milles sent them on their first patrol down Pannaan with a squadron armed only with machetes, picks, shovels, and hand saws. Unlike the maintained cart path through Bronaan Pass, Pannaan was traversed by a little-used hunting trail that hadn't been employed for months. It fell to them to clear the trail of brush and fallen trees and construct defenses.

"Damn it!" Jahani cursed, sticking a bleeding finger into his mouth. "Why are we hacking our way through brambles when we could make the enemy do it instead?"

"Good question," Delilah said, echoing Jahani's irritation. "If it's easy for us to patrol it, it's easy for the Alganians to pass through. We should've let the laurels and roses be our sentries!"

Noem swung his machete, muttering prayers of apology to the spirits for disturbing the growth. But even his prayers were strained—he was no less irritated by the task. "My giver wants an outpost down below. It makes sense," he said with two more fierce slashes to vent his frustration.

"Giver's boy, as always," Jahani complained.

The rest of their squad followed, strung out a hundred paces behind, moving the fallen limbs and cut brush. When it neared nightfall, they cleared a camp, posted sentries, and rested for the night. The next day was the same slog, but by midafternoon they reached the bottom of the gap, where the old trail was more evident and followed the creek that drained the pass. Here they went to work over the next two days, building and repairing defenses. They worked their way back up the pass, constructing ambushes, blinds, slot trenches, and setting booby traps: mines and IEDs, spiked pit traps, and deadfalls.

"I still think the brambles would have been more effective," Jahani groused as they plodded back into the camp at Blagstaan. The other two sighed in wordless agreement.

They enjoyed two days of rest before Milles put them into the regular rotation of patrols. Every day, runners came with news of more Alganian raids to the south, and tension rose in the camp as one fighter after another learned of kin killed and captured. The tension shaped into an appetite for revenge and a collective desire that the Alganians would appear and fall into their hands. Jahani was foremost among the belligerent.

"Do not be so eager to shed blood, young man," Milles admonished him. "You know nothing of the horror of it!"

But Jahani sniffed and stormed away, and within the hour he could be heard arguing around a campfire, venting his bloodlust, stoking the rage of his comrades. So Milles pulled his child aside one evening before a night patrol.

"Stay close to Jahani," he said. "He is hotheaded, but he still loves you like a sibling. He will listen to you if you show wisdom."

"I'm not so sure, Giver," Noem replied, shaking his head. "He thinks I'm soft. Even Delilah can't reach him."

Milles sighed. He nodded. "Point taken." The pair stood in silence, thinking, then Milles spoke again. "I am sending your squadron out to patrol the ridge tonight, and I am making you captain."

Noem straightened up in surprise. "You can't do that, Giver! You don't have the authority. The squad must choose its captain!"

"They will choose Jahani, and he is driven by bloodlust. I don't trust his judgment," Milles protested.

"Yes, they might," Noem nodded. "But it is their right, and you know it!"

Milles' face fell. "You're right, of course. I taught you to respect the Old Ways, but sometimes they are terribly... inconvenient."

Noem felt his giver's frustration. Jahani had earned the respect of everyone in the camp. He was tall, good-looking, charismatic, and brave, never shying away from a fight. Because he won almost every fight he was in, many confused his bravery with smarts. Few but Noem and Delilah knew otherwise. Noem hoped it would not take a disaster for people to see that Jahani was dangerous.

Noem, too was tall and strong and good-looking. He, too, rarely lost a fight. But he rarely got in fights, because his soft-spoken wisdom was more effective at diffusing conflict than his fists. Many took this to mean he was less suited for command in war than his more belligerent kinsman. When it came time to choose patrol captains, it had always been Jahani.

And so it was that night. With Jahani in command, they left the camp under the light of a full moon and moved north toward Bronaan Pass. They moved in silence, communicating with hand signals. An hour later they reached the pass, checked in with the outpost, then turned south. They were to complete this circuit a total of four times before handing off the patrol to the next squadron.

They were nearly done with the return leg of their second circuit when Yasan, their radio operator, called for a halt: an incoming radio communication from command.

"Nestling, Nestling, this is Eagle, Eagle, we copy, over," Yasan said after a minute, holding the receiver to his ear, eyes widening. Finally, he reported to the group. "Enemy contact in lower Pannaan sector! No casualties. Orders are to stay sharp!"

Jahani signaled the team to huddle up. Hearts pounding with excitement, they kneeled together by the trail. "So they're taking Pannaan, after all!" Jahani grinned, shaking his head in disbelief. "Guess we'll see whether our garden work paid off!"

The fighters chuckled. Then Jahani whispered again, "I say we take the fight to them. Finally, some action!"

Noem and Delilah glanced at each other in alarm.

"Jahani," Noem replied, "our orders are to patrol the ridge. Let our pickets in Pannaan handle it. We don't even know whether it's a real fight yet!"

"You know perfectly well there's no enemy up here. I'm not spending this war uselessly pacing back and forth through a secure sector. The enemy is down Pannaan. Let's go!"

Jahani ordered Yasan not to radio their position, and before anyone could argue, he jumped to his feet and walked south toward Blagstaan. The rest of the squad fell in. In the dark, Noem could not read their faces, whether they followed with eagerness or apprehension. There was spring in their step as the patrol picked up the pace.

"Shas..." Noem hissed to Delilah.

"Yeah," she agreed. "This won't end well..."

Noem's mind raced. Could they depose Jahani? Once elected, a captain's command was supposed to be absolute. *Milles'* command was supposed to be absolute. Jahani was being insubordinate. Wasn't that cause enough to remove him? *No, it's useless to try without the support of the others. What are they thinking?* He decided to bide his time.

Jahani's hope for action was vindicated minutes later when another communication came through, reporting a sharp firefight in progress, with wounded. As if to punctuate the report, a sharp *boom* echoed up the pass as they crossed through the boulder field.

"One of our IEDs!" someone said. That could only mean the enemy was trying to push its way into the gap.

Jahani grinned and broke into a run. Depression, fear, and foreboding settled over Noem as the group plunged into the steep, winding descent, slowing only when the trees blocked the moonlight. Every few minutes the reports came to Yasan's headset: "We're outgunned! Pinned down and can't withdraw!"

Still, Jahani did not radio back with the squad's position as Milles sent reserves to rescue the outpost. *Why won't he call it in? He could do it now and still get his fight, and the reserves could guard the ridge instead of us!* But Jahani persisted in leaving his commander blind.

The firing rattling and echoing off the surrounding cliffs was hotter and heavier than anything the Donlandans could lay down with their handful of bolt-action rifles. Something wasn't right. Something was different about these guns. But Jahani's blood was up and he pushed on. Was he ignoring what everyone else could plainly hear? Finally, Noem sensed hesitation in his comrades' steps.

But they were committed to the engagement, blindly following Jahani. Soon they'd spread out into the defenses they'd dug themselves a week before. Noem and Delilah, sticking close to Jahani, crouched in a blind and waited in the din of gunfire. Between them, they possessed an old rifle and crossbow, knives, and war clubs. That and their bare hands against whatever guns the Alganians were unloading into their comrades' positions.

The Alganian fire slackened at the fresh opposition from Jahani's squadron, allowing the beaten and bloodied Donlandan pickets to withdraw, carrying wounded and dead. Those who could still fight hunkered down to help cover the retreat.

"How many are there?" Jahani asked the other squad's captain.

"Can't tell," she replied. "Dozens, probably. But their guns... like something out of the ancient stories. It's like they never have to reload. We can't get close to fight them. At this rate, they'll roll us up and go straight to Kroas!"

Noem could tell that even Jahani was nervous now. Then another message from headquarters: assault in progress on Bronaan Pass road! Outnumbered, outgunned! Lost comms with forward outposts!

Jahani's face blanched. Noem trembled with fury. The enemy in front of them was just a diversion! The Donlandan reserves were coming down the gap behind them, and Milles did not know that Jahani had left his post. There were no reinforcements available for Bronaan Pass. They'd been tricked, in their own territory, no less. As if in confirmation, the firing stopped altogether.

"Jahani" Noem whispered. "We need to radio the camp and fall back."

The muscles in Jahani's jaw rippled, and his light complexion turned red as the gravity of the situation sunk in. But rather than admit failure, he doubled down.

"No. We counterattack. We can do nothing about the camp. We take our revenge!"

This time Delilah tried to intervene, gripping his arm before he could rise.

"Take your hands off me!" Jahani snapped, shoving her away before she could speak. He rose and moved forward at a crouch, waving his fighters on. The others glanced around nervously but obeyed. Noem looked at Delilah fearfully. He knew what she was thinking: it was time to relieve Jahani of command.

Reaching into his tobacco pouch with one hand, he took Delilah's hand with the other. "Spirits, forgive our foolishness and help us to defend your lands," he prayed, scattering the offering before him. They moved. Jahani had already advanced several paces. His fighters had risen to follow, but now they looked to Noem and Delilah. One of the fighters nodded, and as they did, Noem saw their eyes glint in the moonlight and understood. They were ready to invoke *impiegann*, the prerogative of a Donlandan squadron to impeach a captain who has proven incompetent or incapacitated. A desperate decision for a desperate moment.

As the unsuspecting Jahani was within their grasp, the forest erupted. Bullets ripped and popped around them, sending splinters flying off the trees and shards from the rocks. The fighters dove for cover. The one who had nodded a moment before landed like a sack in the middle of the trail, clutching their stomach in agony. Noem crawled to them, gripped their arm, and dragged them under cover as bullets clipped around their ears.

The three of them lay flat in their blind as it was slowly disassembled by the unrelenting hail. Pinned, they could only fire blindly in return. Noem heard screams as more comrades were hit. His eyes locked on Delilah's in fury.

"They'll pick us off one by one!" he shouted.

"I know." Her normally calm face was taut with fear. Then it changed. Was it resolution? Resignation? She had made a silent decision. Trembling, she closed her eyes and dug her fingers into the soil, clinging to it like a child clutching her bearer. Her body tensed.

"Delilah?" he shouted over the din, shaking her. "Delilah!"

She turned to him, eyes entranced. Slowly, calmly, she rose.

"Delilah, no!" he seized her arm, pulling her down. Ignoring him, she stood again.

"Delilah!" He grabbed her desperately.

"No. It's okay." She replied with an otherworldly, placid calm. A voice distant, almost not her own. Her glazed eyes looked through him into an unseen realm.

Noem watched with desperate, futile despair as she emerged from cover and stepped onto the trail, fully exposed. But she remained unhurt, as though invisible to the enemy. The bullets flew around and about her, but none sought *her*. She floated down the trail and disappeared into the shadows. Noem rose to follow and regretted it: he was met with a hail of fire and dove to safety as the bullets continued chipping away at his fortifications.

Suddenly, the firing stopped. Noem heard shouts in a foreign tongue: Alganian. Then the shouts turned to screams. Noem signaled his comrades to advance. They obeyed and rose to the attack. Jahani, stunned, followed.

They met no opposition. Only dead and wounded enemies, their bodies broken and crumpled. The Donlandans emerged into the open area where the creek flowed out the gap toward the Shendoa Desert. More Alganians wearing strange, drab uniforms lay broken, cut, and bludgeoned. Noem snatched up one of the enemy guns and examined it: a .30-06 semi-automatic, eight-round magazine. Factory made? *No wonder...*

Noem motioned for the fighters to fan out. "Find Delilah!" he commanded.

Noem went alone, following a strange intuition that sent him tramping through the woods, across the creek, and toward a rock formation up a slope to his left. He found Delilah sitting under the overhang, cross-legged. Her eyes were glass, entranced. Her hands and arms and torso, spattered in enemy blood. In her right hand, a naked blade, her war club in her left.

"Delilah," Noem said softly, kneeling in front of her, touching her shoulder. Her body was rigid, unresponsive, unseeing eyes still glazed. "Delilah, it's over, please come back to us!" He shook her gently. He looked over his shoulder for his comrades. Their voices called in the distance, but none were near. When he turned back, her eyes had rolled back in her head. She slumped to the ground.

"Oh my spirits, Delilah!" he shouted, catching her by the shoulders, patting her cheeks. "Delilah, come on. Please, come back to me! Stay with me. Medic," he shouted. "Medic!"

He scooped her up in his arms and cradled her on his lap as her weapons clattered to the ground. *She's dying! Oh, spirits, please not now. Don't let her die.*

"Medic! Help us!" he shouted again and again.

Minute after intolerable minute passed before the medic found them and scrambled up under the overhang. She crawled over and checked Delilah's vitals.

"Her heart's racing, her breathing's erratic, but I can't find anything else wrong," she said, shaking her head. "We should move her back to camp. I can monitor her better there."

"Okay." Noem nodded jerkily, catching a terrified sob. "Let's go!"

As they regrouped, Noem saw Jahani and charged. "You! This is on you. You did this to her!" Before anyone could stop him, Noem leveled Jahani with a thunderous punch to the jaw. For once, Jahani did not fight back. He lay and took the beating until their comrades pulled Noem away, flailing and screaming.

"Noem! Noem!" Yasan called as he ran up, radio in hand. "Shut up for a second and listen." He handed over the receiver. The channel was open, and Noem fell silent, his body still taut and trembling.

"...she's tearing them apart! Some kind of ghost! The whole Alganian force is going down!"

"Wolfhound, this is Nestling. Please repeat."

"Nestling, this is Wolfhound. Someone just tore into them. Looks like one of ours, a woman, but we can't see who. She's fighting like a ghost! They can't hit her!"

Noem lowered the receiver.

Yasan looked back at him with wide eyes. "Someone just saved our asses," he said.

"Yeah, someone..." Noem looked at Delilah. *Could it be?*

Delilah lay on a stretcher in her catatonic state for the entire climb back to the camp. They returned to news of a miraculous

victory. The Alganians had overrun their outposts on the Bronaan
Pass road, pushing to within a mile of the summit only to be cut
to pieces and sent headlong back to the desert. But nobody could
agree on what hit them, it depended on who you asked. Some
said it was nothing more than one of their IEDs throwing the
enemy into confusion in the dark, causing them to attack each
other. Others said it was a heroic rearguard stand by one of the
outposts, all of whom had since died of wounds. But the surviving
eyewitnesses claimed the enemy was turned back by a single
woman who fought with the strength and speed of many, who
whirled through the enemy column like a tornado, cutting them
down with club and knife, appearing in one place, then another,
so that no blow could land, no bullet could find its mark. Those
who weren't there dismissed this last account as shell-shocked
ravings.

But Noem dismissed nothing as he kept vigil by his lover's
bedside back in Kroas. When they carried her home and lay her in
her bed, she briefly awoke. Her eyes focused and rested on Noem.
"Aphara Wari!" she whispered. "The spirits of the land fight for
us." With these words, all of the strength left her, and she fell into
a deep sleep.

But strangely, Noem was no longer afraid. Remembering the
epic of Aphara Wari, he looked on Delilah with wonder. Could
it be real? The intuition that drew him to her under the rock
strengthened, and as the healers prayed and made offerings day
in and day out, he felt the comforting, protective presence of the
spirits around and about her sleeping form.

***

Delilah's eyes fluttered back to Noem on a still morning in early
spring, four months later, while he lay curled by her side. He said
nothing. He only pulled her against him and held her.

"Noem?" she whispered.

He raised himself on one elbow and leaned over her. "I'm here."

"What happened? Was I hit? I don't feel any pain."

"No, my love, you are not injured."

"Then why am I home? What happened?"

"What do you remember?"

Delilah thought hard, puzzlement knitting her brow. "Jahani leading us down the gap, and I was about to knock him out. After that, it's like a dream, like the spirits took my hand. I remember fighting, the Alganians' screams, how helpless they seemed. My body felt like it was burning." She looked up at Noem, afraid, eyes searching for answers.

What do I tell her?

Noem told her what he'd seen, what the witnesses had said.

Delilah looked disoriented, agitated, confused. "I... I don't understand... no, I couldn't have been... how?"

"It's okay," Noem said, calming her. "We don't have to explain it. It's enough that we are safe. The spirits of the land fought through you."

Delilah sighed and rested her head on Noem's shoulder. Outside, the warriors of Kroas cleaned their rifles, sharpened their knives, and packed rations. The Alganians had raided a village to the north. If the Donlandans were fast, they could intercept the raiders before they crossed the Shendoa Desert.

"Noem!" someone shouted through the window. "You're captain again! Let's go!"

Noem sighed wearily, kissed Delilah, and rose from the bed. Something in him knew this would be a long war. The times of fighting had returned. Delilah would need all the rest she could get.

An Accident on Louisa Road

K.G. GARDNER

THE JOURNEY TO D.C. started early. The alarm shrieked at 5:15, and Ed scurried into the shower, the burst of cold water waking him faster than coffee could. He shaved with a straight razor then put a little putty in his thick, dark hair to combat the cowlick on top. The Charlottesville office was relaxed; most of his co-workers wore jeans, and some would even show up in shorts as soon as it hit sixty degrees. The D.C. staff put the business in business casual, and Ed wanted to make a good impression on the new hires. He laid out his clothes the night before, but in the jaundiced glow of the ceiling fan light, the new jeans seemed unworthy of the blue button-down. He opened the accordion doors on his closet and exchanged the jeans for crisp chinos, the ones Debra had always liked on him.

What would Debra make of his life here? Would she be awed by the mist rising from the Rivanna River as it cut its path through Albemarle County? Ed tried to picture her in one of the spindly chairs at his kitchen table, her blond hair tucked behind her ears, holding a coffee mug and gazing out the window at the low clouds clinging to the lush mountaintops. The view was the only striking feature of the apartment he rented. The eat-in kitchen was a bit cramped, and the backsplash and cabinets needed updating. The outlets were placed in odd areas, and the faucet in the bathroom was temperamental. But it was all his, and it was all he could afford without the extra income from Debra. Ed wondered what she was doing, whether she still rose early to run in Rock Creek Park in that high-viz vest. He shook his head. At some point, he would stop caring. Only been a few months. He needed time to settle in.

Ed had scoped out some running clubs, but he didn't feel ready to commit to anything, not even a running club. Each weekend he would go somewhere to get to know the area—a winery, Skyline Drive, the Downtown Mall. He thrummed with that tension between the freedom and the loneliness of being unattached, seesawing between the two. What grounded him was doing the same job for the same firm. Lucky that Esther agreed to his move in exchange for this twice-monthly trip to D.C. to bond with his co-workers. A small price to pay for escaping the politics, the people, the traffic.

He padded into the kitchen in sock feet to brew coffee and smear cream cheese on a plain bagel. No time to linger over breakfast. He would get on the road early and eat en route. Last time, he encountered a backup on I-66 and didn't make it to his desk until 9:25. Esther dealt him the stare of death that day and orchestrated a big show of having to move meetings around. He didn't want to jeopardize his agreement by coming in late again. He poured hot coffee into a Spy Museum travel mug and grabbed the bottle of red wine from Keswick Vineyards, a peace offering for Esther. Maybe he could persuade some of his D.C. friends to come down for winery tours when the weather perked up.

Waze told him the optimal route would be via Keswick to Gordonsville and Orange. It was a scenic route, although now that the clocks had sprung forward, he wouldn't be able to see the horse farms with their immaculate white fences or the sleeping vines that would feed the wineries. Promptly at six, he queued up the latest episode of his favorite podcast, *Ali on the Run*, and steered his Kia Sportage east on 250. He made the left onto Louisa Road as the sky was turning a deep navy blue, still dark enough to hide the redbud explosions that marked the beginning of spring. He slipped under a sleepy I-64 and slowly took the curve near the Keswick Post Office, which, squat and plain in the glare of the headlights, resembled an abandoned bomb shelter. Ed passed the turn for Black Cat Road, wondering about the name and if it was bad luck to cross it. What a silly, random thought. He needed more caffeine. He flipped open his travel mug, the aroma of coffee enveloping the car.

As Ali Feller chatted with Meb Keflezighi at the Boston Marathon, Ed rounded another bend in the road, slowing to thirty-five miles an hour. Someone darted in front of the car. A face frozen with fear hovered before him, eyes wide and bloodshot, mouth open in a scream. The face of a woman. Ed slammed on the brakes and wrenched the steering wheel to the right. The Sportage squealed to a stop, inches from an ancient ash tree covered in ivy. Ed's heart knocked against his ribcage as if desperate to escape. He put his hand over his chest and tried to slow his ragged breathing. Pain shot through his right knee. The car seemed to be closing in on him, so he pushed open the door and stumbled outside, his knee buckling. He sucked in the cool air again and again. Steadying himself with one hand on the hood, he limped to the front of the car.

The woman lay motionless where she had rolled to rest at the foot of the ash. A scarf covered her head, and she wore a plain cotton dress with a billowing skirt. Sweat glistened on her dark skin. Her full lips were parted, her pink tongue just visible.

Ed moved as quickly as his knee allowed and collapsed beside her. He had never seen a dead body up close, and he had certainly never killed anyone before.

Oh my God, I killed someone!

As he crouched to see if she was breathing, she sat upright, nearly knocking Ed over. She stared into the headlights, panting, terror rolling off her in waves. Blood and dirt marred her young face, her clothes. The way she was dressed, she could be part of some religious sect, one that abhorred electronics and modern ways. Or maybe she had been imprisoned in someone's basement and tortured or abused over a long period, only to free herself when the opportunity arose.

He held up his hands, his palms toward her. "My name is Ed. What's your name?"

Fear twisted her face and hands into knots as she stared at him. "Sarah."

"I want to help you, Sarah. Stay here." He jerked a thumb at the Sportage. She gazed at it in wonder, like she'd never seen a car before. What would she make of his smartphone? "I'm going to get... something... out of my car." He sensed her eyes on him as he hobbled backward to the open door of the car. He grabbed his phone from the console. Not one bar. A downside of living in a semi-rural area was the patchy phone service. He'd have to wait to call 9-1-1 until he reached Gordonsville. Ed shoved the useless phone into his pocket and stood. He tested his knee, putting more weight on it. Still tender, but not as bad as he feared. He shuffled to the front of the car.

Sarah was gone. Ed blinked and shook his head. Where could she be? He walked gingerly to the ash, looking to either side of the trunk. The ground between the tree and the road looked disturbed. Had she run off? Or was that a skid mark from the car? She must be injured from the impact. He had to find her, get her help.

"Sarah?" At first, he called softly in case she was near. Then, as dread unfurled in his chest, he raised his voice. "Sarah?"

Ed scanned the horizon. The Southwest Mountains had emerged from the darkness, menacing against the lightening sky. He could make out other dark shapes in the field beyond the post and rail fence: a gazebo, a small wooden bridge, a row of apple trees lining the drive leading to a large farmhouse a hundred yards away. Dogs barked in the distance. Someone must have woken up and come out to investigate. Ed crossed the road and scrambled over the fence, moving toward the sound while minding his knee. The dogs must have scared the woman into hiding. Three other figures walked from the direction of the farmhouse, carrying torches—actual flaming torches. One figure headed toward the gazebo with the dogs, and the other men toward Ed. Like the woman, they looked straight out of the nineteenth century in their billowing white shirts, tied at the neck. One was tall, about six foot two, clean-shaven, fair hair. The other man looked older, his dark beard flecked with steel gray. Clean-shaven carried a rifle. Dark Beard had a pistol on one hip, a coil of rope on the other. Fiery light and shadow played across their taut faces.

"You there." Clean-shaven raised his torch. "Who are you?"

Ed slowly raised his empty hands. He took a breath, willing his voice to be calm and steady even if his insides were not. "My name is Ed. I was out driving and I—I think I hit a woman. But it was an accident. She ran out into the road—"

"Sarah." Dark Beard's voice dripped with venom. "Where is she?"

"I don't know. She ran off, and I was looking for her, and then I saw you. I thought you might be able to get help."

The two exchanged glances, their faces cast in angry relief by the dancing light of the torches. If these were the men who had imprisoned her—Ed shuddered at the thought—then he didn't want to be responsible for sending her back with them.

"What is this place?" Ed asked, his eyes bouncing between the two men.

"Mildmay Plantation," Dark Beard said. "Everyone around knows Mildmay. Are you newly come here?"

"I am new to the area, yes. Is this a historical reenactment? That's one of the reasons I moved here, for the history, you know, Monticello and all that. It's pretty early in the day for that, but you're really impressive—"

"You sound like a Yankee."

"And your dress is strange."

Ed stifled a laugh. They were really committed to the act. "I grew up in Jersey, but I lived in D.C. for five years before moving here."

Dark Beard lurched forward, moving the torch between himself and Ed. His eyes blazed. "You wouldn't be one of them Yankees that's stealing our property, would you?"

"What? No."

At the mention of stealing, Ed thought of the car and looked back to see that it was gone. In its place, mist oozed along the road, snaking around a large bush. The ash had disappeared, too. Was this some elaborate distraction while someone stole the Sportage?

"Hey! What did you do with my car?"

"What're you talking about? Ain't no train for miles."

"It's not a train, it's a—"

"Maybe it's that Underground Railroad," Clean-shaven said.

Dark Beard's teeth glowed yellow in the firelight. "Tell us what you did with the girl."

"Nothing. I told you, I was trying to help her but—"

"You admit you helped her escape?"

Fear tickled the inside of Ed's throat. "I hit her with the car. She was hurt. I was trying to get her medical help, a doctor."

"She don't need a doctor. Well, she might, after we get her back. Where is she?"

The barking grew louder. The third man headed their way, three dogs bounding ahead of him.

"Where is she?" Dark Beard demanded.

"I told you, I don't know." Curiosity overcame wariness. "You accused me of stealing property. What property?"

Dark Beard released a harsh, guttural laugh. "The girl." He looked at his companion. "Can you believe him, Cliff? He don't know where he is, never heard of Mildmay, he dresses like... like that. And then he acts like he don't know the girl belongs to Mildmay."

Cliff snorted. "Where else does a Negro girl running around here belong?"

They didn't just dress like it was the nineteenth century; they were mentally stuck in the nineteenth century. And in a profoundly horrifying way.

Ed shook his head and held up his hands again. "Look, I don't know what twisted LARPer fantasy I wandered into, but I'm going to go find Sarah, find my car, and get her some help. And I'm going to tell the cops about you people out here. What you're doing is disgusting."

He took a few steps before Cliff said, "You better come with us, mister. Have a little talk."

Ed spun. Dark Beard sprang forward, his free hand moving toward the pistol in his belt. Was it a prop in their sick role-playing, or was it real? Before terror could fog his mind, he remembered his phone. He drew it from his pocket like a gun and pressed the flashlight icon, shooting light into their eyes. As their hands flew up to cover their faces, he turned and ran like it was the last half mile of the marathon and his personal best was within reach. His knee ached, but it didn't collapse. From behind, swear words and shouts for the man with the dogs.

The car was his only hope of escape, but it had vanished. Impossible. The keys were in his pocket. No one could have driven off without him hearing, and no one could have moved the car far enough to hide it. A cold panic washed through him. Where should he run? Every breath was a battle as he barreled toward the fence. He scrambled over it and stumbled down the sloping embankment to the road.

The road! He looked at the pale peach tint on the horizon, the treetops blazing in the early morning light. Must be close to 6:30. More cars would be out. He would flag one down and get those sons of bitches arrested for what they had done to that woman, for threatening him and stealing his car. He ran into the road, gravel crunching beneath his feet.

Gravel? Where asphalt and a double yellow line should be was nothing but gravel. He turned in a circle. The landscape was different, with fewer trees and no grapevines. What happened?

A hiss came from a large rhododendron bush near where the ash had been. A woman peered from the side, waving Ed toward her. He dove behind the bush. A short, thin woman dressed like the one he had hit with his car stared at him with fury.

"You," she whispered. "You fool! Now I have to send you back."

"Who—"

"Shh!" She put a bony finger to her lips. Her eyes, black as night, held his.

Ed nodded once. The dogs grew louder. A shiver raked his spine. It sounded like they were sniffing around the road, so close to where they were. Boots scraped on the gravel road.

"I don't see him, Cliff."

"Damn it, George, that's three now. Mr. Madigan is going to string us up."

"If he gets rid of us, he'll have a helluva time hiring more hands." Another voice, deeper, likely that of the man with the dogs. "He's already losing people who think the place is haunted. Or under some sort of spell."

"That damn witch. When I get my hands on her..."

Ed risked a glance at the woman, who struck him with the full force of her black eyes.

"Well, let's go back to the house," Cliff said. "Maybe they found her."

They dragged their feet across the road, and the fence creaked as they climbed over it. Ed was sweating under the intense gaze of the woman, his breath shallow and quick. He dared not move until she did.

She slapped him across the face.

"Ow!"

"You fool! How'd you get here? Why'd you mess up my plan, boy?"

"I—I didn't mean to. What plan?"

"I sent Sarah away, to be free. Free in another time. Your time. And you"—she pointed at his wildly beating heart—"you went through the door. Now you're here when you should be there." She threw up her hands.

"Uh, you sent her through time?"

"Yeah." From the folds of her skirt, she pulled out a small leather pouch.

"And who are you?"

"Mama Angela." A feral smile cut across her round face. "The witch."

Ed cringed. "You're a witch?"

Mama Angela shrugged and fussed with her pouch.

"Do you live here? At Mildmay?"

"Yes. A hateful place, this is."

"What... what do they do here?"

"They work us. Men, women, children. In the field, in the house. They beat us. Treat us like animals. Worse than animals! Dogs and horses get better than we do."

"So, you're all slaves on a plantation?"

Mama Angela glared at Ed. "*They* call me slave. You"—again, that finger like an arrow to his heart—"call me Mama Angela."

"Mama Angela." Ed swallowed. "You're freeing people, sending them to the future. How?"

From her pouch she drew a smooth, flat stone. She pressed it into Ed's hand. It throbbed, warm and soothing. "You take this. Keep it in your left hand. With your right hand, draw a circle with your middle finger in the center of the road. Stand in the circle, close your eyes, and say, 'Send me, send me, set me free.' " She poked Ed, and he flinched. "Go on. Get out there. Before the door closes."

"What door?"

"The one I opened for Sarah. Go!"

She shoved Ed, and he sprawled onto the road, breaking a branch off the bush. With Mama Angela's fierce eyes on him, he did as instructed. Grit ground under his fingernail as he drew the circle.

He stood in the center, shifting his weight from one foot to the other, and inhaled deeply.

"Send me, send me, set me free."

"Believe it!" Mama Angela hissed.

"Send me, send me, set me free." The stone throbbed in Ed's hand. A warm sense of calm spread through his hand, his arm, his chest. "Send me, send me, set me free."

A gust of wind stirred Ed's hair and clothes. The light blinked out of the world, coating him in inky darkness. A familiar sound drifted toward him from a distance. A car. His eyes flew open, and he ran to the grassy verge moments before an SUV rolled by. He looked around. The sun was up, its golden light stroking the spines of the Southwest Mountains and the bare, woody grapevines at their feet. The Sportage was parked across the road, near the ash. Ed touched his face, his chest. Slowly, he put one foot in front of the other, listening for other cars, until his hand yanked open the door. He poured himself inside and took a shuddering breath. He strapped himself in, started the car, and eased out onto the road. The clock on the dashboard said 7:12. His hands shook on the wheel, but his foot was firm on the gas pedal.

Two hours and twenty-six minutes later, Ed slid into his assigned workstation and docked his laptop. Beside him, Esther finished typing an email and turned to him, her fleshy face hard.

"I rescheduled the meeting with the new hires for ten-thirty. You promised you were going to leave earlier this time."

Ed spun slowly in his chair. In his haste to get to his desk, he'd left the wine in the car. He hung his head and sighed.

Esther's pursed lips fell open, her plucked eyebrows rising over her deep-set eyes as she leaned forward. "You all right, Ed? You look pale."

She wouldn't believe a word of it. He wasn't sure he believed any of it. He'd used the drive to think it over and over, and by the time he parked, he knew that he would never tell anyone. But he might try to find Sarah.

"Ed?" Esther's brows reached new heights. "What happened?"

He decided to take the path of greatest plausibility.

"There was an accident on Louisa Road. A major one."

The Girl in the Stream

PARKER MCINTOSH

THE GIRL IN THE stream wasn't dead.

Amanda didn't think she looked alive, either, floating half submerged on her back in a still pool near the bank. Pale skin, so thin it bordered on translucent. The suggestion of muddy veins spiderwebbed across her cheeks and down her throat. Black hair, a deadened cataract that connected the girl's skull to the water. She wore a long white shift that hid her feet and trailed off into the current. And she stared with pupils so big they covered most of her eyes, following Amanda's progress on the streambank.

Amanda's throat closed. She'd been walking up the bank, trying to lose herself in the stream's mindless babble when she found the girl. It wasn't fear like when she'd been confronted by the neighbor's loose dog. Standing frozen at the mailbox while it snarled and inched closer until her father scared it away with a shotgun blast. And it wasn't like when her mother caught her sneaking cookies from the pantry before lunch and slapped her fingers with the yardstick. In the girl's bottomless eyes, Amanda recognized depthless violence.

The girl looked at her, motionless, as if she were cut from bedrock. Eyes the color of lake water beneath a storm. Amanda's feet sank in the damp sand, her toes turning to stone. Icy fingers of water seeped up and gripped her feet. The cool air turned frigid.

Amanda rubbed her arms for warmth and the girl struck, lunging from the water up the riverbank. Amanda, arms pin-wheeling, fell backward. Her shoes stuck in the grip of the sand. Amanda pulled her feet free and up into the arms of the ivy on the bank, her eyes closed and her teeth gritted. She hadn't even managed to scream.

Nothing happened. Amanda opened her eyes. The girl was close. So close she could trace the pulseless black veins in her neck. The hem of the girl's shift was in the water. The rest of her body stretched up the bank, not quite long enough to reach Amanda.

The girl's veins receded into the marble of her skin; her snarl softened into bowed white lips. Her eyes lost their depth and hardened like drying mud. Behind the girl's body, Amanda's shoes sank beneath the sand.

"Can you leave the water?" Amanda said when she found her voice. *I should be running,* she thought. *I should be crying out for help.* Something kept her quiet. While her heart still pumped in her throat, she fought the insane urge to step forward, into the reach of the Girl in the Stream.

The girl tilted her head but did not answer.

"Do you live here?"

The girl crawled backward, retracting into the water, her eyes never leaving Amanda's. Her body fell beneath the surface of the water, the tip of her nose the last to submerge. Amanda waited until the cloud of the girl's billowing white shift settled like sediment and fell invisible before she took her eyes from the stream. She shivered, true cold coming on now, and turned downstream to head for home. Stepping through the brush, Amanda was careful, even with the steepness of the bank and her bare feet, to keep a good distance between herself and the water.

***

The waterways of Albemarle County proved deadly that summer. A college student taking remedial classes drowned at the head of the Rivanna Reservoir, his car abandoned on a low bridge traversing a nameless branch. He had stopped, the paper reported, to relieve himself.

"Drunk idiot," Amanda's father said. "Shows all the commonsense schooling earns you."

A group of adults tubing down the Mechums River were caught in a crosscurrent. Their inner tubes flipped, and two women were forced beneath a natural dam near a stream outlet.

"Weren't even wearing their life preservers," Amanda's mother said.

Amanda wanted to know which outlet they'd been trapped by.

A fly fisherman disappeared in the state park. His friends searched for him when his dog returned home alone. They found his truck and tent, but the ash in the firepit was cold. His rod was discovered on a boulder a quarter mile downstream, the hook missing and the line hanging limp over the water like a thin strand of hair.

Amanda collected these cutout stories from the local papers. She wrote down the details in a journal she kept in her closet. When the shouting in the house felt like it would overwhelm her, she took them out and read them like clues she could piece together. She dreamed of the Girl in the Stream and woke each morning with the afterburn of the girl's icy hands cold on her throat.

***

The Girl in the Stream stared at Amanda with narrowed eyes. *Is she confused that I would come back?* The girl stood in the middle of the stream, which should have been over her head in depth but only covered her ankles. Shirttails dripped down below the surface. Her body floated there, bobbing in the current. Face rounder than Amanda remembered, cheekbones hidden by a fullness that hadn't been present a week before. She smiled, her teeth stained with mud like weatherworn gravestones. Then she dropped below the surface. Amanda hiked on, heart racing like she'd stared down a wild animal.

Amanda wasn't sure why she'd come back to the stream or why she'd been seeking the girl that lived in it. After seeing her again, locking eyes with her wildness and power, she knew she'd return.

Amanda explored the woods surrounding the stream until she had a name for every tree. She discovered calm pools where water bugs skated, an oxbow of a lake where a fat orange salamander scurried away from her feet, and fishing holes where brook trout bobbed below the surface, their slim, torpedo-like bodies pulsing shadows fighting against the current. She stumbled on remains of campsites, firepits, fast food wrappers, and Styrofoam cups. When Amanda saw these discarded items, she picked them up. She ignored the more precious abandoned items: a fishing pole, a camera with a cracked lens, a rusting Jeep at the end of an overgrown trail. She didn't dwell on the fate of their owners.

The Girl in the Stream didn't always appear. Sometimes, Amanda caught a flash of white billowing beneath the surface. Others, a feeling of watchfulness permeating the babbling brook sounds. And sometimes, it wasn't present at all. Amanda grew to understand these feelings. To know when it was safe and when to keep the water at arm's length.

When she didn't feel the girl's presence, Amanda explored closer to the stream itself. She grew bold and ventured into the water. Once, she stripped to her underwear and jumped in, imagining she was the Girl in the Stream. The water closed in above Amanda, and she never touched the bottom. Her lungs constricted in an icy grip, and she clambered from the water covered in goose pimples. She felt clean, though. As if some impurity had been temporarily washed from her skin.

As Amanda shivered, shaking the water from her body and pulling her clothes on, she caught sight of the girl's eyes watching her from above a small waterfall. They froze with a predatory hardness that made Amanda's stomach twist.

***

Amanda was old enough to suspect her parents were headed for divorce, so when they announced it before the end of summer, she wasn't surprised. Their arguments shifted in the last year from petty nitpicking to full-blown screaming matches that sent her scurrying to her closet or sprinting out of the house.

Amanda left her home on Gillums Ridge to live with her mother in a one-bedroom apartment in Staunton. She started high school and her memory of the Girl in the Stream diluted like oil over water. The image of the girl would clarify for brief moments if Amanda focused, before rippling as if a stone had been dropped into a watery reflection. She dreamed about the girl often, though, and wondered if that's all she'd ever been. A dream in the woods to distract her from other ugliness.

Something happened during the divorce that Amanda's mother wouldn't speak about, and Amanda did not live with her father over the summer. Visits to his house were short and supervised. She didn't explore the woods again on her own.

High school passed in a blur. Friends from her old school reached out less and less, and she found it easier to keep to herself.

Amanda only applied to colleges out of state. She felt water-logged at home, like roots were pulling her into muck. If she didn't sever them, she might drown. When she received a full ride to Southern Oregon University, it felt like a world away. She hoped it was far enough.

She didn't return to Virginia for fifteen years.

***

"It looks the same, only smaller," Amanda said.

She and her mother stood in front of the house on Gillums Ridge like children hesitating before jumping into the ocean. Her statement wasn't entirely true. The driveway was more potholed than she remembered, and the gray-green moss that shadowed the eaves had spread in swathes across the north-facing wall. Despite the summer heat, the house made Amanda shiver.

"We better get to it," Amanda's mother said.

She was smaller than Amanda remembered, too. Bent and wrinkled, like fifteen years had been fifty.

Amanda's father was dead. Something about a life lived hard catching up to him, and the house needed to be cleaned out. She wasn't sure how she felt about this. The last time she'd spoken to her father, she still lived in Virginia. Still, the house was an undeniable part of her life, a tether or an anchor.

Amanda's bedroom looked like it hadn't been touched or cleaned since she left it. The comforter was the same, purple and green pattern muted by dust. She bagged half-remembered trinkets for Goodwill or the dump, holding herself aloof from the memories they evoked. And then she found her journal.

When she opened the pages, the newspaper clippings were yellow and curled into little cocoons. The careful, looping letters written in cursive looked like someone else had written them. Amanda stared at the history of forgotten violence in the stream and shuddered. For years, she'd covered disappearances and unsolved cases for her local Oregon paper. Puff pieces and snippets to garner eyeballs, and she'd never connected them to her time in this house. To the Girl in the Stream. The shadow of the Cascades chilled her life just like the shadow of the Blue Ridge, and she never noticed.

Icy fingers of thought clawed at Amanda's throat. Oily memories bubbled like an evil spring with poison waters. The walls closed in. The house, disinfected by their cleaning, was still haunted. She fled and entered the woods.

***

The stream barely trickled. It resembled an inconvenient path through the woods rather than the healthy flow she remembered, the streambed now a collection of polished rocks and knee-high weeds. She started to walk, keeping away from the water's edge out of instinct rather than the fear that something lurked in the pitiful flow. It made for rough hiking. Amanda didn't remember the telltale differences between poison ivy and common. In trying to avoid anything green, she ended up covered in mud, her shoes half-sucked off her feet with each step.

She wasn't thinking about the girl until she saw her. Above a boulder that was once a waterfall and now little more than a seep, she expected a wide pool filled with brook trout. She found an empty bowl of rock and gravel. In the middle lay the girl, one pale and clammy foot firmly in the remaining trickle of water

She was smaller than Amanda remembered. A child bride struck dead, still wearing her long white shift. Her skin was pale, her hair a tangled mess of reeds and moss. Cheekbones stuck out like the knees of a cypress tree.

Amanda approached cautiously, her body half-turned and ready to run away. A dozen macabre headlines spilled across her mind. But the girl looked at Amanda, her eyes glassy, the rest of her still. Her eyes had the pale vacuousness of window-filtered sunlight on a cloudy day. She reached out, a finger pointing, before her hand fell limp in the mud.

The forest around the stream crowded close in the absence of flowing water. The girl was dying, whatever that meant for her, like the fish and frogs and salamanders before her.

There was a sullenness to this ignominious end for such a force in Amanda's life. That the one powerful thing she had held at bay could be broken in her absence brought back every oily fingerprint of those summer days and humid nights. The weight of memory choked her, and she fell to her knees.

Amanda saw herself reflected in the girl's pupils, a shadowed, oblong body. Amanda stood and stepped forward and picked the girl up. She thought there might be some connection that wouldn't break. That the shirt would hold tight to the water that was the girl's home, and she wouldn't be able to pull her away. The shirt dragged in the mud. The girl lifted like an empty husk. Cold and hollow. Only her eyes, watery and wondering, betrayed any sign of life.

Amanda abandoned hope of avoiding poison ivy. She carried the shell of the girl downstream through the mud and vegetation. Past the dried-up pools where fishermen once cast for trout. Down the polished slopes where water once fell. She trudged through reeds and kicked her feet free of weeds, all the way to the river.

Compared to the stream, even at its height in her memory, the breadth of the river was stunning. Branches tumbled by, drawn on by a flow as powerful as time. Amanda stared, holding the girl for a while. Wondering why she never came to this wide-open space when she was younger. It felt freer. The air wasn't so viscous.

She set the girl at the edge of the water, submerging her legs. Amanda stood to go.

The girl's arm shot out, grabbing Amanda's hand. Her skin was cold and rough, but strong. The tendons of her wrist stood out like roots, and Amanda's stomach clenched with fear. The strength was like the current. It could pull her in and under and hold her there forever.

The girl's eyes were hungry, but there was something else there, too. They shone with uncertainty. Her brow creased in question. Amanda stopped pulling away and squeezed the girl's hand until her own knuckles turned white to match the girl's skin. She felt the coldness in her grip. She saw herself beneath the water, kicking and struggling, her heavy clothes dragging her down. The water filled her nose and mouth. Amanda's feet touched a hard bottom and she kicked up, jerking her whole body.

She opened her eyes. A black tongue touched gray teeth, and blue lips circled.

Let me go.

The girl's fingers hung loose. Amanda was safe and dry on the riverbank, her own grip on the girl's hand the only thing holding them together.

Amanda opened her fingers, and the girl drifted back. Her shift was caught in the current and her body was drawn away. Before she slipped beneath the surface, the girl's mouth creased into a smile, her eyes glittered, and her head turned toward the unknown, around the bend.

Amanda hiked up to the road. The house, when it emerged from the trees, was just a house. Her mother, just another person. The ghosts, not excised, but separated from the waterways of her life. Shallow branches that did not warrant a second exploration. Amanda drifted up the driveway, her legs scratched, her hands muddy, her clothes soaked. She had never felt cleaner in her life.

The Untethered Visions of Henry G. in Cville

Karen M Kumor

THREE YOUNG MEN LOUNGED in The Whiskey Jar, each with a flight of three mostly empty glasses of whiskey in front of them. They had drunk beer at the Oktoberfest in a nearby park in the late afternoon and decided on some food and whiskey to finish off the night.

The time was late and also early morning when they finished joking, drinking, and telling tales. The laughter dimmed as their senses clouded. In the cozy, old brick tavern—wooden slat walls and spindle backed chairs—the warmth cocooned them. For a few minutes, each retreated inside themselves to exist in that lovely, drunken space.

Henry G., a tall, skinny man of twenty-four with dark, unruly hair, stood, checked his last glass for a last drop, and set it down too hard on the wooden table with a thump. "Time to go. Up, my men."

The other two nodded, inspected their empty glasses, and waved to the waiter as they stood. The three rambled on unsteady legs out toward the chill October night. Henry paused his six-foot five frame at the doorway and held up a hand, pointing inside. Stumbling back in, he grabbed his old UVA hoodie with *Cavalier* scripted on it and struggled into it.

His friends waited outside. One lit a cigarette.

As Henry exited the doorway, his shoulder collided with the door jamb, knocking him off balance. His body wheeled in a pirouette and he fell like a rag doll.

***

When he woke, Henry was shuffling through the Downtown Mall not too steadily. He passed The Fitzroy and remembered a wonderful dinner he shared with Tessa. *Where was she now? Did she marry that jerk? What did she see in him? She wore that yellow sundress with the flowers on the trim that day.*

He kept walking past that stupid, unfinished hotel, eight stories of rebar and steel I-beam Babylon open to the weather. *Been that way for what, ten years, maybe?* He rested against the big, black planter across from the hotel and shook his head. "Stupid, stupid," he mused out loud. No one noticed.

The Mall was crowded with people, everyone in shorts and short sleeves. Henry squinted at the sun, feeling the heat of late morning on his back. He wondered about it being daylight. *Musta' passed out.*

He struggled out of his jacket. Band music and fireworks echoed in the distance. In his fog, he dropped his jacket on the planter and wobbled down the Mall toward Ting Pavilion. *Must be a concert.*

Approaching Ting Pavilion, he realized the music was not in that direction. He puzzled for a moment, still brain-fogged. The noise was coming from UVA campus. Reorienting himself, he turned toward campus.

Oddly, Henry didn't recall crossing the bridge. He found himself approaching the Lawn with the old dorms lining it. People were milling around, families loitering and students rocking in the chairs outside their open doors. Lawnees and Lawnee parents.

He remembered Phil, two years younger, still lived in Room 11. He managed to find it. The door was open. Phil and Bart, his Whiskey Jar buddies, sat on the daybed with a couple glasses of beer. Henry thumped the door frame, and the two looked up briefly then raised their drinks.

"To Henry." And they drank.

Henry laughed and nearly lost his balance again. Phil gazed briefly toward Henry. His friends started talking about old times, reminiscing. Henry was not able to follow the conversation in his confused state, so he turned back toward the Lawn and decided he should find the toilet.

"I need a piss. It's this way, yeah?" Henry signaled to his left but did not wait for his friends' replies.

Henry felt damp sweat on his back and under his arms. He looked at the sun, covering his eyes with his hands as a shield. After seconds, he found he could take his hands away and look directly at the sun. It didn't hurt. He was amazed and stared at it a long time. It was white hot but did not hurt. He realized that it should be painful and was dangerous and looked away.

After his eyes readjusted to the light, he saw that there were about twenty large, white tents out on the Lawn. *When were those set up? It's not graduation, is it?*

He strolled the columned corridor searching for the toilet, but there were no signs. The people in the corridor were all in costumes: Civil War era costumes. The band, a small group of men in gray uniforms, dusty and ragged, played "Dixie."

Ha! A Civil War reenactment. Civil War, he sing-songed in his head. *C'ville. Civil. Uncivil. Civil. C'ville.*

But this was different. People were hustling in and out of the tents, carrying food trays, bowls, chamber pots, and linens. A bearded man exited one tent and lit up a cigar. Blood covered his apron and sleeves. *Very realistic.* The man sat heavily onto a bench by the tent.

Henry forgot about finding the toilet. He roamed, passing more dorm rooms. The doors were open, and inside were two or three men lying on cots. In one room, a man was moaning. Other rooms were quiet, the men inside sleeping, maybe.

The nice furniture was gone! That's going far for a reenactment!

A Black woman in white with a kerchief on her head exited a room carrying a chamber pot. She passed him, and the ripe smell of urine rose around him. He stopped a moment to clear his head and think.

A slender, wiry-muscled Black man, dressed in plain, weathered, rustic clothes approached him, his back bent under a heavy load of chopped wood. Sweat streamed down his face, and his shirt, dark with sweat, clung to his chest.

Outraged, Henry accosted him. "Sir, this is too much. You should not be participating in this as a slave. What kind of performance is this? It's, it's demeaning."

The man halted and looked up. He frowned and searched the air about him. He waved the air like shooing a fly, shifted his load, and continued past Henry.

Henry was dumbfounded. *What the hell! Have people lost their minds!?*

He gazed at the tents as he descended some steps to the Lawn. The band had stopped and was receiving instructions from the director.

A group of Black children, perhaps five to seven years old, were playing on the ground. They were playing a game with stones and were dressed in threadbare clothes, some clothes too small and some too big.

A Black woman hurried out of a nearby tent, tapped one child, and handed him something. She barked a half-heard order to him. He nodded, and she sent him running barefoot up and around the Rotunda.

Henry stared at the sun reflexively, shielding his eyes with his hands. Oddly, he could see the sun perfectly through his hands. He studied his hands in wonder. They were almost transparent. Henry was horrified. Momentarily, reality wheeled away from him in a surreal disconnect.

He laughed to himself. *I'm dreaming. That's why it's day and summer. It's really October. I just need to tell myself to wake up.*

"Wake up. Wake up."

But nothing happened.

Guess I have to wait.

He walked down the Lawn, away from the Rotunda, passing campfires and tents. Peeking into one, he wished he had not. The smell was revolting. Blood, rancid sweat, shit and piss. Soldiers held a man down as the surgeons prepared to sever an arm, an arm that was blue to the shoulder. The patient stiffened, awaiting the pain, but he was already in agony, his face contorted. Sweat soaked through the surgeons' shirts as they focused on the task. No words of kindness. A white woman in bright white attended the surgeons and a large, elderly Black woman attended her.

Henry turned away, not wanting to see more. Moans and a squelched scream split the air. Now, Henry needed to piss. A chamber pot stood outside a tent. He relieved himself, secure that this was a dream, anyway.

A group of soldiers wandered onto the Lawn opposite the Rotunda. He gasped as he realized that Old Cabell Hall was not there. The Lawn end was open, and the whole area was dust. Dust swirled and blew over the tents, unsaddled horses and children, and himself. And there were flies, lots of them, attracted by the rare fragrances.

The men were soldiers because they carried rifles, yet they wore dusty shirts, loose, tan pants, and battered, brimmed hats. Little they wore was gray, though one had a rebel cap. Rugged looking and weary, they rambled past him toward the largest tent. The tent flaps were open. Henry heard some talking but could not hear the exchange.

He marveled at all that surrounded him. How could he be here, in this place, seeing this so clearly?

More enslaved people busied about, carrying, loading, serving. He felt tired, very tired. It was as though the weary, burdened people around him made him tired. He felt their fatigue and sorrow as his own. His legs were heavy. Again, he tried to will himself awake.

"Wake up. Wake up!" he yelled as loud as he could. One person looked in his direction but then away.

It's not working. Maybe if I can find my way back to Phil's room?

He climbed up to the colonnade in front of the dorm. As he approached Phil's room, a woman in the distance walked toward him.

He knew that walk. Only one woman walked like that: Tessa. The woman carried a basket on her head and was dressed in a loose-fitting, indigo cotton dress and a kerchief. Her breasts shifted in cadence with her gait. Her rich, honey-brown skin was perfect. He felt desire like a live wire down his back.

Tessa walked regally. She was six feet two inches of woman. Not skinny, built strong. Perfect for him.

Maybe this dream was of Tessa's ancestor. He waited until she was quite close. The fragrance of the fresh bread in her basket conflicted with the ugly smells and, for a moment or two, won. Her blue dress and apron turned to yellow as she strode toward him.

It was Tessa! The small, oblique scar across her eyebrow was there. It was her.

It's not real, but...?

He yelled, "Tessa, Tessa!"

She stopped and searched the air vaguely. He wanted to kiss the scar on her brow. Instead, he reached out and gently touched it. She smiled, her black eyes mirthful. Her full mouth and beautiful teeth took his breath away. For a moment, he thought she saw him, looked into his eyes. But no, she walked right through him.

"Tessa, wait!"

When he turned, she was gone.

A scary thought bubbled up. *Was he a ghost? Something had happened. He couldn't remember.*

He dismissed the thought. After all, Tessa was not dead, he reasoned with broken logic.

He felt sad and drained, lost with a feeling that he'd forgotten something important. Something was missing.

Henry trudged up the stairs, passing enslaved and white people, men and women all engaged in urgent tasks. On the colonnade he found Phil's room. Inside, all the furnishings were gone. Just empty cots with clean, rustic covers on them, waiting for new patients. He was not able to stand any longer, his legs resisted movement. With relief, he laid down on one of the cots. All he wanted was sleep.

Ah, for some sleep. A thought swam up. He had fallen, but then nothing. It occurred to him that maybe it wasn't a dream. Maybe he was...

He felt hands on him. The hands were not gentle and not rough but firm, purposeful. His vision cleared, and he saw himself from above, lying on the concrete. Calmness enveloped him as he floated. He watched with interest but no emotion.

Ah ha! It's not a dream. I am messed up bad.

Yet he felt no distress. He watched, fascinated. He heard but could not see Phil crying.

His body lay on the ground in front of The Whiskey Jar, his face battered and bloody. A collar supported his neck. Two EMTs lifted him onto a gurney and into an ambulance. He saw Phil and Bart and gawkers.

He grasped that he was suspended somewhere in a mind space. One EMT examined him. The other was placing a catheter in his arm.

"Twenty-something year old man, face fracture from a fall. Vital signs: BP 200/100, pulse 110, respirations irregular, 12-20. Ox level ninety... five. Alcohol level 0.17. Unconscious, does withdraw to painful stimuli. Looks like broken left orbit with content extrusion into nasal cavity on left. Left eye vitreous hemorrhage."

"Yes... Okay. Will start head-trauma protocol... Yes. Moving now. Ready ER."

He felt nothing. No pain. No distress. He thought about Tessa again. *Tessa with the small scar across her left eyebrow. Beautiful Tessa. Her black eyebrows and beautiful skin.*

Stupid. He was so stupid. She wanted to settle down. But he let her go. Did he let her go, or did she dump him? Can't remember.

But Jezuz, she met the guy in a bar. She married some guy she met in a bar! And not a UVA bar, but some dive in town. I could walk into a hundred bars and never find someone like Tessa, funny and smart. Witty, but with a smiling wink.

He didn't like the guy or trust him.

Was he a Virginia Tech guy? Dopie Hokies... Or Richmond Spider? Stupid Richmond, don't know a spider from tick or a mite. Maybe it's spider-mite. A chigger! Vermin. Idiots!

Then he remembered feeling squeamish about introducing her to his Georgia gentry parents. But it never came to that, though he'd met her mother.

Where did they go for lunch? The winery with the ice cream? Where was that? She was a nice woman.

He heard they have a baby on the way.

No wasting time. Maybe that was it. He didn't want kids. He didn't. He thought maybe he would have, if... But Tessa.

Now he felt something. Loss. *Tessa was gone. Forever.*

Henry felt hands on him again. His senses returned. Now, that was pain! Big, roaring beast pain. His eye, his face. Voices talking surrounded him. He wore a white gown and was strapped down in an operating suite.

A woman spoke to him kindly. "Okay, now. We are taking you to surgery. You have suffered a bad head injury. We are taking care of you. Everything will be alright. We will get you through this. Just be calm." She put a mask over his face. "Breathe."

After hesitating, he did as he was told. But before the blackness enveloped him, he saw Tessa in her yellow, flower-trimmed sundress as he faded.

A swift thought flitted across his mind.

Where did I leave my jacket?

Thaw

E.F. BUCKLES

I WAS THE LAST dragon on Earth. My mistress found and raised me, but when I grew to the height of a pony and breathed my first flame, the citizens of our remote island home of Embonear became fearful of me. Their leaders claimed I was too dangerous to live and scheduled me to die at the hands of paid competitors. A mob wrenched me away from my mistress with chains into a sandy arena where I stood alone, trembling and frightened. But my mistress defied her country and stood up for me. She broke away from her captors, ran to my side, and used the magic she'd hidden from her own people for years to defend me from the warriors. With a flick of her hand, she blocked their arrows with a wall of ice, then blinded them with a flash of brilliant white. While they were still blinking and groping, I implored her to climb on my back, and we fled. Fled my attackers, the arena, and our island.

I flew over the water for days with her on my back. We reached a new continent, losing ourselves over a great sea of trees until my young wings could no longer bear the strain. I crashed at the bottom of a valley, skidding painfully on my belly through mud and underbrush.

My mistress's arm snapped from the impact. Blood soaked her sleeve. She needed help, and bonfires glowed in the distance. But we had no way of knowing if these strangers would try to kill me like the people of our homeland.

"I must hide you," she said. "But I swear I will return." Despite my pleading, she refused to allow anyone the chance to harm me again.

The scent of her anxiety was strong as she placed her good hand on my chest. Magic poured from her palm, freezing my every joint and scale in stone. Only my eyes, ears, and mind remained working, and I watched her walk away until she vanished from my life.

Hours turned into days, and I fought panic. Mistress would never abandon me. Not after all we'd been through. She must have fallen ill and would come for me as soon as she was well. But after years of solitude, my heart froze to stone, too.

***

Decades slipped away, and I watched in unfeeling silence as the seasons changed and the forest grew. Ivy crept up my legs until it covered me, but I could still peer through gaps between the leaves, especially when the wind blew. The green veil protected me from wind and rain while also shielding me from the gazes of the rare human that came through the area. In the early years, I mainly watched humans with brown skin and dark hair pass as they carried out their lives hunting, traveling, and gathering wood. I understood their language, though it was different from that of Embonear. Perhaps my mistress included a gift of translation in her spell, believing that I would need the knowledge had she been able to return and unfreeze me. These people spoke of many things: farming, war, gods, invasions, exploration. Sometimes their talk caused me worry that one of them, in their curiosity, might discover me. And what would their response be? I was little more than a strange decoration in this state, so they had no reason to fear. But perhaps I had a reason to fear them. Would they gawk at me? Move me? Break me to pieces? Best not to ponder that last option...

A child came close to finding me once while he and his friends passed by in their animal skin clothes and shoes. They tossed a small brown ball between themselves until one of them missed and it rolled to my feet. But he scooped up the ball and kept running.

Eventually, pale humans arrived. Explorers and hunters, carrying sacks of supplies on their backs and long gray sticks that flashed light and thundered, ending the lives of animals as effectively as any knife or arrow. But they never came near me. Until...

One day, a family passed by. Husband, wife, and two small children riding in their horse-drawn wagon. They climbed out of the wagon, paying my location no mind, and walked onward until they were out of view. Women were a rare sight. The wife reminded me of my mistress with her wavy brown hair, dark eyes, and slim figure, but the face was all wrong. It had been long since I last thought of her, yet my frozen heart couldn't even dredge up a twang of sentiment or other emotion. Over several months, they cleared a large swath of land until they had room to build a little cabin and plant some gardens.

I remained undiscovered under the trees, but the reduced foliage allowed me to observe the settlers' lives. They survived off the land for years and grew their family until they had six children. When the youngest was mature enough, she explored their land alone. Judging by her height, she was about twelve, the same age as my mistress when she hatched me from an egg and decided to raise me.

At first, the girl's exploration remained limited to the fields her family planted, but one day, she came to the edge of the forest, checked to make sure no one was looking, and slipped in. She climbed everything: rocks, trees, and vines, reminding me more of the monkeys of my homeland than a child. Finally, she ran past my location and tripped and fell in front of me. Her knee bled, and she grimaced, but then she turned toward me and any distress evaporated. I don't know what drew her attention. Was my claw poking out of the leaves? Whatever the reason, she came close, parted the ivy, and stared at my face with wonder. All those old questions from years ago came flooding back. If she told her family, what would they do with me?

After the girl cleared the debris off me, she studied me from nose to tail then ran off. She visited me almost daily after that, climbing on my back and running around me with her arms outstretched like she was flying. Once, she even brought a book out and drew my likeness, but she never brought another person to see me. I was her secret. But it didn't last. Barely a month later, the girl ran to me so fast that she was panting by the time she stopped. Much to my befuddlement, she took the ivy vines that she'd left around my shoulders like a shawl and covered me up the way I'd been when she first found me. Her mother strode out onto the porch of their house, shading her eyes with her hand and scanning the land for her daughter.

"Emma Grace!" the woman shouted. "Where are you, child?" A wagon sat in front of the house, and the girl's father and siblings loaded their belongings onto it.

Emma Grace shouted back, "Coming!" Once she had me covered, she lowered her voice to a whisper. "Goodbye, Dragon. Goodbye, house. Goodbye, land. I'll... I'll miss you." A tear trickled down her face. She swiped it away and took off at a run back to her family.

They were leaving? A part of me thought they would always stay. If my frozen heart had any feeling left, I would almost miss them.

Without the family to watch, time blurred again. The occasional human would happen by to examine the house, but they soon abandoned it to degrade until only the stone chimney stood.

The trees returned to where the fields had been, and the lonely years marched on, broken only by the random and infrequent passerby. Clothing styles evolved, as did the bags carried on their backs, but they all wore the heavy boots eternally common amongst travelers.

This winter marked my four hundredth as a statue. Snow crowned my head, and dripping water gave me icicle fangs. One of my few comforts was when the trees lost their leaves to reveal the stars. Over time, moving lights joined them in the heavens, some pulsing, others constant. I wondered if mine was not truly the last dragon egg. Perhaps others hatched and roamed free, unhindered by the fear-driven mob that sought to destroy me and my mistress. But the lights remained ever distant. Unreachable.

Spring blossomed, and with it, the first change that happened in a long while when a woman passed through. She wore greenish trousers, a light brown shirt, and a tan wide-brimmed hat. An embroidered patch was sewn onto the shoulder of her left sleeve, and a gold badge sat over her chest pocket. She hiked through with a pack on her back and walking sticks in her hands until she located the abandoned farmstead. Upon spotting the lonely chimney, she pulled out a black box of some sort, held it up to her eye, and made it flash a light from a small square on the front. She tucked the box away and continued on.

Over the course of the next month, more humans came. They trickled in slowly at first. One human, in the same uniform as the first, marched through with a container that squirted a bright pink stream of liquid on certain rocks, saplings, and other plants. Of all the random accouterments humans carried, this was the strangest yet. It reminded me of animals marking their territory.

A group of about ten humans arrived a few days later. They were quite diverse. Male and female, old and young, brown, black, and white. The two older ones wore the uniform that I recognized, and the younger ones wore matching shirts of the same light tan color and a large, circular green-and-blue symbol on the chest. They carried axes and hand saws, rakes and machetes, and they cleared the underbrush and debris marked with pink spray, creating a narrow but walkable trail that wound up toward the old chimney and stretched into the forest.

One younger girl drew my attention. She was maybe a couple of years older than Emma Grace had been but with curlier hair. The moment she spotted that chimney, she slowed her work and dropped behind the group until she was the last in line. She let them get so far ahead that they were out of sight.

Strange girl. What was she doing? She ducked behind a shrub that blocked her from the view of the other humans but not me. There, she pulled a book from her pack. Its brown leather cover was creased and the pages yellowed, but it appeared well cared for. The girl flipped the pages to a certain point then turned her back to me and held the book in such a way that the charcoal sketch within was visible. I couldn't believe it. It showed the little cabin that Emma Grace's family had built on this land so long ago.

The girl held the book like she was trying to line up the sketch with the abandoned chimney. "This is it!" My sensitive ears caught her lowered voice across the distance. "I can't believe I found it!"

Found it? Why was she interested in the remains of the old house?

"That means..." She lowered the book and flipped a few more pages, turned so I could no longer see the contents. "The stone dragon must be..." Her words trailed off.

She was looking for me. If my heart worked, it would have leapt into high speed. She wandered closer and closer, her gaze sweeping the underbrush.

"Nia?" called a female voice. One of the uniformed women from the group searched for her. They spotted each other at the same time. The woman placed her hands on her hips. "You need to stay with the corps. There's more work to do, and we don't want you to get lost."

"Sorry." Nia grinned sheepishly and shut the book.

The woman relaxed and walked over to her. "These abandoned homesteads are pretty interesting, huh? What do you have there?" She jerked her chin at Nia's book. "That thing looks almost as old as the chimney."

Nia's face lit up. "It is. This was my great-grandmother's. Her family lived here until she was twelve, when the government made this land a park and all the residents had to leave. She wrote all about their old house and what it was like to grow up here. She even drew it from memory when she was older. See?" She showed the woman the sketch.

"Wow." The woman's voice held genuine admiration. "She was quite the artist."

"She found out where in the park her house used to be and wrote all the information down here. I just knew I had to find it."

Nia shut the book and said nothing about me. Interesting.

"That book is a treasure," said the woman. "Take good care of it, okay?"

Nia smiled. "I will."

The woman put her arm around Nia's shoulders and led her back to the group.

Nia tossed one last glance in my direction. I knew she would be back.

***

For three days, I watched and waited, and one evening, there she was. The sun cast long shadows through the forest. Nia followed the new trail to the old chimney, where she'd been before. She took out that old book again, turned toward my location, and worked her way through the underbrush, her gaze sweeping this way and that. "She said it was taller than her," she muttered.

Indeed, Nia was a little taller than Emma Grace, but a head shorter than me.

Evening birds sang in the canopy while Nia searched. If I had breath, I would have held it. What did she plan to do when she found me? Was I another object of fascination, like the old homestead?

Nia nearly walked past, but then her eyes widened. Again, I wondered if a part of my stone body was poking through the ivy to draw her attention, or if, perhaps, the sun was at the right angle to show some gray skin through the gaps in the leaves. She stuck a finger through the leaves, poking my nose. Rock hard, of course. She did a little dance of excitement, parted the vines, and looked me full in the face, her mouth in a perfect *O*.

Great. Now she would tell those uniformed people about me. They didn't strike me as the types to break me down for stone so much as the types to turn me into a landmark or museum oddity to be gawked at for eternity.

Instead, her gaze skimmed my form with such awe that the deepest depth of my core shivered.

Voices echoed from the path, getting ever closer. She covered me up and ran. How strange.

***

Nia further surprised me by visiting daily during the lonely twilight hours. Each time, she parted the ivy tenderly, as if I were glass.

She studied and sketched me along with the woods, adding her drawings to a journal that was new but styled like her ancestor's. One day, she leaned close and purplish blotches peeked out from under the edges of her long sleeves and high collars. Bruises? That explained why she sometimes arrived with wet cheeks and puffy eyes and even sat on my feet and wept.

My mistress used to sit with me like that when she needed to unburden her heart. I would wrap myself around her and let her talk. The memory made my stone chest ache. I wanted to tell Nia that whoever caused her pain would be nothing more than cinders if I had anything to say about it. If sitting with me soothed her, I was happy to keep vigil.

My centuries as stone had blurred together in endless numbness, but that day, something changed. I couldn't put my claw on it. All I knew was that I felt warmer inside than since my furnace had last burned.

The warmth increased each day until a week passed, and I awoke one morning to sensations in my extremities. My legs were still frozen in stone, but for the first time in four hundred years, I felt them attached to me—joints, bone, and muscle. I was thawing out of my prison! My mistress's magic wasn't permanent. How long until I would have freedom?

Free. The word was sweet and frightening. Where would I go? What if humans still feared me? What if Nia did? I didn't want her to be afraid.

Soon, my legs thawed from stone to flesh. As I reveled in wiggling my toes, my mind churned, wondering how Nia would react.

The moment she arrived for her next visit, her gaze dropped to my red scales. She squeaked with surprise, but curiosity overcame fear, and she brushed my foot with her fingers. Her hand jerked away from the radiating heat of my thawed furnace.

An insect crawled over my knuckles, tickling awfully. I flicked it off without thinking.

Nia gasped. "You're alive! Can you hear me?"

She realized the truth, yet she stayed. A fragile hope rose within me, and I wiggled a claw in response.

"You can." Nia fanned herself. "Great Gran wrote that she always thought the dragon statue was special, but she didn't know why. I never imagined this! I'll find some way to help you, I promise." She ran a few steps away then returned like she'd forgotten something. "My name is Nia, by the way. Don't worry, this is our secret. Oh my gosh, I found a real dragon!" She bounded off, skipping every few steps.

This was going to be interesting.

***

By week's end, only my head, shoulders, and tail remained stone. While we waited, Nia continued visiting and talking to me. I sat in a place called Shenandoah National Park, in a country called the United States of America. Nia lived near the park, and her father didn't allow her to hike in by herself, but she'd joined a group called the Youth Conservation Corps so she would have an excuse to explore her ancestors' homestead and find the mysterious dragon statue. Now that she'd found me, she was ignoring her father's rule about hiking alone.

"He gets sad sometimes and drinks to feel better. But it only makes him angry." She rubbed at one of her bruises. "It's... better to be out of the house when he's like that."

We established a system where she asked me yes-and-no questions and I scratched the ground with my claw to answer: one scratch for "yes" and two for "no." When she learned that I could see, she used a small flat box she called a "smart phone" to show me pictures of her modern life and catch me up on much of the history I missed.

Turned out that dragons weren't "a thing," as she phrased it, in the modern world. Most believed we were only myths, though, over the years, there had been people all over the world who claimed to have spotted dragons. These sightings were dismissed as fake, but once I was free, Nia hoped she might investigate these claims further. After all, if I existed, perhaps there really were other dragons hiding in the world.

She ensured my shining scales stayed covered with ivy between visits in case any random hikers stumbled across me, explaining that the people who didn't believe in dragons or magic would "freak out" if they saw me like this. Excited as I was about my thawing body, my stomach bubbled like lava. Nia might put herself in danger by helping me. If humans still feared dragons and Nia tried to protect me, they might come after her the way they attacked my old mistress. I couldn't allow that. It would break me to leave Nia, but I would follow my mistress's example and protect her, even if it meant hiding in the loneliest corners of the Earth.

***

By the next night, I had only the tip of my nose and tail left to thaw. My tail was still stuck to the ground, so I fidgeted with my claws while I waited for Nia.

Dread filled me at having to tell her goodbye, and the feeling only intensified as the stars peeked out overhead. She was late. Something was wrong.

A man's shout rang through the trees. I pulled the ivy veil over myself and resumed my old pose. Nia sped out of the trees and fell at my feet, her left eye swollen shut. "Dragon, help! I've never seen him this angry. Help, please!"

Panic immobilized me. What awful beast could drive a girl who did not fear dragons to such terror?

A husky man with rumpled clothes and mussed hair stomped into view, his bulging eyes fixed on Nia. The stench of alcohol hit me like the first gust of a storm, much like when that drunken crowd dragged me and my mistress to the arena so many centuries ago.

"You heard me calling." His words slurred together. "Don't you run from me again!"

He dragged Nia to her feet by the wrist, and my confusion gave way to burning fury. "Is this where you've been coming at night?" Spittle flew from his lips. "You told me you were at Sarah's house!"

Nia squeezed her eyes shut and turned her face away. "Dad, you don't understand."

"No excuses! I'll teach you to lie to me." He raised a fist.

A roar burst from my throat with such volume, the man fell on his rear. I leapt forward, wings outstretched in their full glory. The tongues of fire licking my lips reflected in his widened eyes.

"How dare you touch her? Leave here and never return," I bellowed in my most authoritative voice.

The sorry excuse for a human scrambled backward. "What the..."

"LEAVE, NOW!"

He struggled to get his legs under himself then ran, spewing curses in his wake.

I swallowed my fire, but Nia cowered, tears streaming. No, no, no. I rolled over to expose my belly. "Don't be frightened. It's still me, your statue."

She wrapped quivering arms around my neck and sobbed. "What do I do, Dragon? I can't go home, I can't."

In that moment, I understood. My mistress meant to protect me when she cast her spell, but she sealed her own fate when she left. We should have stayed together. Protected each other. Nia was my friend now, and I would not let fear make me abandon her. I wrapped my body around her, laying my chin on her lap while she cried.

"Nia? Nia!" called a familiar female voice. That uniformed woman with Nia the day she found the old homestead came running down the trail with one of those metal light sticks in hand. She skidded to a halt and nearly screamed at the sight of me.

Nia stopped her. "Candace, wait! This is a friend."

Candace blinked rapidly, her hands pressed to her chest like her heart might fail her. I stretched out my nose and allowed her to touch it. She gaped in wonder but shook it off and kneeled in the dirt. "Nia, what happened? I heard shouting. Your dad was running like a ghost was after him, and he screamed something about a dragon eating you." She squinted at Nia in the dying light and gasped. "He hit you?"

Nia turned away.

I smelled her fear. If she wouldn't speak up for herself, I would. "This is not the only time he has hurt her. I have seen the bruises."

"You talk?" Candace's voice squeaked.

I fixed her with a stare. "You accept that I am a dragon, but my ability to speak surprises you?" So skeptical, these humans. Belief seemed to come more easily to the youths.

Nia let out a small laugh and Candace smiled, though sadness quickly dimmed it. She wiped away Nia's tears with her thumb. "Why didn't you tell me?"

Nia shrugged. "I don't know. He wasn't always like this. It was only after Mom died that he started drinking. I just... I felt so alone."

I knew that feeling better than most. For four hundred years, I'd believed I had no more friends. No help. No hope. But it wasn't true. "No one is ever alone, Nia. Even I, as a statue, was never truly alone."

"She's right," said Candace. "Er... You are a girl, aren't you?"

I suppose the feminine sound of my voice gave it away. I nodded.

"Anyway..." Candace continued. "I'm here. Our new dragon friend is here. You don't have to be alone anymore. Your dad needs help as much as you do, and I swear I'm going to do everything within my power to help you both get it."

I nuzzled my nose against Nia's cheek. "Whatever happens, we'll face it. Together."

Nia threw one arm around me and the other around Candace. "Thank you."

The Tree That Smiled

JAMES VERLON

MAX ASCENDED THE FIRST flight of stairs toward Rose's Tea Shop and was welcomed by the fragrance of masala chai. On the second flight, he made eye contact with Ganesh floating on a bed of clouds. According to legend, if you blink too soon, you'll miss the wink from the elephant deity—and with it, the good luck it brings. Then again, Ganesh was merely on wallpaper.

Max reached the landing and entered the shop. Two customers were nestled behind a half-closed veil, cross-legged atop exquisite Persian cushions. Other tea patrons perched on wicker chairs from Southeast Asia while discussing their latest read. Behind the counter, Rose brushed back her wavy blond hair as she unpacked tea. Fast but smooth Bossa Nova melodies danced in the air with the smell of herbs, spices, and aged tea leaves.

Rose's Tea Shop was a place to wind down and meet fellow travelers of life's long and sometimes arduous journey.

***

Rose tightened the lid on a jar of Darjeeling then turned at the creaking of the aged wooden floor. Max, sporting a navy blue and orange UVA sweater, stood at the counter.

"Nice to see you again." She placed the jar on a shelf that held an assortment of teas, incense holders, and figurines. "What can I get you this lovely evening?"

"Hmmm... a pot of jasmine, please."

"That'll be nine dollars."

"It's nice to know some things haven't changed." Max paid as he looked for a place to sit near the windows overlooking the street below.

Rose set a kettle of water on the stove then retrieved a jar of jasmine that provided shade for one of the many Buddha statues within the shop. She lifted the lid, and the aroma of the jasmine leapt out, finding its way to her. With a keen eye, she measured scoops of dry leaves and transferred them to a light blue teapot.

The kettle hissed while Rose prepared a serving tray. Then, in ritualistic fashion, she grabbed the kettle and slowly poured hot water into the teapot. The water awoke the dry, shriveled tea leaves, and the jasmine petals unfurled, blossomed, and floated like a lotus in a pond.

Rose glided over to Max, who sat on a wicker chair at a glass table supported by a circle of wooden elephants.

Max lifted the pot from the tray. "Everywhere I go, shops have raised their prices, yet yours remain the same. What's your secret?" He poured the jasmine into his cup. Misty veils of steam partially concealed their faces like the Persian curtains in the lounge area.

"Hope. I believe things will turn around for the better. Like most things on the mend, I'm just giving it some time."

"Ah... an innocent answer. I was expecting something more like, 'Well, comrade Max, there are certain overlaps between the tea-making and poison-making business,' " Max quipped, delivering his best Cold War-era Soviet spy impression before taking a sip.

"Well, since you've already taken a sip, time will tell if you're correct or not." Rose angled her left shoulder toward him, miming a drag from an invisible cigarette.

"Let me guess, you also sell the antidote?" Max held the cup to his lips as he looked at her helplessly. Accent no longer present, he asked "How much will that set me back?"

"No money, only a positive Google review."

"Right... I'll give you five stars," Max scoffed. He confidently took another sip, and they both chuckled.

A simple trade. A friendly review for an antidote. Rose wished it were truly that easy to stop another kind of poison, the kind that slowly kills shops.

***

Charlottesville's popularity surged in recent years, but with that growth came higher costs. Five months ago, Rose's landlord had informed her of a twenty percent rent increase. To make matters worse, a recent drought, coupled with rising demand, caused tea prices to skyrocket. She dipped into her savings, even considering a loan as she watched long-time local businesses shutter their doors.

Rose was reviewing the day's receipts when Aurora, her longest-serving shift manager, finished sweeping the shop. Aurora placed the broom into the supply cabinet, which bore a playful warning: "Do not enter! Disney's *Fantasia* mops WILL ATTACK!"

"Something wrong?" Rose asked as Aurora slowly approached.

"Rose, I'm worried about my job. I'm worried about this shop. I'm worried about you. I don't even know how you're staying in business."

"I have a close friend who got into the tea leaf business."

Rose's close-knit tea family of loyal local regulars and her cherished staff of five had grown over the years, and she couldn't imagine what life would be like without them. In fact, her employees often spent their time off enjoying the eclectic ambiance of the tea shop and each other's company. But for several months, Rose had tap danced around conversations about finances, often half-jokingly telling curious customers she was "being courted by a Duke from Liechtenstein" or she "received a large donation from a generous philanthropist who wished to remain anonymous."

"There haven't been any changes to tea suppliers," Aurora responded, a hint of annoyance in her voice.

"It's in my new ledger..."

"Rose, stop."

"What do you want me to say?"

"I want to know that we're going in the right direction."

Rose recalled words from her sailor friend during their month's long journey on a sailboat before opening her tea shop. "Sometimes, a sailboat must drift off course before finding the wind that moves it in the correct direction."

Rose hoped her conjured wisdom was enough to soothe Aurora, who suddenly fell silent before leaving to toss out the trash. When Aurora returned, she grabbed her bag and headed toward the door.

"Have a nice..." Rose began, but Aurora didn't look back as she shut the door.

Rose finished reviewing the day's receipts before gathering her belongings and locking the shop for the night. As she strolled through the Downtown Mall, she passed a handful of empty businesses, some displaying notices that read:

It is with great sadness...

Due to historic supply chain issues and rent inflation, we have decided to close our doors...

Thank you for all the support over the years...

She paused near a building that blended in with the others, indistinguishable in its neglect. The place might have been forgotten by time, but not by Rose. She reminisced about when it was a warm, welcoming space, filled with the aroma of delicious baked goods, the sounds of live music, and the voices of poets. As the memory faded, Rose caught sight of her forlorn reflection in the window. She stepped back from the shop, now less than a shadow, an empty husk adorned with a "For Lease" sign.

At home, Rose deliberately ignored the bank notices scattered across her coffee table—daily reminders of overdraft fees and mounting credit card debt. She wondered how much longer she could maintain the facade. No dukes or philanthropists lining up to save her.

She sipped chamomile tea, hoping it would ease the restless night ahead. As she sank into bed, she imagined herself floating on still water.

"I could use a little hope," she muttered.

She drifted like a piece of wood in a river. A river flowing upstream.

Rose slowly opened her eyes and discovered herself levitating above the bed, caught in a blue, translucent stream gently pulling her toward the bedroom window. She reached for the nearest bedpost, but her fingers slipped through it, as if they were made of smoke. The stream propelled her toward the closed window, and she braced herself for impact with her eyes tightly shut. But the collision never came. When she opened her eyes, she was outside, high above her home. The treetops like tiny shrubs as she ascended rapidly, flitting through the clouds like a ghost in a jet stream.

Rose descended onto an expansive field of teal grass. The light in the sky didn't stem from a single source, like the sun or moon, but from swirls of radiance. Rolling waves of color oscillated like the ebb and flow on a calm shore. The blue stream carrying her connected to a wide basin near a majestic oak tree. A gentle breeze brushed her face as another cluster of luminescence approached.

The tall grass brushed against her as the light guided her toward the tree. Rose felt a heartbeat rhythm pulsate beneath her as she neared the trunk. As she drew closer, she recognized it from her youth—the Earlysville Oak. Instead of journaling, young Rose confided in the tree, spending countless days nestled beneath its canopy, sharing her thoughts whenever books filled her with intrigue, joy, or sadness. Her heart warmed as she once again settled beneath the Oak's sheltering branches.

"Hello, old friend." She caressed the rugged bark, and the tree gently shifted.

The wood subtly creaked, reminiscent of the floor in Rose's Tea Shop, before a crescendo of thunder echoed. She swayed as the ground rumbled beneath her. The Oak twisted, unfurling from its dormant state like tea leaves blooming in water. When it settled, chestnut brown irises the size of tires gazed down at her.

"Oh my!" Rose's heel caught on a protruding root. As she stumbled, a tree limb intercepted her fall. A deep crease spread across the Oak's trunk, accompanied by the symphony of a thousand snapping toothpicks.

Rose had wondered what a tree might sound like if it spoke, imagining a sonorous grumbling that would take an hour per sentence, like Tolkien's Entmoot. She also imagined *how* a tree might speak: its throat a hollowed trunk, an esophagus of flexible wooden fibers, lungs formed by roots deep in the earth, and breaths powered by geysers pushing water and gas into the air.

"Apologies," the Oak said in a comforting, grandfatherly voice.

"Nice to see you again."

"You've grown," the Oak observed.

"Six inches," Rose replied, trying to glimpse inside its cavernous mouth.

"But your roots have grown deep within those around you."

"You brought me here, didn't you?" she asked as the Oak smiled.

Rose noticed another vibrant blue stream emanating from the Oak's trunk, stretching beyond the fields and disappearing over the horizon. Though the distance and direction were hard to grasp, she felt certain the stream led to the heart of Charlottesville.

"That... That's to my tea shop, isn't it?"

"We're connected. We've always been connected," the Oak said.

The Oak's bark shifted again, revealing a glossy mirror embedded in its trunk. Through a hazy hue, Rose glimpsed the eclectic fixtures of her shop and her equally eclectic staff. She watched as they served customers, returned to the counter, and chatted with one another. Though she couldn't hear their words, the mirror showed her the faces they often hid from her—filled with worry and doubt.

"They're concerned about you," the Oak said.

Rose's cheek twitched as her eyes welled up. "It's not easy running the shop. I don't mean to lie," she confessed, her voice cracking. "I keep waiting for hope to arrive." She fought back the tears, regained her composure, and looked up at the Oak's enormous eyes. The pupils were so large she wondered if they were eyes or portals to another realm.

"And you... have you a name?" she asked.

"You've already given me one." The glossy mirror dimmed, shifting to a muted hue. Rose saw the reflection of her heart-broken teenage self in the mirror, burdened by the weight of the world as she sought solace under the Oak's canopy. But young

Rose found only a stump, its tree rings decimated by termites, its bark rotted away.

"You were my only hope!" young Rose shouted, kicking off some loose bark.

The mirror faded, and present-day Rose looked up to see the Oak smiling at her.

"Rose, your words breathed life into my stump, and I sprouted anew here, in a different field of existence," Hope said.

"Sorry about kicking you." Rose felt embarrassed, glancing down and away to avoid the tree's gargantuan eyes.

"I didn't feel a thing," Hope chuckled. "Now, would you like a cup of tea?"

"Oh, Hope... Your finest rooibos, please." Rose smiled.

"One cup of our finest rooibos, coming right up."

She looked beyond the Oak and noticed shriveled plants and trees with a few brown leaves clinging to collapsing branches.

"What happened to them?"

"Over the years, it's grown quieter. The trees, the plants, my friends—they've all been affected by a drought. A drought of dreams. We need more people like you, people who believe."

A hulking branch descended from the Oak's canopy, like an elephant's trunk offering a gift. Small twigs held a wooden tray adorned with intricate depictions of trees. Rose picked up a cup crafted from wooden leaves spiraling together like a vortex. The amber tea within swirled in a mesmerizing motion, as if plucked from an elven land. She toasted the tree then sipped, savoring the chocolate and earthy flavors. With each sip of the warm, invigorating drink, her worries evaporated into the air.

"I've felt your unease and the unease of those around you," Hope said.

"I think it'll work out in the end. It just needs time," Rose replied calmly.

"Rose, your tea shop is like a tree that nourishes your community with its fruit and canopy. But without water, it will wither."

She was reminded of the slew of closing announcements from local shops. Those fruit trees would be missed, like lost loved ones.

"I've yearned to reach you, to help you as you helped me," Hope continued. "Many friends once thrived here but perished because too few humans believed in them, cherished them. I couldn't save them, but I can help you now."

"How?" Rose asked as she finished her drink, but she suddenly felt herself being pulled away. Her last glimpse of Hope and the field of grass shrank like a portrait falling down a well, growing smaller and smaller. No gliding through the clouds this time; her vision blurred at the edges. In an instant, her eyes flew open, and she found herself staring at a tree outside her bedroom window.

For a moment, she was filled with confusion, wondering if it had all been a dream. Then she noticed the small wooden cup in her hand, and determination surged within her. The next day, Rose awoke refreshed and driven, the vision of Hope lingering in her mind.

***

Behind the front counter, Rose spent her downtime drawing while sipping from her new wooden cup. Aurora and the staff watched curiously as she filled the trash bins with crumpled, quickly discarded sketches. When Rose went to the back patio to collect dishes, she returned to find Aurora smoothing out one of the scrunched-up papers.

"What are you drawing?" Aurora asked.

"I'm creating Hope," Rose explained, showing Aurora her latest drawing—a vague depiction of a twisting tree branch holding a pot of tea.

Aurora's expression grew puzzled and concerned. Rose turned away, reaching for a new sheet of paper before brewing more rooibos.

With each passing day, Rose grew more aloof, one foot in reality and the other in a place unseen by those around her. She continuously sipped from her wooden cup, gazing at her finished drawing of Hope the Oak. The more she relived the memory of the ethereal fields, the closer she felt to Hope.

A few days later, Rose began taking measurements near the shop's front entrance.

"Rose, you've been acting as though the shop is an afterthought," Aurora said.

"Actually, quite the opposite. I'm working on the future of the shop," Rose explained.

"Renovating?" a passing customer asked as Rose stretched measuring tape from the doorway to an empty spot along the wall.

"In a way, yes," she replied.

At the start of the week, Rose placed unsightly construction materials—rolled-up chicken wire, wooden beams, and bags of plaster—near the shop's entrance. She began working on what she called "the skeleton of Hope." Customers and staff observed as Rose measured, cut, and assembled the frame with unnatural speed. The staff mostly left her to it, so long as their paychecks continued. By the end of the week, Rose completed half of the trunk's skeleton.

Monday arrived, and Rose was busy mixing plaster in a bucket.

"Maybe she's building a giant tea fountain that'll perpetually brew the house blend," one customer speculated.

"Actually, it's a booby trap for burglars," Peter, a tea server, joked.

By this time, some customers had left, opting for shops without an active construction site, but others were captivated by Rose's live, performative art. She steadily filled the skeleton of her peculiar project, sculpting the tree's body with her hands. Patrons tiptoed around the chaotic mess and even messier shop owner. Layer by layer, the tree took shape.

"Building regulations probably prohibit growing trees indoors, so Rose is making her own!" a customer remarked.

"A Christmas tree all year round!" another added.

Rose had become the tea shop's obsessive madwoman, often found covered in sweat and plaster, intensely focused on her blossoming creation. By closing time, smatterings of plaster dotted the shop—an annoyance for some staff members who spent extra time cleaning. Rose, however, often pitched in to help.

When the trunk's body was nearly complete, Rose appeared with a mold of her own face and placed it in a divot within the trunk.

"Did our Dear Leader bring a likeness of herself for our altar table?" Peter quipped to Aurora as he pulled a serving tray from the counter.

"Who needs surveillance cameras when Rose's face can watch us all shift?" another tea server joked.

Even Aurora admitted the face was bizarre, but pretty cool.

After a week of work on the trunk, Rose began crafting the tree's limbs, using chicken wire and wood to support the plaster, hoping gravity would cooperate. She applied handfuls of plaster while balancing on a ladder, which occasionally made the old wooden floor creak. Customers and staff nervously watched, fearing Rose might fall, and carefully avoided the fresh plaster overhead, paranoid it might drop into their tea. Gradually, the off-white branches sprawled across the ceiling of Rose's Tea Shop.

When the plaster phase ended, the tea crew breathed a sigh of relief, only for Rose to bring out buckets of paint and brushes, turning their brief respite into another headache. The staff quickly realized that leaving Rose to her own devices led to chaos, so they developed 'preventative' cleaning methods to keep her mess contained. Aurora routinely supplied Rose with paper towels and a bucket of water, minimizing her trips to the kitchen sink.

With each brush stroke, Rose brought life to the once colorless trunk. But as the tree grew more vibrant, Rose herself seemed to drift further away, often lost in thought when she wasn't near it. She would giggle and smile as she added new hues to her Hope tree, and at times, staff and customers overheard her talking to it.

"Yes, yes... that'll do," Rose said, adding dashes of chestnut brown to the cheek of her face in the tree. She then dabbed a little on her own cheek. "Now we match," she laughed. "What did you call it? Brain Wave? Such a strange name. I don't think I've ever heard of that kind of tea."

***

One Friday evening, only a few finishing touches remained. Although Rose spent most of her workday painting, driven by an urge to complete her work, her progress slowed as lingering doubts about what would come next began to surface.

"Aurora, I'll be away for quite some time," Rose said as Aurora was leaving the shop.

"Have you gone mad? Where are you going?" Aurora asked.

"I've been planning a tea pilgrimage with a friend."

"What will I tell the others? Who will run the shop? And the tea deliveries?"

"What I'm telling you now—don't worry, and believe in hope. I trust you to run the shop in my absence. The tea deliveries are arranged. Check the large safe for the other ledger before Monday."

Aurora was the only staff member who knew the combination, as Rose had entrusted her with some of the bookkeeping.

"But there isn't a second ledg—"

"There is." Rose placed a reassuring hand on Aurora's shoulder. "I'll explain in time. If anyone asks, say that Hope provides," Rose gestured toward the tree. "Aurora, I'd like you to have this." She handed her the wooden cup. "If it's alright, I'd like to close the shop one last time."

"Please write," Aurora said through tears, giving her long-time friend a hug that lingered.

"I promise." Rose watched as Aurora slowly walked down the Downtown Mall, giving a final wave before disappearing from sight. Ignoring the subtle mist rising from the bottom of the stairs, Rose locked the shop doors. The mist seeped under the door, drifting toward the majestic tree. Rose picked up a brush, wet it with paint, and added the finishing touches. After a moment, she stepped back to gaze in wonder at her creation.

"It's done." Rose smiled as she gently placed the brush on the front counter, where she happily served her customers and shared laughter with her tea family for many years.

Like a dam breaking, blue streams cracked through the tree's trunk and flowed toward Rose. In an instant, she was whisked away, returning to Hope the Oak in the ethereal field, her small shop visible in the distance. She turned to the once-empty field and saw fresh tea leaves ready for harvest. Rose looked back at Hope the Oak, and they smiled at each other.

***

Aurora tossed and turned all weekend, worrying about how to break the news to the staff. When Monday arrived, she anxiously checked the safe. To her surprise, she found a green leather-bound ledger adorned with leaf patterns similar to those on her new wooden cup. Opening it, she discovered an entry for a delivery from "Hope's Majestic Tea," listing packages of tea to be delivered. Some leaves were familiar, but others were new.

Aurora did her best to reassure the staff as they questioned Rose's sudden disappearance and the future of the shop. She calmed their worries with words of wisdom that seemed to flow naturally—echoes of the guidance Rose had once given her.

A few months later, the staff sampled five new teas that had arrived from Rose's "friend in the tea business"—a story Aurora once believed was just a white lie. Occasionally, letters from Rose were tucked in with the deliveries. In one letter, Aurora learned that Rose had decided to stay and help her "friend" cultivate the tea. Aurora continued managing the shop, always hoping that one day Rose would return.

News spread about the enchanting tree that had sprung to life at Rose's Tea Shop and the new drinks brewing beneath its canopy. The once-dripping branches had merged with the ceiling, providing the cozy comfort of a tree's embrace.

In the following months, the tea staff exclusively sampled the new flavors being shipped to the shop, carefully deciding on flavor profiles. Seeing an opportunity to engage the tea community, Aurora started a public monthly tea club, inviting customers to explore the exotic new teas that mysteriously arrived. As the staff revamped their menu, the tea club became a popular event, allowing the growing number of customers to share in the delightful selections.

Long-time regulars were puzzled by Rose's sudden disappearance after she created one of Charlottesville's most marvelous wonders. Rose's Tea Shop became a hub of curiosity, and the staff soon found themselves in a peculiar situation. Following in the footsteps of their elusive former boss, they crafted colorful answers to the many questions that arose.

When asked how the tree was created, some tea staff kept the mystery alive by telling customers that a hidden seed among tea leaves from the Amazon had sprouted, with roots rapidly growing inside the building. As time passed, the staff adjusted and refined the folk tale of Rose and Hope. When questioned about their former owner's creation and her sudden disappearance, they would say, "Rose was a goddess in disguise. Just as Athena gifted mortals the olive tree, Rose gifted us her Hope tree." For the customers at Rose's Tea Shop, the folk tale gradually became a myth.

***

Over a decade passed since Max last visited Charlottesville. During a business trip, he decided to return to his old college town. As he walked the Downtown Mall, he noticed many businesses had changed since his time at UVA. Passing by Rose's Tea Shop, he saw the name had changed to the Twisted Branch Tea Bazaar. He ascended the familiar stairs, careful not to blink as he passed the painting of Ganesh. The scented air at the top of the stairs unlocked old memories.

As he approached the doorway, his gaze fell on a large, enchanting tree that greeted him. A face was embedded within the tree, but he couldn't quite place it. Max moved toward the front counter, smiling as the familiar creaky wooden floor greeted him. He thumbed through the updated menu, amazed at the expanded selection—what had once been ten teas had grown to over fifty, with intriguing blends like High Atlas Sage and Brain Wave. Amidst all the changes in the past decade, Max noticed one thing that hadn't changed.

"Excuse me, how have your prices remained the same after all these years?" Max asked.

"Oh, it's because of Hope," Aurora said, gesturing toward the tree at the entrance.

The response caught Max off guard; he faintly remembered Rose mentioning something similar long ago. He looked at the tree again and recognized Rose's smiling face.

When someone enters the Twisted Branch Tea Bazaar, they are greeted by the tree. According to legend, if you blink too soon, you'll miss the tree's smile—and with it, the good luck it brings.

Then again, it's just a plaster tree.

Amphibi-Squatch: A Blue Ridge Tunnel Story

KURT JOHNSON

5:15 a.m. Thursday, March 14, 1850 — Nelson County

JOHN RENFROE LEFT HIS sturdy, hand-built cabin before dawn. A light rain overnight primed the soft ground for tracking. Ten minutes later his well-trained eyes picked up the familiar signs of a black bear: smaller, wider front tracks and rear prints resembling human feet. For two hours he tailed the bear and for two hours the hair on the back of his neck prickled in high alert, as if he were the one being stalked. John feared that once he killed the bear, someone would steal what was rightfully his: a valuable barter piece for supplies in Basic City. His thoughts swirling, he reconsidered—*could this be an animal?* That didn't make sense. An animal would have either attacked or fled in the opposite direction, driven away by fear. It wouldn't have taken this much time for an animal to act.

Despite nagging anxiety, John continued the hunt. Another hour passed, and the target successfully eluded him. However, the sense that someone or something still followed him grew stronger.

A twig snapped. John whirled and glimpsed a hazy figure thirty yards to his left. He was certain something moved, but as his eyes settled on a now still area of the forest he wondered if his brain was playing tricks. Doubtful... it was full daylight, not clouded with the usual morning fog, and he'd had a full night's sleep. John continued to rationalize what was happening until a low, guttural grunt recaptured his attention. Turning toward the sound provided no clues... the camouflage was flawless. If it were a man, he'd have to be at least a foot taller than John. Plus, he'd never seen any clothing that could hide a person this well, particularly considering its size. His eyes remained fixed on the contrast of the lush green fern undergrowth of the forest and the deep brown trunks of the surrounding trees.

With a low growl, a mountain lion leapt from the rocky crag and darted into the woods. Shaken, John knew he had been moments from being attacked. *Why run off now? You had me.* John reset his awareness of the woods and the dangerous animals lurking therein. As an experienced hunter, he had remained completely still thousands of times while baiting his quarry. Abandoning the bear hunt, he was prepared to outwait this thing—whatever it was—until it showed itself.

4:02 p.m. Friday, March 15 — South of the Tunnel

Patrick McMahon volunteered to lead three men in search of a new encampment. Thanks to Claudius Crozet, Patrick knew more of the wilderness surrounding the tunnel than any of the other workers, so it seemed the right thing to do. Over a year ago, Crozet, the head railroad engineer, selected Patrick to assist with the planning of the project, including surveying the tunnel site and determining the encampment location.

As he trudged up the mountain, Patrick pondered their plight. The work to create a mile long rail tunnel was taking its toll on everyone's morale, including his. Exhaustion and disease had claimed several of his friends. Now, the water was bad. Blasting through solid granite took an immense amount of powder, powder that used sulfur as a stabilizing agent. *Was sulfur the culprit? Of course, all one had to do was smell the creek.*

The excursion was taking too long... two hours until sunset. Patrick's lungs burned as he took yet another step up the mountain. Higher was the only option. The higher above the tunnel, the fresher the air and water. The team plodded on. Another step resulted in another cramped muscle; another step, one more blister.

"This is it!" Patrick bellowed as they crested to a flat piece of land. The search for shelter, clean water, and abundant food was complete. "Look, the creek runs pure... see there, fresh animal tracks. We've found our new home."

The scout team was more subdued and the boldest of the trio spoke up, "You realize this means we're up at three instead of four? The days are already long enough, and now this?"

Patrick countered, "Stay put and continue to drink the tainted water. Would you like that better? You've seen what's happening. It's a new camp or sickness. What say you?"

The bravest lost his bravado... not another word was spoken.

Patrick dispatched the men to inform Crozet of the new settlement. He considered it his duty to stay to research the water supply and hunting sightlines. He was confident in front of the group, but unsure deep inside. *Is this the right decision? I know nothing about this part of the woods.* While still light, he gathered large branches, moss, and fern fronds for a crude lean-to. Water next, and finally a fire. Patrick had discharged a rifle several times and was worse than average with a fishing pole. He knew he would need both for protection and food.

Prior to working on the Blue Ridge Tunnel, Patrick led a railroad construction project in western Texas. He shot his share of armadillos infiltrating their food supplies. Armadillos weren't much of a challenge; they moved slowly and made little effort to sidle off when approached. He could walk up and place a bullet where it counted from three feet away. *A monkey could kill an armadillo with a rifle.*

Patrick's angling knowledge amounted to a tree limb pole with an old boot string... fifteen years ago for fun with his father. Fish, or water for that matter, were in short supply during his last assignment. The Texas that he knew was barren. He'd not wielded a pole for over a decade.

Out here... this was different. Surrounded by dense woods with no one to help, he was scared, unsure, and struggling to keep his wits. He wished he had done more hunting and fishing.

A lot of it.

8:03 a.m. Saturday, March 16 — The New Camp

As smoke rose from the woods, John packed up supplies and left to investigate. An hour later he approached a clearing that housed someone's camp. Smoldering embers dotted the ground, but no sign of life. He spotted the remnants of a temporary shelter. Branches and ferns lay strewn about, and he noticed a soft mat of moss that might have made a substitute bed. Searching further, he found the body... thirty feet from the moss mat. *Must have been food nearby or in the lean-to. A common and often fatal mistake in the wilderness.* He'd not seen this man before but assumed he was a worker from the railroad, as no local would camp in these unforgiving woods. *What was he doing out here by himself?*

John scoured the site for clues. On closer inspection of the body, he bristled at the blood pooled under an awkwardly bent leg, but the lethal blow must have been the gash that ran from shoulder to waist. Something felt off. John searched nearby for any weapon used for defense but found nothing. What he did find was a smooth, dark green substance under the dead man's fingernails. *Is that algae?* John inspected the creek, and it was running strong... no algae.

As he returned to the camp, John passed the burned-out fire and recognized the familiar black bear tracks. Struggling to make sense of this unlikely scene, he searched farther. Footprints marked the earth, but much, much larger than a man's. John's feet were enormous, but his foot, including the boot, fit easily inside these deep indentations. A small trail of blood mixed with the "algae" marked the footsteps to the north. Confused and mind reeling, John could only ask—*What happened here?*

***

"You there... hands up!"

John was so preoccupied with the mystery at hand that he did not see nor hear the men. Twice in two days caught off guard. *I'm better than this!* With hands raised he turned to face six rifle sights.

"I mean no harm... arrived a few minutes ago and everything was as you see it now. All I want is to know what happened to this man."

The men stepped out of the nearby ravine. Weathered faces topped sinewy physiques... *likely from years of manual labor.* Pushing forward, the most imposing of the men glanced at John while pointing to the body.

"This man was our friend, Mr. Patrick McMahon. More importantly, he was my brother. I'm Mason, Mason McMahon. Who are you and why did you come here?"

John sized up each man. Mason displayed the most confidence... the only one without a tremor in his hands.

"John Renfroe's the name. I saw smoke. Not many people out this way so I came to investigate. Sorry about your brother. What about you, Mason, and your friends here?"

As others began to speak, Mason shushed them. "We're from the railroad... building the new tunnel. Powder blasts are spoiling our water so we're looking to settle on higher ground. Patrick volunteered to set up this temporary camp. We came today to prepare it for the entire work crew. Can't believe Patrick is dead!"

"See here." John pointed. "I found these bear tracks near Patrick's body, so I assumed that's it... bear got him. But look at these..."

"What in the...? Did you make these?"

Stepping in the large imprints, John captured their attention. "My boots fit in there with room to spare. Wasn't me or any man I ever saw."

Eyes fixed on John's boots, Mason asked without looking up, "You think this thing that made these prints killed Patrick and the bear?"

"I don't know. Things aren't adding up."

John and the group stood silently over Patrick's body. John started, "Patrick's wounds are likely from a bear... seen it before.

What I've not seen is a bear just drop dead after killin' a man. Look under his nails."

Dropping to one knee, Mason inspected Patrick's fingernails. "Algae and blood?"

"Yep, definitely blood and likely algae."

"But, from where?" Pointing to the creek, Mason continued, "It's running fast. No algae there, or anywhere around here."

"I think the algae and the blood must have come from the animal that made those huge prints. One way to be sure..." John led the group to the body of the bear. Mason's men shuffled over, heads hanging low, as if not making eye contact would dissipate their despair. "No marks on this bear, not a scratch. So, how'd blood and algae get under Patrick's nails?"

Shaking his head, Mason had no response. The others silent, frozen with fear.

John posited his theory. "This bear was drawn by something here... probably fish, now seeing that pole over there. Patrick evidently got in the way."

Shrugging, Mason added, "Makes sense, but what happened to the bear?"

"I'm getting to that. Something interrupted the bear. Whatever it was made those prints and limped away... see that trail of blood and *algae?*"

Mason shook his head in disbelief. His crew gawked at the bloody trail and stood slack-jawed as he spoke. "You're saying that thing killed a black bear?"

"I think so. See how it's sprawled out like that, the way its body is contorted? I think it broke its back."

"Sure, the bear attacked Patrick and fell and broke its back. Not a chance, John!" Picking up on Mason's sarcasm, the others joined in by muttering nonsense. Mason again shut them down with a quick shush.

John's patience was waning. "That's what I'm saying. It had to be the mysterious creature. And, if I'm right, this creature is bigger and stronger than anything that has ever lived in these woods. This is a five-hundred-pound adult black bear with a crushed spine!"

"If you're so sure about that, then it probably killed Patrick, too. No way to know that Patrick's wounds are from that bear. You said it yourself... *likely* from a bear. Lots of creatures out here, John. We'll get it."

"You're not listening, Mason. I don't think this creature killed Patrick."

Turning their backs before John could finish, Mason and crew desired no further evidence or discussion. John's argument held no sway. "The creature is responsible. Head home, now... we'll take it from here."

Mason turned and barked orders for the rest to settle the camp for the night. Frustrated, John trekked back to the cabin. They were wrong. He knew it.

The notion that a creature unlike any other was walking these woods kept John's mind racing. *Is it possible that the bear rambled into Patrick's camp and the creature intervened? Is there a wild animal out there that wants to help humans?* John pushed through the cabin door immersed in his thoughts, the walk home not even registering.

Night had fallen and the low rumblings signaled an empty stomach. Famished, John reached for the dried venison from the cupboard. He sat, savored the salty meat between his teeth, and recalled, over and over, the events at Patrick's camp. Sleep would not come easily.

6:23 p.m. Friday, March 15 — The New Camp

The human fished the stream for dinner and eventually caught two trout. He ate one fish and left the other by the fire before he fetched water from the creek. He was away for a minute, but a minute was all the bear needed. Turning from the creek, the man took one step and, like a blur, the first swipe snapped the leg backward, felling the human. Razor sharp claws ripped the flesh from the torso with the second, and final, blow. Watching from a safe distance and with great hesitation and anguish, the creature felt torn about intervening. Its drive to protect the human prevailed, and it emerged from its cloaked canopy. *Am I too late?*

The bear sensed the presence of a competitor, left the mangled body, and raced toward the creature with shocking speed. With no time to think, the creature had to fight. Using the speed of its foe as an advantage, it sidestepped as the bear lunged with lethal force. Missing its target, the bear rolled to the ground, and the creature pounced. Off balance and disoriented, the bear could not defend itself as the creature hefted the beast and slammed it to the ground, severing its spine and bringing its life to a premature end.

Approaching the tent area, the curious creature found the human clinging to life. With a last gasp for air, the man lurched forward, grabbed its legs, and tried to pull it closer. Startled by the physical contact, the creature tore away from the human's grasp, leaving deep gashes in both legs from knee to ankle. A small trail of blood, the dead human, and a shattered bear were left behind as the creature sped through the woods.

By the time the creature entered its cave, the bleeding had stopped and its legs were healed. Since the physical changes began, its body mended remarkably fast. These injuries were preventable, though. Curiosity had won out over safety. Its fascination with the other two-legged animals was dangerous and the unnecessary death of the bear was avoidable, but the pull toward these humans was incredibly strong. From the first incident with the man and the mountain lion, the nurturing instinct prevailed; so much so that this behavior was becoming a danger to survival. The creature closed its eyes and rested while pondering its erratic behavior.

Am I the same type of being as those I'm compelled to protect?

3:02 p.m. Thursday, March 14 — Afton Mountain

The creature eyed the mountain lion stalking the human. It despised the lightning-quick cats, not because they were a competitor for food, but because they indiscriminately killed everything that moved—whether for food or fun. The creature did not believe itself to be like that, though it was confused about the other two-legged creature in the woods. *Why do I feel the need to shield him from the dangers of the big cat?*

The breeze shifted. Head up and nostrils twitching, the cat picked up the creature's scent then raced away, sparing the human. Returning to the search for its meal, the creature dispatched the bear and dragged it back to the cave. Exhaustion took over. Leaving the cave now and venturing into daylight was dangerous.

The bear carcass would be unattended, but the creature had no choice. It desperately needed light.

Emerging from the cave, the chameleon-like creature was bathed by the ultraviolet rays. The jolt of warm energy was immediate, and the pale green skin folds morphed into the much darker olive-green color of the surrounding ferns in the forest undergrowth. The creature stood motionless, virtually undetectable in the canvas of the woods.

December 1849 — The Creature's Cave

The tingling woke the creature each morning. Starting at the toes, the sensation crept up the legs day by day. The creature shuffled to the usual spot and emptied its stomach with a flood of yesterday's meals. Stepping past the growing pile of fur on the cave floor, the creature knelt on all fours... the sickness was getting worse.

It must be the water.

The taste was odd, but palatable for a time when combined with the cache of frog eggs. Now that the nausea was getting worse, the creature knew it could no longer drink the creek's poison.

The transformation occurred so slowly that it never seemed odd. Winter beckoned and the creature felt the cold more acutely. Where fur once was, crisp breezes chilled to the bone. At night, the creature lowered itself into the cave's shallow pit, backfilled with leaves and pine needles. It watched and noticed... the slithery four-legged critters running the forest floor did the same thing.

In daylight, the strange blend of unsavory water and eggs provided an energetic boost. The smooth, green, hairless skin folds that covered it from the waist down turned a brighter green, but the hue varied depending upon the landscape. The upper body remained unchanged. The coarse, mahogany brown hair provided the warmth and protection it needed to survive the harsh winter nights when snow could fall at a tremendous rate.

Beyond the physical, the metamorphosis resulted in changes to instinctive behaviors, like curiosity overriding fear. Over the last several months, the creature ventured closer to the other two-legged creatures in the woods.

What are these things and what are they doing out here? Why am I not afraid?

5:53 a.m. Sunday, March 17, 1850 — The Renfroe Cabin

John woke to a thundering boom. He shot out of bed, rushed to the entryway, and threw open the door. "Mason?"

He was bigger than John remembered from the day before... thick forearms accentuated by the rolled-up sleeves; meaty hands clenched in fists ready for battle. His motley crew shuffled their feet directly behind him.

"Renfroe, have you seen it?"

"Seen what? You just woke me up so, no, I haven't seen anything."

"That creature. If you've seen it, you need to tell us."

Perturbed now, John curtly answered, "Look, once I left the camp last night I came straight here, ate, and went to sleep. If you're so keen on hunting this thing, I suggest that you calm down because someone is going to get hurt. You're not thinking straight."

Mason bristled and clenched his fists tighter. Veins popped from his neck while his face turned a scarlet red. "Listen, John, if you don't want to help us that's fine, but we will find the creature, and before the end of the day we will have its head on a spear."

Off they went, cursing and yelling. Anger was getting the best of Mason and his posse of six. John understood, though he believed the creature not to be responsible. If the same thing happened to one of his brothers, he wouldn't behave level-headed either.

John considered his past interaction with that odd animal that blended seamlessly with the woods. Could this be the same creature that killed Patrick and the bear at Patrick's camp? The size of the animal would fit with what he believed happened. And since it did not seem interested in doing harm to John, might it make sense that it attempted to help Patrick, not kill him? *Could this creature be more man-like than wild animal? Or it doesn't see man as a natural enemy?*

In his mind, John retraced his steps, first while tracking the bear and second while making his way to Patrick's camp. If his bearings were correct, in both encounters the creature appeared to be travelling in the same direction. *It must have a den or lair west of here.* He gathered supplies and a rifle then departed to search for this mysterious creature.

8:42 a.m. Sunday, March 17 — The Search

The posse's pursuit was fruitless... several sightings of squirrels and rabbits: nothing unusual.

Undeterred, Mason gathered the group under a shade tree to plot their next steps. "We will not stop until this creature is dead. Men, we must avenge Patrick's death!"

Mason commanded they change course and head west. That's when they picked up the markings of something unusual. And big! Broken lower branches and large footprints led them on their hunt. Mason felt the growing anxiety and excitement exuding from his men. His body tingled, too...they were closing on their prey.

***

What was that? John set his sights on the location of the sound and movement but was thwarted yet again. He was certain he saw something. Not wanting to again play a waiting game that he surely would lose, he rose and crept to where he expected the creature would be... still, nothing. He took a few more steps and paused. Behind him, growing louder and louder, the rantings of seven men, hell bent on revenge, sent chills up his spine. The posse neared.

The startled creature must have heard it too, and John at last was able to see its movement firsthand. This animal was huge! It made sense now as to why it was so well hidden. The upper half of this beast was dark brown and woolly, with an ape-like face and head. The color against the surrounding tree trunks was nearly indistinguishable. But the lower half is what amazed John. Like the skin of a salamander, the shade of green blended perfectly with the fern undergrowth. *This must have been what was under Patrick's fingernails.* This creature was a master chameleon.

***

Holding the rifle steady, Mason approached. "John Renfroe! What are you doing out here?"

Frustrated, John replied, "Food doesn't just show up at my door, Mason. A man needs to go out and get it. I'm hunting squirrel," he lied. John needed to buy time. "I know what you and your men are after, Mason, and I can help. I saw prints, like we saw yesterday, about a hundred yards south of here. I didn't follow them because I need food more than I need to chase a ghost."

"Appreciate the tip, Renfroe, but don't you think it odd that we followed similar prints... that led us to you?" Mason's posse found this hysterical. Head jerking toward them, the steely glare from their leader instantly silenced their guffaws.

Smugly, John said, "Don't know about those. Only told you what I saw."

Mason's stare locked on John. "We're heading south! That's where John Renfroe says we'll pick up the creature's markings again!" he mockingly shouted orders to the men. "Don't know what you're up to, Renfroe, but you'll thank us later for ridding the woods of this killer."

The posse retreated in the direction of John's falsehood.

***

Rifle raised, John turned and eased toward the creature. He had paced twenty yards in when the creature slowly emerged from hiding. Standing from a crouch, it lumbered toward a rocky area obscured behind the forest growth. *Should I shoot? Why would it walk right out in the open?* Stunned, he gawked at the physical deformities, if they even were deformities? Whatever this creature was, it had adapted quite nicely to the surroundings. The green and brown body resembled a cross between a large amphibian and a northeast sighting known as Sasquatch!

John was convinced that the creature would not harm him. The Amphibi-Squatch seemed to know that John purposefully pointed the posse in the opposite direction. Any doubts about what happened at Patrick's camp were extinguished. This creature was not only curious about humans but also felt compelled to protect them.

John lowered the rifle and spread his arms wide, defenseless. The Amphibi-Squatch kept its eyes on John and took two steps backward, and two more, until it stopped directly in front of the rocky area. John followed to match the pace. As he got closer, an opening became visible... *a cave.* The creature inched toward it as a wailing-like sound ricocheted off the cave walls and echoed in the woods; a throaty frog croak mixed with a baby ape crying. Never had John heard a sound like it. He suspected that the creature was protecting its child and might do so at any cost. Pleading eyes locked with John's.

Neither meant harm to the other, but the tension hung in the air like Afton morning fog. The baby continued to cry, and John knew the Amphibi-Squatch desperately wanted to go to it. Still, it was protective enough that it would not lead John to the cave.

Sensing this, John looked empathetically into the creature's eyes and gave a slight nod of his head to show compassion and let the creature and its family be. The creature returned the gesture. John turned his back and disappeared into the dense forest.

At their next encounter, John would lie again to Mason McMahon and the other men working on the tunnel. They'd gather around as he tells the wild tale of the day he shot and killed the Amphi-Squatch that took the life of a brother and friend.

***

Author's note: Claudius Crozet was a real person who led the Blue Ridge Tunnel construction project in the mid-19th century.

Join the Journey

JAMES BLAKEY

SEDONA WILLISTON TOTTERED ON three-inch heels as she skulked between the rows of apple trees. Her black suede Steve Madden ankle boots made an ideal fall fashion statement until it came to walking on uneven terrain. Style again the victor over practicality in their never-ending battle.

Always the professional—unlike that Kayla from Old Dominion Adventurers, *ugh, those eyebrows*—Sedona submitted a formal request to record at Carter Mountain Orchard. Ownership dismissed any question of collaboration and replied with their standard videographer rates. That price—any price—was too high for Sedona, Media Studies major at UVA and aspiring influencer. Brands and businesses were supposed to pay *her*.

On a busy Saturday, she parked her car near the Monticello Trail, waited for late afternoon, then scrambled to the orchard at the top. With the air filled with the scent of ripe apples and the sounds of twittering birds, Sedona searched for the ideal backdrop to record against.

She turned left. *Perfect!*

An old-timey scarecrow affixed to a sturdy wooden post with the Blue Ridge Mountains in the background. The straw man's arms were outstretched, one slightly higher than the other, as if caught mid-gesture, dirt-stained gardening gloves fitted over the ends. Overalls bleached by the sun and patched with scraps of cloth. Underneath a plaid flannel shirt, red with streaks of black and white, the fabric fraying at the cuffs. Around the neck hung a piece of old rope—more noose-like than makeshift scarf. On its head a wide-brimmed straw hat, a few strands sticking out at odd angles.

Sedona slipped off her backpack, retrieved and assembled her tripod. The influencer clamped her phone into place, hit record, and stepped in front of the camera. A pair of Gucci sunglasses, the logo visible, hung from her collar. Sedona's signature accessory, a lime-green fedora, sat jauntily atop her honey blond hair.

She stared at the camera and unfocused her eyes. A trick she learned from the Coyle Twins, her best friends at UVA and All-ACC First Team volleyballers/influencers.

"Hey, everyone. It's Sedona from Exploring Virginia." She gave a friendly wave. "Today I'm coming to you from spectacular Carter Orch—Mountain. Crap." She took a deep breath, silently counted to five, then began again.

Bright smile. "Hi, everyone! Sedona from Exploring Virginia, coming to you from breathtaking Carter Mountain. Today, we're exploring the magic and charm of the orchard, starting with this incredible view behind me. Maybe later, we'll share an apple pie recipe." She invoked her catch phrase. "Join the Journey!"

Sedona tossed her hat out of camera range, shook out her hair, and repeated her spiel. "Hi, everyone! Sedona from Exploring Virginia..."

After completing the second intro, Sedona compared the videos. In the low, natural light, shade from the brim obscured her eyes. Sans hat, her blue irises really popped. But the fedora was a huge part of her personal branding. She would hate not to use it. Sedona replayed the videos, uncertain which was better.

Huh? The scarecrow's right arm moved during the first intro. Started straight out, then raised slightly. Finally, the hand turned, as if to beckon her.

Sedona glanced around. The orchard was quiet, undisturbed except for the gentle rustle of leaves. Wind wasn't strong enough today to move the scarecrow, was it? Certainly no one nearby to mess with its arm.

Curiosity piqued, Sedona tapped record and stepped in front of the phone.

"This is a bit creepy, folks," Sedona said, her voice a mixture of amusement and nervousness. "Our fashion-challenged straw friend seems to have a mind of his own. Can we figure out what's going on?"

Humming "If I Only Had a Brain," Sedona approached the scarecrow and scrunched up her nose at the odor of mold and mildew. Its straw hat cast a shadow over its burlap face. Two dark buttons for eyes, dull and mismatched, one slightly larger than the other. For a nose, a knotted piece of rope protruded. The mouth was a simple stitched line, turned downward in a somber expression.

Sedona pushed against the post, pulled at the ropes binding the straw man's limbs. Everything seemed normal, yet the scarecrow seemingly moved on its own. She tugged on the right arm. Soft, filled with straw, but it remained in place.

A voice, like the rustle of cornstalks, said, "Please don't touch me without permission."

Sedona jerked her head, pulled back her arm, lost her balance. She tumbled backward, falling to the grass on her butt.

Laughter erupted from the scarecrow. Its downward mouth transformed into a wide grin.

The one thing Sedona didn't stand for was being made fun of. She scrambled to her feet, brushed off her clothes, and marched up to the scarecrow. She poked his straw chest. "That wasn't very nice."

To her astonishment, the raspy voice responded, though the mouth didn't move. "My apologies, dear girl. It was not my intention to frighten you."

"I wasn't scared," Sedona lied. "What are you? Some kind of rejected Disney World animatron?"

The scarecrow chuckled. "Nothing so elaborate. Just your standard cursed soul who, after he offended an overly sensitive witch, was condemned to spend an eternity in this orchard warding off unwanted critters."

"Do you have a hidden camera and a microphone in there?" Sedona leaned closer, peering at the burlap face. "Look, I'm sorry I snuck in, but I'm just a college student and can't afford the recording fee. I know I'm trespassing, but can't we work out some sort of arrangement? My friend made a deal with this resort in the British Virgin Islands. She gave them a dope review with loads of killer videos, and they comped her stay and all her meals."

"I understood about ten percent of that," the scarecrow said. "Let me assure you, this is no technological trick. I am indeed a cursed soul."

Witches and curses? Was that possible? Still, the interaction with a talking scarecrow—whatever its origin—would be a game changer from her other videos. Sedona slipped into influencer mode. "Join the Journey. How long have you been imprisoned?"

The scarecrow didn't answer.

"How did you offend the witch that cursed you?"

No response.

"Hey, I'm talking to you." She flicked the brim of his hat. "I need some engagement here."

The scarecrow remained silent and unmoving. Did Sedona imagine this? She replayed the encounter on her phone. The recording showed her falling over backward for no apparent reason. Only her side of the conversation was audible.

Outrage overwhelming her uncertainty, Sedona marched up to the straw man. "What happened to my video? Why isn't your voice on there?"

Did the scarecrow subtly shrug his shoulders?

"Vampires can't see their reflection in mirrors. Poltergeists lose cohesion if they travel at speeds greater than fifty miles per hour. I have the power to choose whether to be heard on your device. I could allow it, but what's in it for me?"

"Weren't you listening? I can't afford to pay. Can we work out some cross-promotion?"

"Cross-promotion?"

Sedona swore the scarecrow furrowed his burlap brow.

She gave an exaggerated sigh. "Okay, what do you suggest?"

Everybody wants something, even haunted scarecrows.

"Assist me in escaping this prison of straw."

Sedona thought through the implications. "And after you're released, this"—she tugged at the overalls—"would become an ordinary scarecrow?"

"Correct. My soul will have finally passed on to heaven, hell, wherever souls go."

"But I need video of you talking and moving. Let's do an interview, *then* I'll help."

The smile on the burlap face curled into a frown. "But once you have the recording, what's stopping you from leaving me here? How can I trust you to hold up your end of the bargain?"

Sedona stomped her foot. "It's literally in my job title." She retrieved a gold-and-aqua business card from her purse and held it to the scarecrow's button eyes. "See? Sedona Williston, Trusted Influencer." *Could it even read?*

"Do you promise, Sedona Williston, to help free me from this curse and imprisonment?"

"I promise." Sedona crossed her fingers. A one-off interview with a cursed soul inside a body of straw was sure to go viral and spike her follower count. But how could she top that and retain her new viewers? Keep the soul or whatever inside the scarecrow—for now—and string it along for a few vlogs?

"Join the Journey." Sedona grabbed the tripod and carried it closer to the scarecrow. "What's your name and where are you from?"

"My name is Zachariah Showalter, and I was born in 1908 in the town of Scottsville."

"And what did you do to this witch that she placed a curse on you?"

"One day I was out hunting, and I stumbled onto her land, into her garden. Stepped on her carrots. I didn't think I did much damage. But that's not how she perceived it."

Sedona stopped recording. "We need some action. Move your arms. Do something with your face. We're making a vlog, not a podcast." She tapped her phone. "Okay, you pissed off the witch. Now what?"

The scarecrow raised his right hand and tilted his head. "I apologized. Offered recompense. But the witch would have none of that. She cast her spell on me. I still remember the words." The mouth line on the burlap face contorted into an unsettling grin.

From flesh to straw, the switch is cast,
In this scarecrow, your soul is fast.
Bound by straw, beneath the summer sun's glow,
Your soul shall dwell where crows dare not go.

As the scarecrow's recitation ended, the skies darkened, birds scattered in panic, and a gale-force swept through the orchard, shaking apples from their branches.

A burst of blue light enveloped Sedona, blinding her. She felt like she was falling and thrust out her hands. But she didn't hit the ground. Sedona kept falling and spinning. Slowly, her vision returned, but the images were misshapen, distorted, like peering through broken glass. She tried to blink but couldn't.

Laughter filled the air. Not raspy like the scarecrow, but light and feminine. With great effort, Sedona turned her head in the direction of the voice.

A blond girl in black suede ankle boots picked up a green fedora from the ground and slipped it on her head.

Not a girl! That's me!

"What did you do?" Sedona screamed, but it came out as a series of grunts.

The girl in the fedora smiled. "It will take some time before you can figure out how to talk. Close to ten years for me. Fifteen for the soul before that." She walked to the tripod and fiddled with the phone. "Your—I mean my—blue eyes really pop in the late afternoon light."

New Sedona tossed the fedora aside and stepped before the camera. "Greetings fans, ready to Join the Journey? Sedona from Exploring Virginia here at Carter Mountain Orchard, and look what we found." With a sinister grin, she half-turned and pointed. "An old-timey scarecrow..."

Transfer Status: In Progress

LIZ P

Transfer 3892, Lot M

SourceGate 38.029084° N, 78.476056° W

See, this is what I get, agreeing to a Tinder date on a Tuesday evening. In *Charlottesville.*

There's nothing to do here on a Tuesday evening, so I should have been suspicious when he insisted it be tonight, and I should have gone ahead and blocked him altogether when he insisted we meet after ten. *"Because of work,"* he said, which sounded like a lie, even then. He's a grad student at the University of Virginia—physics, presumably—and it's early January, the middle of winter break. What could he possibly be doing until so late at night? Is there a secret particle accelerator under the 250 bypass?

I should have been suspicious, but armchair quarterbacking my own creepy date crisis isn't going to do me much good. I have to keep my wits about me.

"I dunno if I'm comfortable with this." My voice sounds a little shaky, and I try to give it a more jovial, less panicky tone as I continue. "I don't want to end up on a murder podcast."

His brows draw together in what appears to be genuine confusion. "You think I'm a murderer?"

I gesture vaguely at his whole vibe—his coaxing a woman into a dark tunnel at the stroke of midnight vibe. "If the shoe fits."

He looks down at his worn sneakers then back up at me. "Are these murderer shoes?" he whispers.

You know... this is why I agreed to the date in the first place. He seemed cute. Earnest. Smart but also pleasantly dense, if you know what I mean. Like he could fix my laptop but wouldn't use the opportunity to install spyware. Like he could make me laugh without being smug about it. Like he'd ask if I already knew something before trying to explain it to me. And dammit, I'd been right. The date was great, right up until it took this bizarre, murderish turn.

"Your shoes are fine." I gesture, this time more deliberately, behind him to the soon-to-be murder scene. "Luring me into a dark tunnel is not fine."

He looks behind him at the tunnel then back at me, and for a moment—just a moment—his face hardens with determination. Inside my coat pocket, I manipulate the nozzle of my pepper spray from 'safe' to 'fire.'

But instead of attacking me, he walks to a nearby low wall and slumps onto it, dropping his face into his hands.

"You're right," he says, his voice muffled, and my heart leaps into my throat.

I'm right? About what, specifically? The murdery bit, or the *seems* murdery bit?

I've taken two steps back when he continues, an edge of despair in his voice. "This is impossible."

"What's impossible?"

This is my problem. I can never seem to walk away, even when I should. It drives my friends crazy, the way I commit to mediocre jobs and mediocre boyfriends. And now, apparently, deadly, disastrous dates. I just get this sense, sometimes, that I have to follow through. That I'll never find a more exciting job or a less vanilla boyfriend, so I might as well learn to love it. That if I walk away from this date before I'm one hundred percent sure this man is a serial killer, I'll be walking into some kind of hopeless, loveless, lifeless vacuum.

He lifts his face and studies mine, eyes glittering in the ambient light of the empty pavilion. The quiet is so big under here. I guess that's intentional. Acoustics and whatnot. It is a performance space, after all. Still, the silence is vast, and even the hush of our breath seems to fill it and rebound back to us, amplified to a roar. I've been to concerts here that weren't as loud.

"I'm not supposed to tell you about it until you see it."

I take another step back. I might be stubborn, but I'm not a complete idiot. I can recognize the semaphore message he's waving at me with his collection of little red flags. The Tuesday night date. Meeting so late. Insisting on the Downtown Mall, even though we both work at the university and The Corner would've been closer. The sparse Tinder bio. The "want to walk for a bit?" in the middle of a cold night on the empty mall. Now, the increasingly senseless ramblings.

I-A-M-A-M-U-R-D-E-R-E-R, spelled out clear as day, now that I'm seeing it all together with the benefit of hindsight.

If only he hadn't seemed so *nice*. But what kind of excuse is that? Every girl knows you have to be extra wary of nice guys. Not every seems-nice guy is a lure-you-into-a-tunnel-at-midnight guy. But every lure-you-into-a-tunnel-at-midnight guy is a seems-nice guy. It's basic math.

"Okay," I say. "I'm gonna be honest. I really enjoyed our date, and you seem like a really nice guy, and you're funny and cute, and I want to go out with you again." *Lie*, but that's a bridge to cross later. "But I *really* don't want to go into that tunnel with you."

He stands when I begin to back away. If I run, could I escape him? I'm pretty fit, but he looks fast. And strong. I've got the pepper spray in my left hand, my phone unlocked in my right. Can I dial 9-1-1 fast enough? What should I prioritize? Dialing or running? If I pepper spray him, maybe I'll have time for both.

"Wait," he says, holding out his hands just as I try to whip out the pepper spray, and—

I freeze.

No. I am frozen. Trapped.

Strong arms surround me, pinning my arms and holding me in place. But he's still standing several feet away. I look down and see nothing. I dare to look behind me and see only empty air. But there are definitely arms bear-hugging me from behind.

Ah. I see.

Clearly, I am dreaming.

I make a few cursory efforts to wake up before realizing it's hopeless. I must have taken a melatonin or something. My best bet is to commit and ride this out.

"I know you're scared," my date says, still holding his hands up in placation while sleep paralysis holds me immobile.

How should I play this? I think fictional heroines are meant to be sassy, but I am neither fictional nor a heroine. I don't even *like* fiction. I'm just a regular, real-life girl, trapped in a weird dream.

"I am scared," I admit, taking a disjointed breath and letting it out on a shaky exhalation. "This isn't creepy anymore, it's scary. Are you holding my arms? It feels like somebody is holding my arms."

His face twists, his own hands still held up in the air. His fingers flex slightly, and I feel the invisible arms tighten in tandem with the movement. If I'm being honest, none of this is dreamlike. I have a cramp in my neck, and the disembodied arms are pinching the strap of my purse between my arm and my ribs. The cold is stinging my sinuses, and my toes are going numb. All these little hurts. All these very real, very *awake* little hurts...

I might not be dreaming.

Blood rushes loudly in my ears, and my vision starts to go gray and foggy around the edges.

"I think I might pass out," I say, even though it seems pretty stupid to voice my weakness. But there's not a lot of blood left in my brain for thinking. All of it is in my ears, roaring a useless warning.

The invisible hands nudge me, and my feet stumble along obediently as I am guided to the low wall my date was sitting on. A new invisible force settles on my shoulders, pushing me down. I lean forward, bracing my elbows on my knees, and all the disembodied hands leave me. Maybe I ought to take the opportunity to run, but I don't. I'm too busy trying to will away the cold sweat and the encroaching darkness.

Maybe if I faint, I'll wake up in my bed.

Maybe if I faint, I'll wake up dead.

It seems like a big gamble, so I try very hard not to faint.

When the swooning sensation finally passes, I sit up and find The Worst Date Ever studying me with deep grooves of concern carved into his forehead. Behind him, two figures, too shadowed and distant to identify, shamble across the distant mall, crossing from the bus station to the courthouse. I open my mouth to scream, and nothing comes out. The air itself is muffling me.

I am no longer in danger of passing out. My blood has left my ears and is racing hot and panicked through my body.

"Please don't be afraid," my date says as the dark figures—my salvation—disappear into the darkness. "I'm not going to hurt you."

"This is crazy." I go to slide my hands into my pockets, aiming for the pepper spray that I should have used the second we wandered down here, dammit, but cool, unseen fingers gently wrap around my wrists in subtle discouragement. I clench my fingers around the hem of my jacket instead and will myself to think. "Please let me go."

"I can't." But he looks like he wants to.

"Yes, you can."

"No." He sinks into a crouch so we're roughly at eye level. "I can't."

I can't believe I'm going to die here. Here, of all places. I used to come here with my friends when I was in high school. We all agreed this place was the kind of place where you'd go to get murdered late at night. With the resounding emptiness of the pavilion on one side and the school-after-hours quiet of the office building on the other, this tunnel was like a portal to a horror movie. Only an absolute moron would come here with a stranger in the middle of the night.

The irony of it all is going to kill me before the ghost hands even get the chance.

"Please." I raise my shaking hands and clasp them together in pitiful, desperate entreaty. "I won't tell anyone about this. I promise. Please, just let me go."

He glances at the tunnel, then at his watch, then at me. And then, of all things, he sits down on the concrete, all casual with his arms braced on his bent knees, like we're about to discuss poetry together on The Lawn.

"Look," he says with a deep, heavy sigh. "I can't just let you go. You're too important. But I can try to explain. It's a stupid rule, anyway, not telling you." His eyes glaze a little, like his mind has gone elsewhere. "The transfers are easier if you know they're coming. It's common knowledge. The rule is archaic."

Behind him, one of the yellow-coated Ambassadors strolls into view, hands tucked into his coat pockets. Technically, he's here to keep university students safe—an institutional response to a string of tragic murders a while back—but I doubt he'd care that I'm not a student. A thwarted murder is a thwarted murder. I pull in a deep but quiet breath, not wanting to project my intent to scream.

"Don't." The command isn't stern. More resigned, like he knows that *I* know that he can stop me. Like he knows that having that invisible hand close over my mouth again is going to send me into hysterics. "Give him a wave so he knows you're okay."

I'm not okay at all, but I lift my hand and give the Ambassador a wave. He waves back, no doubt seeing a cute couple on a prolonged date—*no need for a walking escort here!* Five minutes ago, that impression would have been accurate.

"I'm going to explain," he says when we're alone again, though how he can tell the Ambassador walked away is beyond me. "But please don't tell anyone that I told you. You'll get my license taken away, and I just got it. You're my first transfer. If I botch it, you'll be my last."

Maybe sassy fictional heroines are only sassy because they're annoyed by the opacity of their circumstances.

"You have to know none of that means anything to me," I say. Sassily.

He sighs and hangs his head between his arms. When he looks up, there's amusement in his eyes. "If you stop arguing with me, I'll explain. Deal?"

The absolute audacity of the man! I raise my eyebrows and give my head a querying little shake to prod him onward.

"Okay, so..." He pulls a small booklet out of his pocket and flips through a few pages before stopping. He looks up. "Are you familiar with the Many-Worlds Theory?"

"The what?"

"What do you know of quantum physics?"

"That it's not my business."

He flips a few more pages forward.

"How about Indra's net?"

"Whose what?"

"Do you have any knowledge of eastern religion? Hinduism? Buddhism?"

"My aunt Claire was a Buddhist."

"And what did Claire teach you?"

"That bringing anti-war sentiment to Grandpa Jeff's dinner table is a good way to get yourself banned from all future family reunions."

He grunts an absent-minded acknowledgment and flips to the back of the booklet. "You were born in '92, right?"

"Excuse you? How do you know that?"

His thumb tracks down the small page as if scanning an index, and then he flips to somewhere in the middle of the booklet.

"Did you ever watch the movie *Donnie Darko?*" he asks, eyes fixed to the page.

"Is that the one with the freaky rabbit thing?"

His expression brightens. "Yes! Do you remember the plot?"

I shake my head. "Nope."

His expression dims. Perhaps I shouldn't take such pleasure in bursting his bubble, but then again, he's the one trying to murder me. I don't think I'm obliged to have good etiquette in this kind of situation.

"What about *Star Trek?* The, uh..." he brings the booklet closer to his face and squints at the page, "the 2009 film adaptation?"

"Never saw it."

We go another few rounds in the same manner before I start to get exasperated.

"Look, I'm just not into sci-fi, okay?"

"You've never read any books, never watched any television shows or any movies that feature worlds other than your own?"

I wrinkle my nose. "Not really. I saw the first few *Harry Potter* movies back when they came out. Does that count?"

He blinks at me. *"Harry Potter?"* Back to the little booklet which he flips through determinedly for a few seconds before muttering something under his breath that sounds like *"useless"* and tucking it back into his pocket.

"I'm assuming since I don't meet your nerd specifications, you're going to let me go?"

I try to stand, but he makes a minute gesture with the fingers of his right hand, and an invisible palm lands on my shoulder, holding me still.

"Please stop doing that," I demand.

"Please stop trying to leave."

"Stop being creepy, and I will."

"I'm not trying to be creepy."

The problem is, I'm becoming steadily less creeped out. Sure, he's got me trapped in a dark, spooky corner of the mall. Sure, he appears to have magical powers of some kind. But also, the more time passes the more I realize that he's not acting deranged. This whole potential murder has a bashful, business-like atmosphere to it. He brought some kind of nerd guidebook to explain his delusions, and the guidebook looks professionally bound.

And *are* they delusions?

If they are, I appear to be having them too, what with all the invisible hands.

"Okay." I sit up a little straighter. "I'll meet you halfway here. I'm getting the impression that there's some kind of central element of all these dorky references that you're wanting to tell me is real."

He straightens, brows raising. "Yes. Exactly."

"Okay, so stop beating around the bush and just explain."

He reaches toward the pocket with the booklet, and I hold up a hand. "Not from your cheat sheet. In your own words."

"It's easier for me to explain if I establish a frame of reference."

"You know what would be even easier? Letting me go."

Leaning back on his hands, he cocks his head and studies me for a moment. "I see why they want you."

Ice twines around my spine. I might've spoken too soon about the declining creepiness. "Let's start with that. Who are *they*?"

He shakes his head. "I can't tell you that."

"Why do they want me?"

"Because your mind is the kind of mind they're looking for."

"Try again. Only this time, pretend I'm an innocent woman you've got trapped in a dark alley who thinks she's going to get murdered, so you're trying to put me at ease."

His lips twist into a little smirk, and I remember grudgingly that I actually wanted him to kiss me, not even ten minutes ago. That's why I came down here with him, moron that I am.

"This is hardly a dark alley, but alright. Are you familiar with the hero's journey?"

"What don't you understand about 'use your own words?'"

"What don't you understand about establishing a frame of reference?" He pauses, waiting for me to argue. When I don't, he huffs out a little breath of relief and continues. "The hero's journey is a sort of narrative structure you see a lot in fiction, which you'd know if you'd ever read a book."

"I read!"

"Fiction?"

"... you were saying?"

"As I was saying, it's a common narrative structure that typically starts with an archetype called the reluctant hero—someone who is living an ordinary life but is called into an unwanted adventure. Still with me?"

"Just because I don't read doesn't mean I'm stupid."

"The point is, they're looking for that archetype. For reluctant heroes."

"I am reluctant. I'll give you that."

He smiles. "So was I. The reluctance is more important than you think. As important as the heroism. Maybe more."

"Why?"

He pulls in a deep breath, shoulders rising and falling as his gaze goes soft and drifts toward the tunnel. "It's difficult to explain *why* without first explaining what, where, and how."

I pretend to consider it, and he watches me as if my response matters. Like I have any real choice in what he says or how he says it, or even what happens to me at the end of the conversation. When he doesn't fill the silence, I cast an exasperated glance up at the white canopy of the pavilion. "Give me the 'what' first, I guess."

His eyes dart back to me and sharpen. "Would you like a literal explanation or a symbolic one? Literal may be easier to believe, but symbolic will be easier to understand."

"Dealer's choice." When his brow wrinkles in confusion, I wave a hand. "You decide."

"May I please use my reference book? For all that our worlds are similar, the language of yours has some departures from that of my own."

"Our *worlds?*"

He winces. "Yes. In a sense. May I please use my reference? This really will be easier if—"

"Fine." I wave a dismissive hand, and he pulls the booklet from his pocket, flipping purposefully through the pages.

"Okay," he says, marking a page with his thumb and making fierce eye contact with me.

I remember—again reluctantly—how much I'd enjoyed the dance of his gentle brown eyes on our date. *Stupid hormones. Stupid heterosexuality. Stupid dating apps.*

"So, imagine you're walking down a path."

When he pauses again, waiting, I nod for him to continue.

"And you come to a fork in the path. So, there's a path to the left and a path to the right."

"I'm familiar with how forks work, vis-à-vis paths. Thank you."

His glare is kind of cute. It's a concerted effort to remind myself he's a madman.

"I'm being thorough. It's an important metaphor."

"So, I'm at a fork in a path..."

"You're at a fork in a path, and you can go either left or right. There is a theory—a demonstrably true theory, as you'll soon discover—that the choice is something of an illusion. There is a world in which you take the path to the left and one in which you take the path to the right. Both worlds exist, and both are equally real."

"What about me? Are both versions of me equally real?"

His grin is a thing of pure joy, and I resent how much it brightens the shadows of this whole situation he's gotten me into. It makes me feel as if I'm still at dinner, being charmed and being charming and wondering if I've finally found a decent, interesting guy.

"That's exactly the right question! It is *the* question. The last true unknown, really, in all the worlds I've traveled. Does our consciousness itself split? If we find ourselves walking the left path, is our right-pathed self any more or less aware than we are? Any more or less real?"

"So... you don't know."

"I do not."

"Why can't men ever just say they don't know?"

"I don't know."

"Cute."

Dammit, though, if he isn't cute. And making a strange sort of sense.

"So... what, then? There's many worlds, and you come from the one where people took the path with magic ghost hands?"

He wiggles his fingers, and a gentle breeze gusts across my cheek. "I come from a world where once, long ago, the human mind gained a modest manipulative power over the natural world. It's no more magical than the ability to sing or sense danger or make a joke."

Before I can respond, he checks his watch and, with a little nod to himself, pops to his feet. I shrink back, reminded all at once that this bizarre, distracting conversation started with my perfectly pleasant Tinder date trying to coax me into a spooky tunnel. My perfectly pleasant Tinder date who also happens to be much bigger than me and who wields magical—*I don't care what he says*—powers.

"I don't want to go to a different world." I'm not even scared he's going to murder me anymore, just scared he's going to kidnap me and take me to another dimension. This Kool-Aid he's serving is powerful stuff.

"You don't have to." He nods his head back toward the mall, toward the relative safety of the security cameras and the occasional yellow-coated Ambassador. "I'll walk you to your car."

"But—"

"The gate is closed," he says. "It's too late now, anyway."

I leap to my feet and we walk together up the shallow concrete incline of the amphitheater. He gestures for me to precede him when we reach the narrower walkway leading back to the mall. When I slip my hands into my pockets, he doesn't stop me, but I find myself nudging the nozzle of my pepper spray back into the 'safe' position. I know it's stupid. I should take the opportunity to incapacitate his disarming, delusional ass and make a run for it. But I feel sort of giddy, now that we're back on the mall, old brick buildings looming over us. I feel safe and excited and unwilling to ruin it all by siccing the cops on this nice man who I think might be telling the truth.

We walk past the darkened storefronts of the mall, past the dry-for-winter fountains, past the comforting bright lights of The Paramount.

"I'm parked by the library," I tell him, and we turn up the side street toward the park.

"Is there a world where this is still Lee Park?" I ask as we walk past the shallow plinth where the statue used to sit.

His answer is quiet, a touch mournful. "Several."

"Oh."

"But there are many more where it was never Lee Park."

We reach my beat-down little Mazda, and I stop, clutching my keys in my pocket. "This is me." But instead of unlocking the car, leaping into the driver's seat, and mowing him down GTA-style in my scramble to flee, I lean back against the door. "I enjoyed our date. Even if it wasn't a real date."

He drops his gaze and smiles at our shoes. I could swear his face flushes, though it's hard to tell in the light.

"I did too."

"So, what happens next?"

His gaze lifts back to mine, and he leans a shoulder against the street sign. "I'd like to take you on another date."

"You mean you'd like another shot at luring me into the tunnel?"

"Both, maybe. I'm not meant to give you a choice in the matter. I'm meant to just bring you. The portals are only open at certain times, so I can justify a week or two of delay, but..." His face tightens into a grimace, and he glances over his shoulder, back toward the distant tunnel. "Like I said, I just got my license, and this is my first transfer. I don't have a ton of professional credit to borrow on, here."

"Well, I still don't know what a transfer is, or what kind of license you're talking about. But I'm getting that my choices are to go on a few fake dates and let you convince me or to run out the clock and have you drag me with your magic ghost hands. Doesn't that seem hypocritical to you, though? Your whole speech was about choices. There's supposed to be a forked path, and I'm supposed to be able to choose which path I take."

"Yes," he agrees, more readily than I expected. "Yes, you are. Which is why I want you to choose."

"Surely there's people who *want* to choose to go with you, though? Why does it have to be me? You never explained that. Why not... why not him?" I gesture at the city bus that just pulled into the stop across from the park. "Maybe he wants to go."

He follows my gesture and studies the backlit silhouette of the bus driver as if earnestly contemplating my question.

"Creative types, adventurous types, your bus driver there... their paths have too many forks."

"Oh. How helpful. Now I understand."

He rolls his eyes at me and tucks his hands deeper into his pockets. "The reluctance we talked about earlier, it affects your path. For whatever reason—and we truly don't know the reason—people like you never seem to find themselves at crossroads. It's as if every version of you chose the same path so many times, life stopped giving you options to do otherwise. Like you turned right and turned right and turned right, and the paths to the left began to grow over."

"Oh my god. You chose me because I'm *boring*?"

He barks out a laugh then falls into a few agonizing moments of thoughtful silence.

"No," he finally says, but it feels like a lie. "And I didn't choose you."

"Ouch."

"It's not meant to be an insult. You were chosen by a council, and they are rigorous in their selection process. It's a greater compliment than I could ever pay you. That said," he scuffs his toe against a tuft of dead grass growing out of the pavement, "I would have chosen you. For a date, that is. I would truly have... swiped right."

"Good lord, just finish the story."

He flushes again and lowers his gaze. "You're not boring. You're steady. You are a straight, strong strand in a busy and tangled web. The constancy of souls like yours has an anchoring effect. You pull the wild souls toward you and keep them from flying off into true chaos. But anchors are meant to be drawn up when it's time to set a new course."

"So you were sent here to draw me up?"

"It's an imperfect metaphor. I was sent here to guide you onto a new path. Not to remove you altogether."

"You were sent here to *force* me onto a new path, you mean."

"Yes. Those were my orders. But, like you, I am a being with free will. I can choose my path, and I choose to let you choose. My simply coming here has created a new path for you where there wouldn't have been one before. I have to trust that's enough."

The trouble is, I'm starting to believe him. I can all but feel that path opening up, that sense of possibility that I so rarely encounter, and this one feels big. Almost too big. Like I've landed a job for which I have no qualifications. "I still don't understand, though. Why *me?* Surely there are more important people you could be snapping up and throwing into better timelines."

"Why *not* you? Remember, you're responsible not only for your own fate but for all the souls to which you're tethered. Your choices determine the course of an entire ship full of individuals, some of whom may be those 'more important' people."

"Okay, fair point. But aren't there people who need it more? Shouldn't you be in Palestine or something?"

His lips tip up at one corner, and he gives a rueful shrug. "The Palestinian jobs tend to go to Arabic-speaking transfer specialists. I am a Virginia native, though it's not called that in my world. I was a natural choice for a Charlottesville transfer."

"That's... logical."

"We are nothing if not logical."

"What's it called, then? In your world? If not Virginia? Is Charlottesville still called Charlottesville?"

"Go out with me next Tuesday and I'll tell you."

"Does it have to be after ten?"

"No. But I would prefer that it end around midnight. As I said, the gates are only open at certain times."

"Do we have to go through the tunnel?"

"If you're ready."

"Where would we be going?"

"Wherever you like. I'd planned to take you to my world, but the destination isn't as important as knowing the travel is possible. I can give you some options over dinner if you like. There are some I believe you'd enjoy."

I unlock my car and pull the door open, but I hesitate before climbing in. "Is the nightlife better in your version of Charlottesville? Is there somewhere quiet we can grab a drink when we get there, or do we have to go to your Livery Stable?"

The sad thing is, if I knew he'd keep smiling at me the way he's smiling now, I'd go with him through the tunnel this instant.

"Of all the infinite Charlottesvilles we could visit," he says as I finally slip behind the wheel, "I assure you there are none with a worse nightlife than yours."

Transfer Status: In Progress

The Gap

Jordan Garris

THE FIRST TIME IT happened, I didn't realize it until afterward. I skidded down the Sketchy Rocks and there it was, a baby deer tucked into a patch of poison ivy. I had seen this deer twenty minutes earlier, on the sloping peak of the Carlos climb, a flicker in the fog of my gasping effort. Now, the forest, refocused by the ease of descending, framed the deer as if to gloat its own magnificence. I smirked at the tingle of déjà vu and scampered down the trail.

It wasn't until my next climb that it struck me: the shadows, the deer's posture, the poison ivy—my two sightings matched like a photograph, but only the second was real. The first time, I was half a mile up the trail from the spot where the deer curled in the leaves. I met my awareness of the peculiar with a mental shrug. I didn't understand yet that I'd sparked a glint of my life still to come.

It's the mountain climbs that bring it out, see. My gift. I haven't decided which part is the gift: the Flashes themselves, or the way I can bring myself to the Gap between life and death, where the Flashes live.

Was I born with the gift, or did it appear? I don't know. I was never into sports as a kid. I started running trails sophomore year with a goal to balance out my excessive Insomnia Cookies intake. I found that I loved to climb. Rocks, roots, views, snakes—I was there for all of it, as long as it was the hardest thing I had ever done. At the end of each run, I had a four- or five-digit number to log in the vert column of my spreadsheet. Nothing fancy. Excel–I'm old school.

I had summitted other climbs, too: Humpback Rocks, The Priest, Jarmans. They were hard, but I craved a more concentrated suffering. Then I found Carlos: the trail with complete disregard for switchbacks and state park boundaries, all culminating in that pitch of 1,026 feet of vert in 0.6 miles. The burning and gasping I lived for. The portal, I would find, to my gift.

Healthy people can't exercise themselves to death. You slow down or stop before you do something jack-shit crazy. I found, when I finally got around to looking for it, that I don't have that emergency brake.

I became aware of both simultaneously: the Flash, always of the future, and the need to be still, to avoid the vacuum of death around me until the groping hands of life could snatch me back. All of this was in a second, maybe less. My confidence in these things isn't something I want to argue about; that's why you're reading this now rather than hearing it.

I climbed Carlos every day, sometimes three, four, five times in a row. I ran and slogged on the skyward dirt, pushing off on the trees that offered handles along the way. I gripped the jagged ledges of the Sketchy Rocks, the one section where the mountain bested the trail, threatening a bumpy slide down to anyone without sure footholds. I never turned around more than a couple seconds at the power lines or the rock outcropping. The views were nice, but staring at them wasn't going to take me up. It wasn't going to bring me to the Gap.

Once I realized what the Flashes were, I sought them out on purpose. Some of the visions have manifested already: the power going off at the moment I cut myself shaving, my roommate's new electric blue mascara, the burned popcorn smell invading the lecture hall. Others I continue to anticipate: a salted caramel macaron cracking between my lips, a strong hand grasping the back of my skull with the pressure of invited but frantic romance.

The Flashes all seem to be events coming in the next few months. There are no images of flying mortarboards, no labor pains, no arthritic hands struggling with a ketchup bottle. I don't think this is a limitation of the gift or the Gap. I think it's a reflection of my remaining lifespan. I don't want to argue about this; that's why I'm writing it instead of telling it.

I can shape them, lead my mind to a topic, an emotion, a person as I start the climb. If I make my mind a shrine to my curiosity, the apparition respects this. There are limits: I've tried to lead my thoughts to find out whose hand that is or where to find that damn macaron. It hasn't worked yet. But I can follow the loose strands of my life as it is now. That's how I found out my grade on my P-Chem final a week early—a 92. It's how I found out about my mom.

I picked her up and took her to the emergency room a week after she appeared in the Flash. I didn't say we were going to the ER; I told her I wanted to go out for coffee. I trusted the Flash, but I wasn't sure about the timing. Turns out I had it exactly right. She had her stroke two minutes before we reached the hospital. I realized as we walked out together two days later: my behavior had changed the future. The visions are not absolute. See, in the Flash, I found her hours later in her kitchen.

You might think I am only returning to Carlos for the Flashes, but it's equally for the climbing. The build-up is what makes the pay-off so rewarding. My calves and quads have ached, hardened, then ached again. I've learned new vocabulary like *iliotibial band* and *posterior tibialis tendonitis*, words furnished by Google as I couldn't bear the thought of going to a doctor who would propose a logical solution: lay off the vert. Worse yet, he might sense what I couldn't talk about: I was on the verge of killing myself.

I had a Flash of my own body sprawled on the Sketchy Rocks. In the Flash, I approached from below, the panic of my would-be rescuer surging. But the vacuum of death was defeated again. The panic left—it had never been my own panic, anyway—as the real world, the real Sketchy Rocks, returned, obscuring the future.

I wasn't as surprised by this as you might think I would be. But still, I did my best to be responsible. I stopped running for a few days. I had learned. I could modify the future. I proved it, studying in the time I would have been running, raising test scores above the Flash's pessimistic predictions.

My tendonitis healed. My back and legs smoothed then tensed with unreleased power. My sunburn peeled then faded to light brown. I ate enough to keep up with my appetite, my stomach content for the first time in months.

I felt awful.

My mind sagged, unplugged from its source of wonder. I created circuitous routes on campus to climb sequential staircases, searching for a glimmer. I talked to my mom, describing my day in hours of homework and dollars of next term's textbooks. I wandered through a frat party, probing for the hands I had seen, forgetting to listen when people spoke to me, pretending the music was too loud for me to hear them.

I left the party, swapped stilettos for lugs, and drove to the base of Carlos. A full moon beckoned; a sideways wind too cold for my bare legs taunted. The mountain was trash-talking me. I surged from the beginning, careening for the Gap, thirsty for even the mundane.

I woke up on the Sketchy Rocks, a lump on my forearm and my temple. The Flash of my body on the rocks: it had happened, but it was modified, just like Mom's stroke. It was night—not day, as it had been in my Flash. No one was finding me in a panic. I had dodged it. I was okay.

I did two more climbs that night, easing myself back in. Only one more Flash as a reward. Cinnamon sprinkled on a latte. I could be patient. More would come.

I sprinkled cinnamon on my latte the next morning and returned to Carlos. That morning, I did four more climbs. I survived three more Flashes. The beach. A swollen toe. My body on the trail again.

My legs still burned from the night before as I drove them into the ground, hands on my quads. The pain I loved was welcoming me back.

Over the next week, I achieved twelve more climbs before I passed out again. I also claimed some scars from briars, a bee sting, the singe of sweat in my eye. And I know the future holds an abysmal putt-putt shot, the thumping wind of the windows down on the interstate, a cramp in my hand while taking notes in class.

I know where this is going. I can't talk to you about it—whoever you are, finding this, reading this.

I'm leaving this in a place where someone will read it when there's a reason to look. My hunch is that loose paper in an otherwise empty nightstand drawer will get someone's attention when it's over. I can't argue with you. I know what you'll tell me, whoever you are.

I've climbed Carlos seventeen times this week. I passed out three times. I know where this is going.

I don't want to argue with you.

Midnight on Rio Road

KENT M. PETERSON

"YOU *STOLE* IT?" LIZ couldn't quite believe what she'd heard. Next to her, Jeff's red plastic cup paused halfway to his lips; he must have been equally surprised.

"Not exactly." Todd grinned at the two of them. "I just happened to be working for the contractor that redid the wiring in that part of the police station. And it just happened to get bumped and fall into one of the trash bags where we were dumping the junk. And somebody in a dark hoodie just happened to go poking through the trash bags early that morning before the garbage crew came by for pickup.

"Of course, *I* don't know anything about that," he added with mock sincerity, hand over his heart. "All I know is that this is very definitely a perfect duplicate that I very definitely had made from scratch. I certainly wouldn't know what happened to the original." He grinned at them again and raised his own cup in mock salute to the eerie-looking clock where it sat on the shelf above his desk.

Jeff leaned closer to better examine it. The clock was made in the likeness of a human skull with a wooden dial set into each eye-socket: the left one was marked for hours, the right one for minutes. A handle sticking out of one ear was clearly for winding it up. The hands were still, stopped a few minutes before twelve.

"Does it, you know, work? As a clock?"

"Oh, yeah, it works fine. I wound it up a bit to make sure. But the ticking got on my nerves, and the jaw opens and closes constantly while it's going. Pretty creepy, so I let it run down."

"Todd! Hey Todd!" someone yelled from the hallway. "Get your ass out here, we got a beer pong game going in the conference room."

"Ah'll be thar!" Todd yelled back in an exaggerated accent. Turning to Liz and Jeff, he added: "Don't stare at it too long. Tends to make you jumpy if you do. Ask me how I know." He grinned again, raised his cup to them, and headed down the hall to rejoin the company office party.

"Come on, Jeff," Liz urged. "That thing gives me the creeps."

"Yeah—in a minute." Jeff was poking at it. "Doesn't feel like plastic. But I guess they can make some pretty hard and rough plastics. It can't be a real skull, can it? What does bone feel like, anyway?"

She groaned. "If you're going to get weird about this—"

"Jeff! Liz! There you are." Carson stuck his head in the door. "Aren't you—oh. You're looking at that thing."

"Jeff keeps staring at it. It really freaks me out," Liz complained. "Did you know Todd says he stole this? Right out of the police evidence room?"

"Yeah. Not the smartest thing he's done."

"Well, yeah! If the cops get wind of it—"

"I don't mean the cops. That thing's supposed to be cursed. You remember that one car crash?"

Jeff looked around at him. "Which one?"

"On Rio Road. The weird one, on that curve where there's nothing around and it's still kinda wild. You don't remember? About a year back, it was all over the news for a while. That's where this thing came from—the cops found it in the crash debris."

Jeff shook his head. "Not ringing a bell. I must've been busy fixing batch jobs for that quarter's mass mailings or something."

"Lucky you. There was this fortune-teller dude on the Downtown Mall about that time—what? Yes, I go see fortune-tellers, they give me all sorts of ideas for my D&D game. Anyway, he used these weird dice with stick-figures instead of cards, and he was pretty good. Kept saying things that turned out to be generally accurate—I kept track."

"Oh, I remember him," Liz said. "With the funny little plywood stall. Wasn't he the one with the rain prediction, that year it just never stopped?"

"That's him." Carson looked at the skull-clock and frowned. "After that crash, I remember seeing him staring at the photo of this clock in the paper, shaking his head. *No way out.* That's what he kept saying. I asked him what he meant. He said he recognized it and it was cursed. Then he changed the subject."

"Gimme a break," Jeff said. "Ominous tidings of doom are the whole point of those guys. And he didn't say there'd be lots of rain, just that it'd be unusual. We could've had a drought, and he'd still have taken credit for it." Jeff looked at the clock again, shrugged, and laughed. "What are we doing in Todd's office, anyway? There's a company party out there, let's get back to it."

It was sometime after 11:30 p.m. when the party wound down. Nerf guns and empty plastic cups lay strewn around the offices, empty pizza boxes were stacked on tables in the break room, and people were making their way out to their cars. Todd had to be carried to his SUV by several friends, only one of whom was sober enough to drive. Liz, Jeff, and Carson watched them pile into the vehicle and then pull out of the parking spot, not too unsteadily.

"At least the traffic isn't a problem at this hour," Jeff said. "It'll be an easy drive."

"And so quiet," Liz replied. "Why don't people stagger work start times through the day? Ten-minute commutes instead of half an hour, every day. Just think of it."

"Nah, you'd just end up with mini-jams through the whole day," Carson said. "Even on 29. Traffic expands to fill the space available. You guys're headed that way, right?"

"Not quite," Jeff said. "Through downtown, Park Street to Rio Road, then just follow the loop around north. Like I said, real easy drive at this hour."

Carson nodded. "Makes sense, I guess. Seeya Monday." He headed off to his own car.

Liz and Jeff went the opposite direction, to where Jeff had parked his red convertible. He unlocked it, looked up at the moon in the night sky, and drew a deep breath of the balmy air. "I'm folding the top back," he said. "Too nice a night to be cooped up in a box."

"Whatever," Liz said, yawning. "You just want to play with your toy."

"Sure, and why not?" He grinned.

He'd taken the top off the car often enough now that the process was quick and smooth. Liz's feet bumped into a canvas bag on the floor as she got into the passenger-side seat, but she just pushed it aside to make room for her purse. The car hummed to life, and they set out. The cruise through downtown was relaxing and quiet, a dramatic difference to the area during the day. Soon enough they were moving along Park Street, lined with gentle green lawns and nice houses. Liz stretched her arms, yawned again, and extended her legs to relax in languor. In doing, she bumped the canvas bag again. There was definitely something in it.

"What is this, anyway?"

"What's what?"

"This bag on the car floor. Where I normally put my purse."

"Gee, I don't know," he said, entirely too casually.

Liz flashed a suspicious look at him, largely wasted in the darkness. She reached down and grabbed the bag, pulling it into her lap. The shape prompted a suspicion she didn't want to think about. She fumbled a bit until she found the top of the bag and pulled it open. In the lights from the dashboard, she could clearly see that it was the skull clock from Todd's office.

Her heart skipped a beat or two.

After a few moments, when she was sure she was breathing again, she managed an almost normal tone of voice. "Jeff, why is Todd's skull clock in your car?"

"Well," he said, "apparently in all the hullaballoo of that party, it seems to have gotten itself knocked off its shelf and into some random bag, and nobody quite knows when or how. Ironic, dontcha think?"

She didn't need to look at him to know he was grinning hugely.

"Jeff, you—you idiot. You can't steal things just because you want them!"

"Why not? Todd did."

"Because stealing is a crime and people go to jail for it!"

"That's the beauty of it," Jeff said. "You saw him. He was totally plastered by the end of the night. He'll have no idea when it walked off, or who did it. And he can't report it missing because he's the one that stole it from the cops in the first place!"

"Jeff, you IDIOT!" she said again. Or maybe yelled. She was too upset to be careful.

"Open the mouth," he told her.

"What? Why?"

"Just do it."

The jaw was held tightly closed by something. "Try winding it up," he suggested, seeing her struggle.

She gripped the handle projecting from one ear and began turning it. Soon enough, a quiet, regular ticking began, and the jaw slowly opened and shut, as though chewing something.

Something shiny was inside the mouth.

"What's that? Is this like an Indiana Jones thing?" She looked at him.

Jeff just grinned, watching the road as they rolled along. She tilted the skull clock; the object moved a little. Next time the mouth opened, she darted two fingers in, pulling it out before the yellowed teeth closed once more.

It was a ring, the gem glittering in the lights from the dashboard.

"Is this...?"

Jeff grinned and shrugged. "Funny thing, I've got one just like it." He held up a hand: the ring finger bore the twin of the one she was holding, just like they'd talked about. She could have sworn his hands had been bare when he got into the car. "It's past time, isn't it?"

"JEFF, YOU IDIOT!" she squealed in an entirely different tone as she slipped the ring onto her finger.

"So that's a yes, then?"

She lunged at him; her seat belt brought her up short. She hit the button to release it, then leaned over, grabbed his shoulders, and kissed him full on the lips. The clock fell to the car floor, unnoticed.

"Hey, hey, watch it," he mumbled, laughing. "I know it's nearly midnight and hardly anybody's on the road, but—" The sound of the wheels on the road changed tone as they crossed a bridge.

She looked away from him, briefly, and demanded, "Did you just blow through that stoplight?"

"It's your fault. I was distracted. Anyway, nobody was there, and it's the only stoplight on this road." He leaned over to resume the kiss.

"Watch the road, Jeff," she said, laughing. She then betrayed herself by joining in with enthusiasm. Her phone rang. "Oh, dammit, what now—" She fumbled for her purse with one hand.

Jeff glanced at it then back toward the road. His eyes widened in horror. The car shuddered, swerved, and someone screamed. There was a great banging sound, followed by smashing branches and tumbling darkness.

***

Liz awoke lying on wet leaves and broken branches. The skin of her arms was a mess of scratches. She felt bruised all over, and a rock was digging into one hip. There was a glow from among more trees and bushes farther down the slope. The convertible's headlights were still on, though the engine was dead.

"Jeff?... Jeff!"

She scrambled to her feet and pushed her way through the bushes where she'd fallen, following the gouges the car had dug in the tangle of vines covering the slope. Jeff was still in the driver's seat, unmoving.

"Jeff! Are you okay?" After shoving her way through something prickly, she pulled the driver's door open and reached for him. He didn't move or respond. Was that a pulse? Breath on his lips? She thought so but wasn't sure. The seatbelt was on. She couldn't see any injuries. "Oh, what do I *do?*" Those CPR and emergency medicine classes had always seemed like a good idea for later. Her purse and phone were nowhere in sight; so much for calling 9-1-1.

"Come *on*, Jeff, wake up!" Still no response. Liz felt his lips again, listened for a heartbeat. There. Maybe. Was there a first aid kit in the back? Torn between rage and fear at her own ignorance, she made her way to the rear of the car and popped the trunk. As she did, something shifted, more branches broke, and the car slid forward and further down the slope by about a foot.

Liz froze, her heart thudding in her chest. Nothing further happened, but leaving Jeff in the car was definitely out of the question. The emergency blanket was still there; she pulled it out, spread it on the ground as close to the driver's door as she could. Nothing about Jeff had changed. She unfastened the seat belt, took him under the shoulders, and pulled.

He was way heavier than she expected, and the utter limpness of his body made everything five times harder than it should have been—she had to shove him partly back into the seat and work his feet out from among the pedals. Still no injuries anywhere that she could find. After dragging him across the broken bushes to the blanket and then brushing away the twigs and leaves caught in his clothing, she knelt by his side, talking to him, hoping he would wake up.

A rustling sound of leaves and breaking twigs caught her attention. She looked up the slope. Someone was struggling downhill, a handheld flashlight unsteadily lighting the way.

"Hello!" she called out. "Can you help? My boyfriend's hurt, and I've lost my phone!"

The figure stopped suddenly, the flashlight shining directly in Liz's face then moving to Jeff on the blanket.

"Hello?" she called again. After a few moments, the figure started moving again with slow, tentative steps. Liz was about to say something else when the figure turned the flashlight on its own face.

It was Jeff.

She didn't remember getting to her feet. The two of them stared at each other across the blanket and the still form lying on it. She couldn't make herself say *who are you;* that seemed too obvious.

Finally, she managed: "How did you get here?"

"There was... there was a phone call." It was definitely Jeff's voice. "I don't remember... what happened. I don't remember the crash. It's all really blurry. I think I blacked out... She found me down there." He gestured vaguely in the direction of the car.

"She. Who?"

He stared at her. "Lizzie. You."

"What?"

"You and I were in the car together. We crashed. You found me..." He gestured helplessly. "Down there."

"What? No, I didn't! *You* just came climbing down that hill, and Jeff—Jeff is right *here!* He had his seat belt on! He was still in the car! Only—" She was on the verge of tears. "Only he won't wake up! Come *on*, Jeff," she pleaded, bending down to the still figure on the blanket, massaging the still hands.

The other Jeff, the mobile one, stood there rubbing his forehead with the back of his hand, still holding the flashlight. He was holding the other arm close to his side, as if it hurt.

She looked up at him. "This doesn't make sense! How could I have gotten you? You were up on the road, you came down from there!"

"Lizzie. I think it wasn't—she was my Lizzie. Like he is your Jeff. She and I were in my car, you and he were in..." He looked at the crash below—the single wrecked car, crumpled against the trees—and frowned.

"Well, where is she now, huh? Maybe if I could talk to myself, things would start making sense!" She was on the verge of hysterical laughter.

"Lizzie. She's dead."

"Huh?"

"We were up on the road, looking for her phone. A car came around the bend. It hit you—her—and I saw—" He gasped, swallowed, took several deep breaths. "It smashed her into the guardrail. I saw that. I'm going to have nightmares about it. I was a bit farther up the road. After it hit her, it must've sideswiped me or something, knocked me down. Stunned me, I guess. I don't know if I got knocked out again? The next clear thing I remember is hearing your voice. Wasn't sure whether that was a dream, or if the other was a nightmare, or—" He shook his head. "So, I came down here and found you. And—him."

"No. No," she said, shaking her head. "This is crazy. I'm not dead. I'm right here. I'm right here! And where's your car, huh? *Where's your car, smartass?* That one's our—his! We just crashed in it! I just pulled *him* out of the driver's seat! And where's yours, huh?"

He started to point at the car with his free hand, winced, like he thought better of it. "I don't know. I don't understand. Maybe this is like some parallel universe stuff. The other you died. Maybe, between him and me, one of us was supposed to—" He stopped, swallowed, made himself say it. "—to die also. Only we didn't. I woke up, and he didn't."

"Except..." She was suddenly cold, staring at him. "Except what if you're not really Jeff?" She couldn't think what had made her say that. Something had put the idea in her head. What? Why?

"Huh?"

"Maybe you're not him. Maybe you just look like him, right now. Maybe you're something else." There was a rock pressing against her calf where she was kneeling on the ground. It felt pretty big—she could probably fit her hand around it. She didn't look at it.

"Lizzie, this is crazy." He looked like he was about to step toward her but stopped when he saw her expression. "We need to call for help. I dropped my phone somewhere, too. Did you check if yours is still in the car? I'll see if I can find it."

He pushed his way through the bushes toward the car, reaching out gingerly with his hurt arm to keep branches out of his eyes. In the beam from the flashlight, she could see his hand was bare. No ring. That was it. A glance at the still figure on the blanket—was that a slight rise and fall of the chest?—yes, that same hand, and on it the ring, twin to her own, the rings they had been laughing and kissing about so recently, so long ago. The oppressive stillness of the night was choking.

"He *will* wake up," she told herself sternly, and she grasped the rock next to her leg.

The other Jeff was leaning over the passenger compartment, playing his flashlight over the inside of the car. She rose to her feet, took three long strides forward. He jerked upright just in time to receive the hurled rock square against the side of his head. The flashlight went flying, there was a tinkling sound, and it went out. The other Jeff's body tumbled down the slope into darkness.

The silence was broken by a groan. She looked around. Jeff—her Jeff—was sitting up on the blanket, holding his head.

"Jeff!" Laughing, crying with relief, she was at his side, arms around him.

"What... what happened?"

"We crashed. You don't remember? Are you all right? I was thrown clear out of the car, I guess you were knocked unconscious. I had to pull you out of all that." She gestured downhill, toward the car, the mess of bushes and broken branches, the trees visible in the still-shining headlights. "I was so worried. Are you sure you're all right?"

"Yeah, I think so. I mean, I've got some sort of headache, but... I seem to be in one piece." He stood up carefully and looked around. "Huh. Some crash. I hope the car's not totaled, I like that car."

"Jeff!" The stress and tensions of the night suddenly threatened to overwhelm her.

"Hey, I'm glad you're in one piece, too." He took her in his arms. "Hey, babe, it's all right, it's all right. Look, we should get up on the road and see if we can get help."

"Okay." She was sniffling from the whiplash of emotions. "And see if we can find my purse."

"And my phone. I lost it. It's not down here."

"Yeah, mine is off somewhere too," he said, checking his pockets. "Here's my flashlight, though. And hey, it works. That'll help. Come on. Our stuff was all lying around loose, probably bounced right out when we—oh wow, look at that." He was pointing the flashlight at the torn guardrail. "We just blew right through that, didn't we? There's probably junk from the car scattered all around here."

There was, indeed, junk from the car all over the place, things that had been in it and pieces that broke off when it hit the guardrail, both on the road and scattered over the ground near the breach.

They spread out, using moonlight and flashlight to look through the debris. After a few minutes, Jeff suddenly spotted something familiar. "Hey, here's my phone."

"Great. Help me find mine. It could be anywhere in this mess. I've got my purse, but half the stuff fell out."

He only half-heard her, focusing on the little glowing screen. "Hey Liz, I'm calling your phone. It should be ringing now. Hear it?"

He looked up just in time to see the blinding glare of headlights come barreling around the curve. Just in time to see Lizzie look up. Just in time to see it smash her into the guardrail. It was headed for him, and for an instant he had the crazy idea that it was a red convertible just like his—

Blackness overtook him. He wasn't sure for how long. When his vision cleared, he became aware of three things: a stabbing pain in one arm whenever he moved it, the moonlight on the broken guardrail, and Lizzie's voice somewhere down the slope, calling his name.

He scrambled to his feet. His flashlight was still working, somehow, but his injured arm kept sending stabbing twinges of pain. That hand, with the ring, was swelling a bit too. He pulled off the ring and put it carefully in his pocket. Heedless of the skull-shaped clock lying on the graveled roadside, he headed down the slope, following the sound of Lizzie's voice.

What's Going on Here?

JAMES COLE

OF ALL THE INTRICATE accidents of human creativity, there is none so resilient as the *pile*. Sometimes, with proper vim and volume, your pile can achieve great things. Get enough people to push some stones together in the desert, and, *boom*, pyramid. What's that, a spot on the Ancient Wonders of the World? Don't mind if I do. Me? I'm not grand enough for pyramids, not pragmatic enough for landscaping, even. My piles are built from paper and procrastination.

I might've paid my bills on time if I remembered what corner of that mess they buttressed. There was a delicate ecosystem to the envelopes and forms, layers in a rainforest that incautious prodding might entirely upset. My previous attempts to shrink the stack usually took the form of a migration, population not so much lessened as seasoning at one end of the desk or another.

"Aha!"

There, just under the birthday cards from the week before, I found the sun-bleached poster of Kiwi the orange tabby, her name and owner's phone number written in thick Sharpie. I tried to smooth some of the creases, as if this would shake off the fuzz of the photocopied image.

"Sorry about the wait," I said, returning to my door. "I'm just glad it was near the top. I'd have needed a shovel otherwise."

My guest perked from his lean against the jamb, smiled warmly, and studied the poster through a pair of thick bifocals. A curious combination of camouflage and Kohl's, his aesthetic might best be summarized as 'suburban survivalist.' Not exactly my ideal cold caller. When I initially saw, through the peephole, the KA-BAR on his hip and headlamp skew across his forehead, I'd serious reservations about answering at all. I'd cracked the door, chain lock letting no more than a couple inches for conversation. Only when he mentioned Kiwi did I allow a true face-to-face.

"Sad thing, this," he said, folding the paper into one of his many pockets. "Unlikely we'll find her totally alive."

"Totally alive?"

"Some Sasquatches have been known to begin eating their small prey while still wriggling. Much like bears."

I stared at the man, replaying the last few seconds, confirming the order of his words. "Did you say Sasquatch?"

"Yes, ma'am. Although, you may be more familiar with the colloquial 'Bigfoot.' Which is a ridiculous name, if you ask me. Their feet are perfectly proportional to their stature."

"You think a gorilla man stole this cat?"

Now he looked at me like I was the unhinged one. Across the hall, my neighbor exited his apartment, all polyestered for street cycling. He noticed the strange, snuff-stinking man and shot me a look as if to ask *should I call the cops again?* I waved him off.

"Sasquatch is hardly a gorilla," my visitor continued. "More likely a descendant of *Gigantopithecus blacki* that crossed the Bering Bridge around a hundred thousand years ago. You might say he is closer to a predatory orangutan."

"I thought Bigfoot lived in, like, northern California, or Canada. What makes you think–"

"Common misconception," he said, widening his stance. "Sightings of giant woodland primates have been reported across the continent. We only associate the species with that area because it remains one of the last great untouched wildernesses in the country. In fact, Blinken et al. proposed in their 1998 paper that westward relocation of the Sasquatch was driven by rapid resettlement of—"

"Okay." I took the reins—he'd drive me mad if I didn't. "Let's reset the needle for a second. You're telling me a big, hairy ape is sneaking into people's yards and snatching their cats? Wouldn't someone have noticed?"

He chewed his lip, rosacea flaring slightly.

"That's why I'm here. We *have* noticed. But don't worry, you can be sure we'll find the beast before it—"

"Thank you, I gotta move some laundry into the dryer. Good luck, though," I said, gently shutting the door.

A sound excuse—and honest, too. Seconds later, I heaped the sopping clothes from one metal hatch to another, set the timer, and took a seat on the dryer as it rumbled. Sometimes, in the first few spins, the door latch would loosen, and a soggy mayhem would come flying out. From my seat, I could see the stranger through the blinds. He waddled with a wide gait all the way to his mud-flecked pickup at the end of the lot, like he was about to lay an egg. Once he'd driven off, I continued to stare at the vacated spot, then a little past it to the white house across the street. It sat on a hill that city surveyors repeatedly warned would one day slide into the road, bringing whoever and whatever it wanted with it.

Not that Ms. Lutger cared.

Knowing her—and I barely did—she'd be in her rocker riding the landspill all the way down, not even bothering to acknowledge the honking cars when her porch ended up in the middle of the lane. I could only dream of such indifference.

She sat there as always, but rather than rocking, Ms. Lutger hung off the seat's edge, kneading the arthritis in her knuckles, head swiveling. Kiwi's absence weighed on her. She sat like this every day for the past week, guilt like Garamond typed across her face. Vigilance often follows a failure of caution. Or was it the other way around?

The dryer twanged into a more manageable rhythm, so I hopped off, let it do its thing, got on with my day.

***

I'd thought the buzz would die there. Cats go missing, people worry, and monsters can't tickle you if you can't see them—these were truths of the valley too obvious to ever record in book or idiom. But where there's a weirdo, there's always a way. In our case there were many weirdos, and, thus, many ways back onto the turnpike toward hysteria.

Two or so days after I received a house call from Wal-mart-brand Bear Grylls, a video started making the rounds. Cville subreddit showed it first, then Instagram. Even CBS19 replayed it a couple times. It wasn't much, no more than four seconds long. These cryptid clips rarely have much more to show. A motion-activated camera in someone's backyard caught a grainy, haggard silhouette rifling through a compost heap, and, suddenly, locals were calling for the National Guard. Reporters on the downtown beat stopped townies and visitors, asked them their opinions on the footage, shoved a mic-cover under their lips, and dreamed of pick-ups from larger networks.

Denver Riggleman, former representative and Sasquatch mat-ing enthusiast, made a sudden reappearance on the public stage. He called for an investigation, pushed for transparency with local law enforcement who, by that point, had responded to at least a dozen ape creature reports. The more cynical and liberal-mind-ed citizens saw this as a bid toward a possible re-election, though Riggleman assured the public he had no interest in running again. Sorry—I suppose I shouldn't malign his critics too much. I'm one of them, after all.

I'd hoped that life might maintain the veneer of normalcy that Charlottesvillians had come to tolerate, but I've learned and keep learning: when mania meets idleness coming down the road, idleness *always* makes way.

"Ms. Baudry!"

I winced at my name, stared at the brick walkway, tried to press through. These strolls along the Downtown Mall were de-signed to give me that dose of *being-in-the-worldness* that kept sanity and Vitamin D in my system. So, you can understand why I'd be a little spooked when I saw my visitor from the day before.

He stood among a crowd of other cryptid eccentrics. Most wore the familiar hunting attire, while others appeared to be from a more psychedelically informed camp. An even smaller subsect dressed like Ghostbusters without the Hollywood bud-get.

"Any word on Kiwi?" he called.

This shouting, even in the middle of a Saturday afternoon, tended to stick out among the late lunchers and dog walkers of the mall. Eyes turned to us, and I did a poor job of *not reacting.*

"The cat, you mean?" an investigator in a caution-tape-yellow turtleneck asked.

"Yes, she's the one who gave me this poster."

He might as well have doused me in chum and kicked me off the back of his boat. The fifteen-plus Sasquatchers (Bigfootists?) eyed me with all the unblinking vacancy of a cereal mascot. I had mere seconds to plot an escape before they came *en masse,* waving cameras, smartphones, even what looked like some kind of long-obsolete temperature probe.

"Ma'am, just a quote for my blog!" one shouted.

"Was this cat known to be a frequent outdoor urinator? I have this theory—"

The rest became so gobbled I could scarcely make out more than a phlegmy exhort.

I bolted for the flashing marquee of The Paramount. It advertised an upcoming showing of *The Third Man,* a continuation of that month's Orson Welles festival. My forehead nearly collided with box office glass.

"One ticket," I said.

The woman at the microphone jumped.

"The show started ten minutes ago. We have another screening tonight at—"

"I don't care!"

I slipped her my card and ran inside before the transaction could even process.

"Ma'am? Your card?"

"I trust you!"

***

I never felt much magnetism from old movies. My sophomore roommate took a pit stop in film studies while going through the ol' major roulette, so the black-and-white transatlantica of the Hollywood Golden Age wasn't completely new to me. *The Third Man* held my attention, but it certainly didn't hold my hand when it came to the plot. Thankfully, Orson's persistent smirking carried me through the runtime.

The lights came on, the aisles pocked with flattened popcorn, and I'd almost forgotten what drove me to this shelter.

"Thank you for coming. Thank you for coming." Ms. Lutger, my neighbor, waited at the door. She wore a maroon vest and nametag, nodding, smiling, making all the disingenuous gestures of appreciation. At first, I thought I'd keep my head down and pass, but then, midway to the bathroom, I one-eightied, excusing myself against the current of the crowd like a salmon making for spawning grounds.

"Ms. Lutger!" I called.

She frowned, not recognizing me in the slightest. The crowd, thankfully a trickle by that point, broke around me as I took station next to my neighbor.

"I just thought I should warn you," I said. "It's about your cat." Still confused.

"You know, Kiwi?" I added.

"Oh dear, yes. So sorry to hear."

"Hear?" I puzzled for a moment. "I was just going to tell you there are some Bigfoot nuts who may come to your door if they haven't already. They seem to think a Sasquatch took your cat."

"Oh." She chuckled softly and produced something like a cough drop or a Werther's. It occurred to me I'd never seen an elderly person eating their own hard candy.

"I know, I guess..." Guilt got the better of me. "I'm actually here to say I'm sorry. About the cat and the fact that I kinda told them about it. I figure I'm likely to blame if they come knocking."

"It's quite alright, dear. I've dealt with my fair share of nuts in my day."

"I'm just glad you aren't allergic."

"Besides, I know Kiwi wasn't taken by any Bigfoot..."

"That's what I tried to tell them," I said, like I could ever be so resolute. "I just don't want them snooping around your property. In fact, I'm only in here—"

"It was a haint."

I blinked. The last moviegoer scraped past me on his walker, and Ms. Lutger thanked him for coming, all while I went through the playback. I was getting a lot of use of my brain's rewind function that week.

"Haint what?" I asked, once we were alone again.

"You know, a spirit. The kind that lives way up in the hills."

"Spirit? Like a ghost?"

"Not every spirit was once alive, flesh and blood, like you or me. Some are just flesh and blood. Some ain't even that! That's what I saw take my Kiwi. But don't you worry yourself about that, young lady. I'm not even lookin' to get that cat back. He was a real devil, that one."

She started to close the main doors to the theater. I hung back a moment, weighing the offered explanations, judging, admittedly, which would garner the wilder looks when I recounted this later with the folks in the paddling club. Then, something even weirder caught in my craw.

"Wait, then why post missing cat posters?"

"Oh, my daughter made a big fuss about it," she said. We started toward the concessions stand, my feet dragging, hers making confident strides. "She gave me that cat, said she was worried about me living alone. But better alone than with that flab-hooker."

"Did—did you just call your cat a whore?"

"No, no, no. Skin the way mine is, claws like that, you do the math..."

It was a little late in the afternoon for that arithmetic, especially with such upsetting variables. I didn't even say goodbye, I just evaporated back onto the Downtown Mall. By that point the evening dinner crowds gathered, foot traffic doubled, the buskers unlatched at their usual corners. The cryptozoologist crowd must've floated to another nucleus of activity. I called my friend Heather to meet me at The Alley Light. I needed to unload some of these details.

***

Two a.m. when I woke up in a sweat. For a moment, all I could do was heave under the comforter, stare up into the vault of shadow, and try to remember the dream that flung me out of sleep.

It felt more like a memory. A summer spent with my grand-parents. A late-night ghost story by grandpa's shed, his wrin-kles made deeper in the flicker of the firepit. Too much s'more sugar and the horrors of co-sleeping with my mouth-breathing cousin.

"So don't you go looking in grandma's cupboard under the stairs. There's two of them boogers living under there. One's all bones, the other all flesh. You'll know 'em by the way they rattle and slop up the stairs. *Click-clack. Squish-squash. Click-clack. Squish-squash.*"

"Harry!" Grandma shrieked from the porch. "Now I told you—I said I told you..."

Long shadows growing longer. Paralysis beneath the great concavity of a presence, a silhouette of living dread always in the corner of the eye.

I checked my phone. Two thirty-eight. I got out of bed and threw off my sweaty clothes. They made a wet flop as they hit the bare wall at the back of my closet. Then I crawled to my couch, watched old-school *Scooby-Doo* in the nude, fell asleep to the paling of dawn.

***

I spent the better part of the following Sunday worrying about Ms. Lutger. Then, most of Monday forgetting about it all to-gether. These kinds of worries tended to well up during the weekends, but thankfully the work week always returned to sober us, consolidate, reset our attentions. Sure, a thought of old mountain phantoms might flicker between the oscillating action of the copy machine, images of cryptids dangling cats over a cauldron might pop into mid-afternoon daydreams. So long as modern living remained its usual numbing sapor, the American mind would find fearful interludes to keep itself out of absolute inertia. The haze of sky in the office win-dow stretched free of pareidolic clouds, leaving only week-old memories to fill in the fantasies. A canvas, or a cave wall.

I'd goofed off most of Wednesday morning, talking favorite *Great British Bake Off* contestants with my cubicle neighbor.

We'd just settled in to get some actual work done when Leif, my brother, called.

"Do you remember that can of bear spray Dad got you for Christmas two years ago?"

That's how he greeted me, no *hello, it's Leif, hope you aren't busy...*

"Uhh, sure. I think it's currently a bookend."

"Bring it."

"Leif, what the hell?"

"Sorry. If you have time."

"Where are you?"

I must've asked a little too loud because my coworkers began poking their heads over the cubicle dividers like worried meerkats. I dropped to a hush.

"Leif, please tell me you aren't up at Bailey's cabin again."

The rubberneckers turned back to their tasks, giving me a split second to dash into the hall. I could tell this conversation would require more than my 'inside voice.'

"What's wrong? Should I call the police?"

A flush of static, some rustling, what sounded like the click of a door.

"Maybe, I'm not... I think I saw it."

"Saw what?"

"Just go home, grab the bear spray, bring it here ASAP. I'll buy you dinner."

"You already owe me for New Year's..."

"I'll buy you *two* dinners. Hell, you can eat 'em at the same time. Just get here quick."

***

It was almost lunch time by that point, so I told my supervisor I'd be taking my break a little early. She gave me that look, the *too-many-questions-no-clear-order-to-ask-them-in* expression which I'm sure had become the default for most in middle management.

I went home, retrieved the can, and made for IX. Leif's car sat angled across two parking spaces, bumper dangerously close to

a light post. The old Range Rover had roved one to many ranges
to be a genuine collectible, the undercarriage showing traces of
rust like the crisped edges of lightly toasted bread. I approached,
trying to twirl the spray on one finger, but the canister proved too
bulky, and I ended up thwapping myself in the chin.

The trunk unlatched, and there Leif cowered under a picnic
blanket. He lay in a sniper's crouch behind a cover of used shop
towel boxes.

"Jesus, dude," I said, handing off the chemical deterrent. "Did
you sleep here last night? Smells like sour pits."

"Sleep? No. Was I here, well..." He lifted the blanket to show a
bedding of Clif Bar wrappers. By my count, he'd torn through a
whole box.

"What's the matter? Besides everything, I mean."

He crawled his way out, wincing against the midday sun. Despite being three years my senior, he'd always been the shortest in
the family. His t-shirt yellowed a bit around the neckline, its front
crisscrossed with tiny threads of paint ejecta.

"Look, I only called because I saw them mention you in
C-VILLE Weekly."

"They what?" My insides somersaulted. It felt like every organ
traded places with its neighbor.

"Said something about you helping with the investigation into
these Bigfoot sightings."

I shook my head so vigorously that my ponytail whipped my
cheeks from both sides. "No, no, no, no, no. I just gave a nutjob a
missing cat poster. I am *not* involved."

Leif blinked at me.

"I'm not!" I shouted. At that time of day, only young moth-
ers and their toddlers wandered the park. The tots dashed from
distraction to distraction, kicking sand, clanging the public xy-
lophone, scraping concrete with chalk. A frightened caucus of
birds zipped around the vine-laced dome. The whole park like a
constant contest of nervous actions.

"I saw it," Leif said. "Last night."

"Leif, please, I don't have—"

"I'm serious. I was installing my new sculpture. You remember:
Love in Lies and Appetites. Anyway, I was getting ready to drill
the pieces together, and I noticed something over by the wall

there." He pointed to the main mural, the sliding door caked under layers of pigment, the list of patrons, the ledge where a mirrored homunculus sat, the bushels of clinging ivy and the target of his gesture, the barrel-shaped sauna.

"It was a little after one thirty in the morning and I thought I was alone, but then I saw this steam cloud over by the sauna. I figured, heck, maybe one of those Fire and Ice guys was out here for a late-night cleanse. But when I looked closer, it's all... fur, like ropey fur, hanging off limbs like a ghillie suit."

"A what?"

"You know, those camouflage things that soldiers wear. Anyway, it started walking toward The Looking Glass, and I just... froze. I couldn't do anything. But of course, I was still holding onto a hefty piece of sculpture and after a while, my arms gave out. It clanged onto the ground, and the thing turned. I couldn't see anything I'd call a face. It was too dark. But I could tell it was looking right at me."

Leif paused to take a hit off his inhaler. Pumps were low, so he tried to shake some residual loose.

"So, there we are: I'm looking at him, he's looking at me. All I can do is try not to piss myself and after a few seconds, he makes a break for it..."

He chewed nervously on the inhaler's mouthpiece. I felt an urge to snatch my bear spray back. It seemed too dangerous for delusional hands. Leif caught on to my skepticism.

"I'm serious," he said. "He vaulted that fence and ran into that closet there."

"Closet?" I repeated, if only to punctuate how ridiculous it sounded.

"I'm pretty sure it's a closet. Like for maintenance or something."

"What's a Bigfoot want with a closet? Hell, what's a Bigfoot want with a steam room?"

Leif threw the empty inhaler over his shoulder into the trunk. He fished around his scatter of unstowed supplies and snacks, pulling forth one last unopened Clif Bar and tearing it with his teeth.

"I know what it sounds like," he said, spitting out a tag of plastic.

"Maybe you should've called someone. Someone, I don't know, other than me. Why wait?"

"Because I never saw him come out..."

"...of the closet," I finished for him.

"Yes. He went in, and I haven't taken my eyes off that door since!"

I turned to the indicated passage. Barely noticeable behind the other IX Park miscellany, its frame almost invisible in the Prussian blue of the wall.

"So, he's still in there," I ventured. "If he didn't come out, he'd have nowhere to go. Right?"

"I don't like that look..."

"Let's see if he's still there."

"Are you crazy? You know what they say about cornered animals."

When I reached the door, Leif tried to yank me back, but I threw off his hand. I pointed to his spray, gestured at the knob, and signed some pseudo-tactical commands like those used by television SWAT officers before a breach. The handle felt unusually cold. A shiver traveled up my funny bone, but I tried not to show it.

Leif shook.

I shrugged.

A countdown with fingers: five to one, and, *woosh*, the door opened. Leif reflexively clicked the trigger, again and again, but he forgot the pin and, thankfully, no noxious jet caught me in the crossfire.

The only detectable movement came from a toppled mop and the buckets onto which it fell. Besides that, the tiny space contained only metal shelves, plaster mix, paint cans, rollers, and a great density of ammonia fumes that, given an exit, gusted out in a nose-wrinkling cloud.

"Bigfoot, huh?" I asked.

"I swear, I saw it," Leif said, lowering his weapon.

"I'm sure you saw something..."

"Don't be like that—smug is no capital quality."

"I'm just sayin..."

"Saying and looking!"

I started toward my car. "I don't know, Leif. Things don't add up. Something's going on in this town."

And in saying that, I realized that—hell, I believed—*something* was happening. Was it a monster? A maniac? Too early and too ludicrous to say. Maybe the heat was reacting with something in the tap water, suspicion on suspicion knotting into one big, city-wide sprain.

"Where are you going?" he called after me.

"Back to work. I suggest you do the same."

"What about the creature?"

"Right, *creature,*" I said. I meant for it to sound sarcastic, but...

"What now?" he asked.

"I don't know much," I said. "And I don't want to sound like a Bailey School book, but I'm pretty sure Bigfoots don't use saunas..."

***

Things always get crazier before they become saner. That's how the old saying goes, right? But if that's true, wouldn't things become infinitely more chaotic? Building up, exponentially, to some limit of disorder, which I suppose would qualify as that inevitable heat death the Science Channel likes to bring up. Or is it that at some critical point the insanity becomes normal, and thus any further concentration of that phenomenon is itself just a commitment to a new normalcy? I'm pretty sure that's how civilizations are made.

Is that what all this was? The seeds of a new culture, a new society?

I hoped not.

A local real-estate baron (though to name him as such seems dreadfully feudal) made an announcement the week after my brother's "encounter." Sixty thousand dollars would be awarded to anyone who could provide physical evidence of the creature. Of course, within twenty-four hours, this bounty came with quite a few asterisks. I imagine only so much could be done with blurry photos of stuffed animals in backyards or lumpy plaster casts that, to the alcohol-aided eye, *might* look somewhat foot-shaped.

Our old pal Riggleman raked in supporters, although everyone kept a wary eye on the frequency of his statements. Background analysis, play-by-plays, and deep rhetorical disputation populated many comment sections across sites and applications, parsing for any trace of political tomfoolery.

More hunters arrived, nightly news segments filled the time slots normally allotted to bumpers, and, wouldn't you know it, money was being made. By whom, from whom, and precisely for which goods or services remained a mystery even to those making the most profit.

As for the people, who could say where any person lay on the spectrum of investment? At work, my boss's assistant chided all would-be ape enthusiasts after one eager investigator knocked over the office recycling bins with his "research van."

An acquaintance from my yoga class showed me a patch of skin on her hip intended for fresh ink. "I'm still debating if I should get the full creature," she said, tracing a vaguely primate shape with her finger. "Or just the head."

"Why not the foot?" I asked, trying to be supportive.

"Don't you think he's probably self-conscious enough about that as is?"

Leif tried calling me a few more times since. He vacillated through states of paranoia and paralysis. One evening, while I was draining pasta, I answered the phone to him hyperventilating into the receiver.

"They're outside my house!" he said.

"Who? The monster?" I meant this as a joke but quickly regretted it.

"I don't know who, but they've been casing me all week. I swear to God. You don't think Bigfoot belongs to the military, do you?"

"I suspect he wouldn't be too good with protocol."

"That's what I'm saying!"

I heard the metallic *slink* of blinds snapping rigid again.

"Are you at least eating?" I asked. "I'll have leftovers here. I could bring them by."

"No, Red Baron's keeping me alive. I haven't gone for three days, but it's keeping me alive..."

"Gross."

When Thursday night rolled around, I'd suffered so much residual anxiety, likely a secondhand absorption from the air, that I decided I'd head down for a pre-weekend drunk. The Whiskey Jar was one of the few places with any real vibe that time of week, so I stationed myself at one end of the bar, draining Old Fashioned after Old Fashioned through those barely capillary cocktail straws.

Matthew O'Donnell, bard and bar-rouser, cycled through a dizzying selection of folk instruments, plucking tunes, leading choruses, encouraging delivery of that de-livering substance. The crowd ebbed in concentration. First some MBAs from the college crowded the main floor, sweaty conferencers in town on business, next the regulars who knew there was no limit to the fashion of their lateness.

"This next one is an original," Matthew said from the stage. "No one else in the world has written this song but me. And even my efforts are a work in progress. Usually," he said, pausing to affix his mic stand, "a song like this takes a few weeks of dedicated com-position, but given the currency of these events, I felt obligated to deliver."

"Christ," I said.

"This one's called 'The Charlottesville Wildman...' "

A few beats and off he went on his bouzouki, strumming up a flurry. I fell into my glass (or it into me?) until the tip of my nose numbed on ice. I didn't pay too close of attention to the lyrics, but it was a jaunty enough reel. I might've picked up the local references had I not been drawn instead to an exchange two stools down.

"Sir," the bartender said. "We can't serve you if you don't have your ID."

"But I don't *have* an ID," the stranger replied.

A sideways glance showed a heavy coat and scarf, Stetson-like hat several sizes too big for its wearer. In fact, the man had to tilt his whole head back just to see beyond the slouching brim. If he leaned any farther, he'd manage a pretty solid Matrix impression.

"Then we can't serve you. We have plenty of dry options."

"Err, no, that's quite alright," he said.

The barkeeper scurried off to take another patron's order. All attention aimed at the stage, or behind the bar, no one except me

and the stranger looking down at the beer-smeared bar top. He
looked left, he looked right. He saw me seeing him. One gloved
finger went to his mouth. Head-on, he appeared even stranger;
how I imagined lepers looked under all those bandages. Although
rather than rashy and decimated, there was a sort of clumpedness
to the flesh around his cheeks, the bridge of his shallow nose,
something like—

"You didn't see nothing," he said, sliding me a five-dollar bill.
He then picked up a glass of someone else's whiskey and downed
it. He put his finger again to his... well, he didn't seem to have lips
either. With a shrug and shake, he stepped back into the crowd
and disappeared.

I spit out an ice cube and flinched when it shattered on the
floor. A catalog of states and adjectives wound through my mind
while I tried to put a label to what I was feeling.

On stage, Matthew entered what must've been the chorus.

And I'm not here to question, I'm not here to convince
That the Wildman of the Mountains has been here ever since
For a long time in the summer, a long time in the snow
But where he's hiding, I'm confiding, we might never know

"Another one?" the bartender asked me.
"Whu—" I stared at her for too long. "No, I—I think I'm good."

***

Mid-morning of my laziest Sunday in months, I pulled one of
those small, Latin-named muscles in my side while rolling under
the blankets. Flexibility, it seemed, another dysfunction for the
day, and besides, the *NYT* crossword app was finally working
again on my phone. A half-hour of frustrated guesses prompted
me to switch over to the usual doomscrolling. One of my work
friends had PMed me something interesting.

"And of course..." I muttered to myself.

The latest article from WVIR told some not so surprising news.

"Donald Sudderland, 38, was arrested early Saturday morning by Charlottesville-area police after a 9-1-1 call from a con-

cerned Belmont resident. Reports indicate that Sudderland was caught trespassing on the Seventh Day Adventist Church property around 3:30 a.m. Although no further details about Sudderland's activities have been released by CPD, a representative for the Church claims that Sudderland was arrested while wearing a full-body ape costume spray-painted brown."

I put my phone to my chest a moment, stared at my motionless ceiling fan, wondered how close I'd been, the other day, to actually giving a crap. The guessing didn't help my headache. I thought maybe reading might.

"Sudderland, an Ohio native, traveled to Charlottesville along with many other Bigfoot researchers after the first sighting on June 4th. Sudderland's social media describes him as an 'avid cryptozoologist and proponent of the Pan-American Primate Conservation Foundation and Bigfoot Field Researchers Organization (BFRO).' A representative from BFRO, Marianne Clisby, was contacted about their affiliation with Sudderland and provided the following comment:

'The BFRO is dedicated to the research and conservation of oft overlooked North American fauna and in no way condones the actions of Mr. Sudderland. Independent affiliates of our organization do not always represent the interests or values of our researchers and we are strongly against Mr. Sudderland's illegal activities. We strive to support actual scientific research into this country's Sasquatch populations and publicity stunts such as these only hurt our collective efforts.' "

Good for BFRO, I guess...

"Mr. Sudderland has made no statement at this time, but locals speculate that Sudderland and others may have falsified the recent sightings to draw attention to their research efforts. Parker Kripke, another visiting cryptozoologist, said the following of Sudderland:

'What was he thinking? That's what the rest of us have been asking. Inevitably, you get some loons in this business who want answers at any cost. They get discouraged and self-conscious when the public mocks them, so they pull stunts like this. It's an ego thing, really. I just wish folks would understand that this doesn't nullify all the hard work real cryptozoologists do.' "

I stopped reading when I got to the provided photo. Yep, there he was, my visitor from the week before. Not a bad headshot, either, though the photographer would've been well advised to have him remove the ballcap. The shadow on Sudderland's eyes left his expression in doubt. He could be feeling anything under there.

Either way, I sensed our Bigfoot *idée fixe* would soon abate. This arrest might just be the Tylenol needed to lower our fever. Speaking of Tylenol...

I went into the bathroom, popped a couple painkillers, and shuffled my way to the kitchen to put some Eggos in the microwave. I had a toaster, mind you, I just liked them that way.

***

It had been almost a week since Sudderland's arrest, and things were starting to ebb toward normal. Well, the new normal. Nothing ever stayed quite the same and if it did, it was only because I wasn't paying attention. Many of the hunters packed up and went home. Media outlets returned to the usual talk of fundraisers, city council drama, and expectations for the coming summer. The university let out and the rest of town, in turn, let out a sigh of relief. Days were longer and hotter, pollen allergies parted for hay fever, all seemed... fine. Just fine. Always and everything. Fine.

I'd fallen into something of an antisocial spiral since the chaos began, and now, after much prodding, Heather had convinced me to join her at the closing party for Live Arts' Waterworks festival. I hadn't seen any of the performances, but in her words: "the plays were heart-wrenching, the lighting captivating, and the poetry forgettable."

I'd have to take her word for it. The party itself was well-attended, though I could confidently say the mingling was only tinged with lucidity.

We'd found our way to the rooftop bar when Heather got to worrying. "It isn't like them to be so late..."

"Uh, huh."

"It's community theater, for god's sake. It's not like he's some Tony winner. Where's he get off shirking the after party?"

I watched two squares of confetti drift, one landing in my tiny plastic cup of rosé, the other catching in the toe of my slingback.

Heather took issue with my distraction but tried to be polite about it. "Everything okay?"

"What's that?"

Voice raised to compensate for the crowd.

"I said: is everything *okay?*" Heather hit those last two syllables hard. It sounded more like an accusation than a question.

"Yeah, no. I—we..."

"Any other opposites you'd like to list?"

"Sorry, I've not been sleeping well this week," I said.

Heather gave me that flat-lipped expression—you know the one, offered when no other will do. She lifted my wine cup to my lips with her finger.

"Come on," she said. "I know you. Two more of these and you'll be calling this the best night of your life."

I choked down a couple sips. I must've made a face.

"Okay, something is definitely wrong," she said.

"I haven't been dreaming much, either..."

"Well, that'll happen when you can't sleep." I think she was trying to sound sympathetic. A ping drew her attention to her phone. "Ah, they're here. Sounds like they're stuck downstairs. I'm going to bring them up. I'll be right back..."

Off she went. I navigated the micelles of partygoers, avoided a string of low-hanging lights, and found a leanable ledge overlooking the side street below. There was no one in the outdoor seating area of Jack Brown's, so I tipped my wine, watched it plummet four stories and splatter on the brick. This made me smile for a second, but it all faded off. I hung my head. My throat burned as though from recent vomit.

I asked myself, seriously, for the first time in weeks: where the hell did this bad mood of mine come from? I thought it could be work. Family. No—nothing so specific.

Perhaps this was what Mom warned me about. The first *stasis* of adulthood. No big goals in sight, no clear hurdles or options to progress. Fewer opportunities to change yourself. And all the old pleasantries, the weekends at the farmer's market, the late-night booze runs, all callusing over into routine. I felt like my chances of becoming an interesting person were melting faster than the

Twix in my purse. It's not that you can stomach less—quite the opposite, in fact. Life was losing its novelty. No great alarms, not even small surprises. Save the Bigfoot stuff, I guess.

But then, something caught my eye. Only the corner of my eye, but still, I turned my head. Down in the alley, I thought I'd seen a dumpster shadow pulling itself free of the wall, taking on a third dimension with a stretch of its inky limbs. No. Wind again, most likely.

A clink. Shuffle. I wasn't crazy! Rolling out from behind the refuse, I spotted a familiar character all wrapped up in a loose-fitting hat and clothes. The very same character who'd locked eyes with me at The Whiskey Jar.

I wanted to call out to him, but instead I perched, all gargoyle-like, and watched as he snaked his way to the fence surrounding the old Dewberry building. A hitherto unseen tear in the chain-link gave him just enough space to squeeze through. He paused only once to look for witnesses. Thankfully, he failed to notice my elevated position. With a twirl and dash, he disappeared into the ruin like some Universal vampire fleeing a mob.

For a moment, I simply gaped, scratched, and felt a second, stronger heart take up the pumping where the old one failed. And...

I guess I can't explain why I, law-abiding, safety conscious—fuck it. I just needed to *do* something. Get it out of my system. Find some answers. Be done with it and cruise on into middle age. Live a little more adventurously, if only so I could regret it later and not live with the guilt of never having tried.

I breezed past Heather and her actor friends on the stairwell. I barely acknowledged Garvey, the volunteer doorman, as I raced to the alley. Once there, I followed the mysterious stranger's movements exactly. First through the fence, the double-take, and off into the dusky site.

The Dewberry had been a shell of a structure for years now, with no signs of ever filling out its form. Sometimes, when the wind picked up and the twilight reflected just so, chains and beams would rattle, flits of moth-ish lights would give a sense of animation to it, as though the whole structure stood on some ancient, mythological creature shifting in its slumber. These sounds, I discovered, echoed all the more terribly on the inside. A rat darted from my eyeline into a cluster of littered shopping bags. I shook on my phone's flashlight to find my bearings.

This was a dangerous place. Hanging cables gonged against concrete pylons, I-beams strained against loose bolts, and celluloid tarps, meant to keep the dust in or out, flapped along fittings like the ghosts of walls never raised. An unrailed central stairway led to higher floors. From this vantage I could see a faint glow, golden, scattered among the trusses of the fifth or sixth floor.

"Are we doing this?" I asked myself.

Something crackled.

A muffled sound.

Talking? Radio chatter?

"Yes, we are," I whispered.

Cockroaches fled my feet as I climbed the first steps. The thought of planting my heel in a nest of the little buggers made me shudder. Up and up I went, cursing myself for choosing fashionable, rather than reliable, footwear.

One floor away from the mysterious light, I could hear the noise with greater clarity. Music. Haunting, staticky, most likely emitted through antique speakers. The final few steps felt tacky underfoot, as though the concrete never quite set, or through some strange summer chemistry, they'd returned to a semi-liquid state. A lone tarp covered the doorway to this penetralium, pulsing slightly with a draft of movement beyond the cold sway of everything else in that gray dereliction.

Hand shaking, I tried to knock on the flimsy barrier. I clenched my teeth to keep them from chattering. "Hello?"

My next step through the portal landed on a Turkish rug. The whole interior, in fact, had been padded in some fashion: a divan with ruptured stuffing, a chaise relaxer, an armoire splattered with too-thick wood stain. The golden light came from a vanity ringed with Edison bulbs and a bevy of cosmetics scattered and crusted with hairspray. Beside this stood a shell with wigs pinned to Styrofoam heads.

Nearby, on an end table, a gramophone played what sounded like a Cab Calloway standard.

...Let her go, let her go, God bless her,
Wherever she may be,

JAMES COLE

She can look this wide world over,
But she'll never find a sweet man like me.

When I die, bury me in straight-lace shoes,
I want a box-back coat and a Stetson hat.
Put a twenty-dollar gold piece on my watch chain,
So the boys'll know that I died standin' pat.

Something hissed near my feet. A shape darted from one heap to another. An orange shape. A furry little—

"Kiwi?" I said, crouching. "Come here, girl." I offered my curled fingers for sniffing. She hissed again, but with a little more coaxing, she crept from her cover for a few experimental strokes. With rapport established, I gathered her into my arms.

"Somebody will be glad I found you," I said. I realized only after standing that this was a lie. I took a moment to survey the rest of the room.

This stranger must've been living there for months. Curiously, there were few other amenities: no kitchen, bed, no discernible outlet for other... natural functions. In fact, aside from the furnishings, the entire space was cluttered with spare clothes. It looked as if every major department store in the state used it for overflow storage. Old thrifted jackets, corduroy slacks, dresses, jumpers, jeans, *JESUS CHRIST!*

I leapt, tripped over my own legs, fell ass-backward into the recliner. Kiwi reared as she bounced off my chest and onto the rug.

A hulking, thick-furred brute loomed in the shadowy corner.

Shoulders so broad they each could individually sport their own set of football pads. A rank, boggy stench wafted from its dreads, as though it'd recently army-crawled through a drainpipe. Not that I'd ever seen a pipe that could accommodate so massive an... ape?

No meaty hands or fangs found my flesh, so I peeked out from the cover of my crossed arms. The creature just stood there, unmoving, unblinking, like it'd been chained to the wall. More rustling came from a rack of clothes to my left.

Door hinges squealed, and then, pushing through a curtain of hanging dress shirts, the stranger emerged. Rather than his former mess of scarves and leather, he wore a long, loose bathrobe of fine terry cloth. He showed no skin aside from his face and... was it even really skin? Looked more like modeling clay set onto a lumpy armature.

The figure blinked at me, looked at the furry beast in the corner, and straightened. "Make yourself at home, why don't ya?"

"Wha—" was all I could manage at first.

"Don't let me stop you from relaxing. Pull that lever there. Put your feet up. Stay awhile."

"Who the hell are you?" I said.

He looked about to answer, but I interrupted with a more pressing question. "What the hell is that?" I pointed to the hairy humanoid.

"That?" He approached the squatch, lifted its arm, placed it around his shoulders. "Don't you recognize him?" he continued. "He's been making quite a stir around town."

"But I thought–"

"Sudderland?" he chuckled. "Didn't expect him to get in on the game. Well, it can't be helped. He did it to himself. I'd feel bad but..."

I wished I'd kept that bear spray.

"No, no. I need some answers," I said. "Can we start over?"

"Now, now. That's a bit rude, don't you think?" He sauntered over to his vanity. His back to me, I could only see the grisly process in the mirror.

He reached up with two white-gloved hands, gripped the lumpy complex around his eye sockets, and, with a few loosening tugs and pokes, popped his face free in one clean strip.

Underneath was bare, bleached bone.

"Ta-da!" he said, turning.

I felt like I should've screamed, but nothing came out. He looked a little disappointed by this.

"Nothing?" he asked.

"I'm sorry, I'm—let's call it too confused to be scared."

"Pfft, typical," he moaned. He went to the record player, lifted the needle, and began hunting for a different vinyl in a stack nearby.

"People just don't scare like they used to. For years it was always: don't you stay out too late, don't you go looking down that

well, don't you go hiding under the stairs, or Bloody Bones will
get ya..."

He picked another album, set it spinning, and began a sort
of awkward bunny-hop dance along to the swing band.

"Bloody Bones?" I repeated. The name rang a bell. Not like
a church bell—maybe a shop bell. "And I suppose that's you?"

He stopped and tapped the breast of his robe. Embroidered
there was an elegant cursive "BB."

"Like Rawhide and Bloody Bones?" I pressed.

"Rawhead," the skeleton corrected. "And yes. Although,
those names don't go so well together anymore."

I nodded. What else could I do?

"So, you've been cooking up a new way to scare people?
Ghost stories ain't cutting it anymore?"

"Stories? Hardly. Scare? We've had to move well past scares,
dear girl."

"Please don't call me that."

"Well, what should I call you?"

I folded my legs into the chair. He was right. I should've been
terrified of a pile of talking bones, but it all seemed so... cliche?

"Okay, so playing off modern interests," I ventured. "I can
understand that. But why here? And what's with stealing people's cats? I figured you'd have eaten Kiwi by now if that was
your goal."

"Stealing—oh, you mean that tabby imp that's somewhere
around here. Always clawing my face off, that one. Literally!"

"I'm just—why? You're a bogeyman. Don't stand there and
tell me bogeymen get lonely."

"Well, it's just that—I'm not—" Bloody Bones toyed with the
belt of his robe. He looked over at the Bigfoot costume, then
to the small mound of slacks where Kiwi made her bedding.
"I've never been a solo act, you see. I was starting to feel a bit
aimless. I can come up with a plan, but I never had the aggres-
sion, the visceral panache at making others' nights miserable.
Not like Rawhead. He could set night terrors in someone with
little more than a snarl and a flex. Me? I'm just a skinless hack."

"Well, so is he," I offered. "You honestly telling me he can do
better on his own? Why break up the band? It's always Rawhead
and Bloody Bones, not Rawhead *or* Bloody Bones."

He tilted his skull. No facial tissue, but I thought I read an expression of guilt.

"We... had a disagreement. Over the last decade, he saw the writing under the bed. Video games, television, the internet? How are we supposed to compete with that? All the horrors of the world, right at their fingertips. Look at you, you barely batted an eye when you found me."

I tried pinching myself, stepping on my own toe, all small assessments of numbness. The world still hurt; the emotion just wasn't there. It seemed hard to feel shocked without surprise, surprised without curiosity. I suppose it didn't matter much that my nightmares were real if I'd lost all contentedness by which to affirm them.

"So he just quit?"

"Worse. He's getting married."

"Congratulations?" I offered. Again, how the hell do you respond to that?

"I disagreed with his decision from the beginning, and now look at me. Trying to replace him with a cat. That thing might be too ornery even for me!" He pointed to Kiwi, who flattened her ears and growled.

"I don't know what to say..." Looking down at my palms. "This is far from the answer I expected."

"Yes, well, I suppose this is the part where you tell me to knock it off."

"No, I—I guess I just don't see the point."

Bloody Bones wagged his finger at me.

"It's not for you to understand."

A pause then. The record scratched. Kiwi rumbled in the silence.

"Can I at least try? Can you?"

He clicked his teeth together. Pupils danced. I wondered if those were real eyes or more prosthetics.

"I am," he said. "I've made my decision."

"Just like that? Just because of me?"

"What? No. Don't flatter yourself." His posture extended into something more resolute. "I've decided I'm going to go support my friend."

"That's great..." I said, then squinted. "How?"

Bloody Bones, gazing off as if on some bright horizon, untied his belt, let the robe fall to his ankles. I instinctively covered my eyes, but curiosity got the better of me. Peeking through my fingers, I saw he wore an elegant dovetailed coat, white bowtie, and vest.

"I'm going to my friend's wedding. He asked me to be his best haint, but I said no. Now that damned hitchhiking ghost is standing in. That specter could fetter himself to anything. If I hurry, I might still make it."

"Jesus Christ, right now?"

"It starts in ten minutes."

"Well, okay, but..."

"But nothing!" he proclaimed, kicking the robe away. He approached, took my hand in his and shook it vigorously. I could feel every knob of knuckle and bony joint through the thin glove. "It is so nice to finally trade words with someone other than that creature."

Kiwi hissed.

"That's right, I'm talking about you!" He turned back to me. "Do return her to the old woman, won't you? I've felt terribly guilty."

"Sure, but... where exactly are you going?"

"There's a little chapel between here and Lovingston. I'm told it'll be a lovely affair."

He strode to the closet, a renewed perk in his step. Upon entering the coat-hung space, he turned to me and bowed.

"You know, Bloody," I said. "I guess you're kind of alright. For a ghoul, that is."

"Oof." He pretended as though I'd struck him in the gut. "You wound me, madame."

"Sorry."

"Don't be sorry," he said. "Be sensible. I'm counting on people like you."

"Like me? I don't understand. Why do–"

But he shut the door. After about thirty seconds, I went to the closet, opened it, and found it completely empty.

Kiwi approached and rubbed her cheek against my leg. Wind sibilated through the rafters a floor above, the cables continued clanging. I looked down at the feline.

"No sleep for me tonight," I said. "Again."

I took Kiwi in my arms. "What about you?"

She groaned in the back of her throat.

"From what I recall, you can sleep through just about anything."

***

Saturday. Summer in full swing. I'd just returned from the Water Street Famer's Market with a paper bag full of maitakes, goat's milk soap, and other produce. That makes for a curious potpourri to pick up in the early afternoon breeze. The mushrooms mixed well with the scent of grass clippings, and the soap made a fine complement to Ms. Lutger's recently scrubbed porch. Her usual chairs sat in a slant of sun across her lawn while the brick steps dried. I whistled to her as she recoiled her garden hose.

"Takes me back, that."

"What?" I said, opening the front gate. "The whistle?"

"You sound like a train."

I laughed. "Should I take offense?"

"Only if you promise to build me a new one."

Ms. Lutger hobbled to one of the sun-heated chairs, plopped down, rubbed her knees, and sighed. I took the one other seat.

"What've you got there?" she asked, eyeing my bag.

I fished out a smaller parcel within.

"I remember how you said you used to go hunting for ramps in the woods. Someone was selling some at the market."

"That's very sweet of you dear, but I don't remember telling you that at all..." After a pause she leaned closer. "What's wrong?"

"Nothing. I'm actually on an upswing this weekend. Things have been... things are strange. But I—hey, look who's back!"

Kiwi came darting from bush cover to attack the paper bag at my feet. Several bats of her paws knocked it over, spilling ramps onto the turf.

"You rat," Ms. Lutger spat at her pet. "Don't you give me that look." To me again. "It's the damnedest thing, you know." She settled back in her chair and looked at a pair of high cirrus just above the roofline of the opposite street. "A haint takes her away from me, and a Bigfoot brings her back. You think this is God trying to give me a hint?"

I smiled, but this was only to stifle another chuckle. "Haints and Bigfoots seem a little more telling than a hint."

"Maybe you're right." She paused, drew in a deep breath. "Would you like to stay for dinner, dear? With those ramps I can make a mighty mountain pesto."

"Thanks, but I can't today. We're giving my brother an intervention."

"Well, I'd hate to intervene in your intervention. Another time."

"Yes, another time."

We sat for a while, then. A few streets over, the whirring of a helicopter touched down on the university hospital roof. Cars crowded nearby Cherry St for a basketball game at the local park.

"What's going on in that head of yours?" Ms. Lutger asked.

"Funny you should ask. What if I told you—" but I stopped. I realized she was speaking to Kiwi, who crouched, pounce-ready, rear end wagging.

"Don't you do it!"

Sprang. Kiwi landed fang-first on Ms. Lutger's shin. As she wrestled the feline free, I stared across at my apartment building, into my window. My living space looked so small from the outside. Especially with the dark hairy shape in the corner.

Somewhere, an ice cream truck started playing its tune.

About the Authors

James Blakey — "Join the Journey"

James Blakey is a three-time finalist for the Short Mystery Fiction Society's Derringer Award, winning in 2019 for his story "The Bicycle Thief." He leads critique groups in Harrisonburg, Charlottesville, and Shenandoah County. His paranormal thriller SUPERSTITION was published by City Owl Press in September of 2024. When James isn't writing, he's on the hiking trail—he's climbed forty of the fifty US state high points—or bike-camping his way up and down the East Coast. He lives in Broadway, Virginia.
Website: JamesBlakeyWrites.com
Instagram: jamesblakeyauthor
Twitter/X: JamesWBlakey
Facebook: JamesWBlakey

Caroline Boras — "My House Mother is a Vampire"

Caroline Boras' sorority house probably wasn't haunted, but she thinks it would have made her college experience much more interesting. When she isn't drafting pleadings and responding to discovery requests at her job as a lawyer, Caroline can be found reading, thinking about writing, and exploring her historic Northern Virginia neighborhood.
Instagram: caro.boras

E.F. Buckles — "Thaw"

E.F. Buckles fell in love with reading at a young age and filled herself with words until they flowed out as stories of her own. Her work has been featured in *Havok Magazine* and the *Fantastic Schools Vol. 6* anthology. She writes her stories in Virginia with her family and dog at her side. When not writing, she enjoys handcrafting items for her Etsy shop, EruvandiCrafts.
Instagram: efbuckleswriter
Pinterest: efbuckleswriter

Julian Close — "The Copper Plates"

Julian Close has lived in Charlottesville since 1975. He graduated from Albemarle High School in 1987, studied Psychology at Davidson College, and received a Masters in Teaching from Mary Baldwin. He has worked in finance and investing, technical writing, and financial journalism, where he developed a passion for teaching essential investing skills. In addition to market analysis, Julian writes short fiction, novels, and drama. His newest passion is playing bass for the Charlottesville rock and blues band "Blue Healer."

James Cole – "What's Going on Here?"

James Cole is a poet, author, filmmaker, and neuroscientist based out of Morgantown, WV. He is currently an Assistant Professor of Psychology and Neuroscience at West Virginia University but was a former resident of Charlottesville from 2018 to 2023.
Website: JamesColeAuthor.com
Facebook: JDColeWrites/about

Tim Freer – "Biodynamic Aeroconducive Gels"

Tim Freer is a full-time writer based in Charlottesville, Virginia. He has worked as a professional grant writer for the past twelve years and helps to organize a local poetry critique group. A two-time winner of the prestigious Charlottesville Writers Critique Circle's Flash Fiction Challenge, his poetry has also been featured in *Tributaries*, an art exhibit at Visible Records Studios. In his spare time, Mr. Dean writes fiction in a variety of genres (his favorites are fantasy, sci-fi, horror, and adventure) and experiments with many different poetic and prosaic forms. He is fascinated by all things surreal, unreal, and just plain odd. He has dreamed of publishing a novel since the days his hobbies included watching *Spider-Man* and memorizing all the different dinosaurs' names.
Facebook: Tim.Freer1
Instagram: timodefreer

K.G. Gardner — "An Accident on Louisa Road"

K.G. Gardner has more than 25 years of experience as a business journalist, a career that enabled her to indulge her curiosity and her passion for words. After writing and editing tens of thousands of news articles and producing a podcast under her legal name, she is excited to return to her first love, fiction. A native of New Jersey, she has lived in five cities on two continents. She lives in Charlottesville with her husband, daughter and two cats. When not writing for work or pleasure, she enjoys travel, yoga, gardening, and reading all genres of fiction. The best ideas come to her during long walks in the woods.
Instagram: kristen_hallam

Jordan Garris — "The Gap"

Jordan Garris is a pediatric neurologist and former ultrarunner with unfinished business on the Carlos climb. Limited as we all are by insufficient hours in the day, she recently traded her time spent running and cycling for a return to her early loves of reading and writing. She lives in Charlottesville with her husband (Nathan) and three children (Fuller, Caleb, and Reid).
Facebook: Jordan.Garris
Twitter/X: JordanFGarris

Ginger Grouse — "Warriors of Kroas"

Ginger Grouse is an anarchist, land defender, trail runner, and occasional blogger who writes short stories, creative memoir, and essays about the intersections of bodily movement, resistance, and decolonization. Ginger loves the mountains of Virginia and Appalachia, and has used trail running as a platform to support Land Back initiatives in Indigenous communities. They live in the ancestral Monacan, Manahoac, Shawnee, and Sappony land of the Shenandoah Valley.
Substack: runarchism.substack.com

Kurt Johnson — "Amphibi-Squatch: A Blue Ridge Tunnel Story"

Kurt Johnson is a career higher education administrator who recently discovered a love for writing fiction. His craft evolved from years of creating humorous rhymes for friends and family to dabbling in children's literature centered on the adventures of his cat. Now, he yearns to share more broadly his writing in historical/fantasy fiction. He lives in the beautiful Shenandoah Valley of Virginia.

Karen M Kumor — "The Untethered Visions of Henry G. in Cville"

Karen M Kumor is a screenwriter for Fish4 Him Entertainment, author, and retired physician. She screenwrites fiction including dramedy, thriller, and sci fi. Her novel is a young adult coming-of-age story. Her son lives in Charlottesville. She and her husband visit often and enjoy the town with their son as a guide. It is a place with a distinctive culture and charm. They are considering to move there to enjoy it full time.
Facebook: Karen.Kumor
imdb: imdb.com/name/nm6777354

Deidra Whitt Lovegren — "Clickbait"

Deidra Whitt Lovegren has written over a hundred short stories and regularly competes in international writing contests. Her novels include *The Medicine Girl*, *The Medicine Woman*, *21 Conversations*, and *The Lady of the Match*, a collection of her works translated into Arabic that premiered at the 2024 Cairo International Book Fair.

Deidra has taught scores of English and writing classes from preschool to college. Currently, she is a humanities instructor at a private high school. She lives in Central Virginia with her husband of 30 years, three sons, and her three rescue cats, General Sherman, Cinna(mon Girl), and Marty.
Website: DeidraWhittLovegren.com

Genevieve Lyons — "The Book Came Back"

Genevieve Lyons wrote and illustrated her first book at the age of six, and she's pursued creative arts ever since. She has studied film photography and she considered a career in music performance, going so far as to pass conservatory-level music theory. Genevieve was too extroverted to spend hours in tiny practice rooms, graduating with degrees in Neuroscience and Biostatistics. She enjoys the connections between ideas, and making connections with others. Curiosity is a hallmark trait that drives her work as a public health statistician and as a reader and writer.

Genevieve is a member of the Women's Fiction Writers Association and a local library writers critique circle. She lives in Virginia with her husband, children, three chickens, and a messy wildflower garden.

Parker McIntosh – "The Girl in the Stream"

Parker McIntosh is a writer and (sometimes) accountant living in southern Oregon with his wife and dog. His short fiction is forthcoming and can be found in the *The Toronto Journal*, *The Garfield Lake Review*, *The Flexible Persona*, among other publications. When not writing or floundering in spreadsheets, he can usually be found exploring the mountains and trails surrounding his home.

Liz P – "Transfer Status: In Progress"

Liz P is a pathological wanderer, in both a literal, geographical sense and a more figurative, spiritual sense. As a result of this drifting, she has lived many lives in many places, and writing has always served as a touchstone—a common thread! a northern star! Liz tends to mix metaphors—to help guide her way. And, of course, no matter how far she wanders there is always Charlottesville's hometown gravity to pull her back into orbit.

Liz mainly writes romance and will happily enter into a street fight with anyone who dares malign the genre by reducing it to its most inane parts. She's not kidding. Meet her outside.

Kent M. Peterson – "Midnight on Rio Road"

Kent M. Peterson grew up in Harrisonburg but got his start as a professional software tester in Charlottesville. Rio Road was his daily commute. All too often the drive home was after working far too late into the evening. After a decade-long exile to northern Virginia, he's back in Harrisonburg, and still comes to Charlottesville for the social dancing. He can't prove the events in this story actually happened—but that doesn't mean they didn't.

Catherine Simpson — "A Hard Bargain"

Catherine Simpson has never made a deal with a fairy, but it's at the top of her to-do list. A writer, editor, and behavior analyst, she lives in Charlottesville with her cat and occasional creative muse, Mauka. When not working on her novel or knee-deep in track changes, Catherine can be found wandering the Rivanna trails or daydreaming in one of Charlottesville's lovely coffee shops.
Website: catsimpsonwrites.com
Instagram: catsimpson_writes

J. Thompson — "Save Our Cryptids - Volunteers Wanted"

J. Thompson is a fantasy enthusiast, tabletop gamer, and aspiring author. He writes boring software documentation as a day job, and fantasy adventures any other time. A native of the Charlottesville area, he grew up in Greene County and has been here ever since, aside from a brief stint over the mountain at JMU. He is currently developing a homebrew role-playing game, and a series of fantasy novels.
Bluesky: jsthompson.bsky.social

James Verlon — "The Tree That Smiled Back"

James Verlon began his creative writing journey as a sort of 'last-person-to-make-money-off-Amazon-is-a-rotten-egg' rat race among friends. Through the years, James discovered that he enjoyed giving life to his imagination and began attending feedback groups and writing workshops. James' accolades include the completion of his Master's in Public Policy, but more importantly winning 'Funniest Film' for his High School English movie project. He hopes to be a debut novelist with his satirical urban fantasy novel about magic folk dealing with bureaucracy, renegade wizards, and nosey HOA neighbors. James can be found attending Charlottesville's Writer's Critique Circle, enjoying WriterHouse happy hours, occasionally participating in New Dominion's open mic, and selling booklets as the vendor 'Nebula Writing' at pop-up markets and local farmer's markets.
Facebook: NebulaWriting
Instagram: nebula_writing
Substack: nebulawriting.substack.com

Caitlin Woodford — "Where Do the Old Things Go?"

Caitlin Woodford is a recent graduate of the University of Virginia program in literary prose. Her writing has appeared in *The Foundationalist* and the *Wild Virginia* blog, and she was the 2023 winner of the Writing Battle Autumn Short Story Contest. When not writing fiction, she works in nonprofit scientific publishing.

From Whitaker Lyon Press

THE CAT WHO LOVED DAVID DUCHOVNY

From the pen of Derringer Award-winning author James Blakey comes three fantastical tales.

THE CAT WHO LOVED DAVID DUCHOVNY

Madame Marie Curie, a Blue Point Siamese, spends her days binge-watching episodes of *The X-Files*. When Marie's owner Jim invites Debbie—the new girl from work—over for dinner, Marie resigns herself to a night of sulking while watching the couple with disdain. But Debbie has set her sights on something more than a free meal, and it will take all of Marie's feline cunning to stop her.

THE WITCH OF SHERMAN OAKS

Jennifer Griffiths, the self-styled Witch of Sherman Oaks, is part life coach, part therapist. Her week isn't going well. The rent is due, and the big-time reality star that Jennifer was counting on as new client just walked out. When the oddly dressed Braxtiaran Darahenij hires Jennifer to do some roleplaying and face off against an evil sorcerer at some junior league Burning Man, she jumps at the chance. Sure LARPers are odd, but Brax is paying with real gold. But the sorcerer isn't playing. He has the power to destroy the Earth. Now it's up to The Witch of Sherman Oaks to stop him.

THE LAST MISSION

John Linn's latest assignment seems simple enough: Reconnaissance of a foreign power's naval base. But the country is hostile. Details about the op don't make a lot of sense. And don't get him started on his handlers. Battling magic and bureaucracy, Linn penetrates the base, but is discovered. It's going to take every trick he's learned his career to make it home. And if Linn isn't careful, this might be his last mission.

Available as an eBook from Amazon or in print from your favorite bookstore.

Whitaker Lyon Press is a small publisher located in Broadway, Virginia specializing in anthologies and short story collections.

For updates on new publications and submission calls, subscribe to our newsletter. As a special bonus, new subscribers will receive James Blakey's short story "Do Not Pass Go..." named one of the Best of the Best by SleuthSayers.org.

Website: WhitakerLyon.com

Instagram: whitakerlyonpress

Twitter/X: whitakerlyon

Read an Excerpt from SUPERSTITION

A PARANORMAL THRILLER FROM JAMES BLAKEY

A mirror shatters. An umbrella is opened indoors. A black cat crosses your path. All omens of bad luck that no one takes seriously. But at Van Buren University when these and other superstitions are broken, students die.

***

Saturday 1:13am

Her headlamp illuminating the way, the college student trudged to the campfire circle and dumped another armful of sticks and leaves.

Satisfied with the pile, she rested on a boulder, her breath visible in the chilly air as she retrieved a bottle of water. To her right, an Adirondack 46er loomed. Above, a cloudless sky of stars twinkled, no city to drown their light.

Easier to try this at the nature preserve back on campus, but even at this late hour that risked awkward encounters with pot-smoking art majors or insomniac townies.

From her overstuffed green-and-gold backpack, she retrieved half a dozen copies of the college newspaper. She
crumpled the pages, placing them strategically amongst the
branches, then marinated the heap with charcoal lighter fluid.

She struck a match and tossed it. Orange flames erupted,
blinding her for a second, enveloping her in a wave of heat.
The hypnotizing fire reminded her of summer camping trips
with her father. *Should have brought marshmallows.*

Her phone chimed. Five minutes until the new moon.

She pulled out the shrink-wrapped lamb chops, on sale
for $9.99 per pound at Price Chopper. The student wouldn't,
couldn't, sacrifice a living animal for the power she craved.
Even the thought of touching raw meat filled her disgust. She
slipped on a pair of latex gloves liberated from biology lab, then
tossed the chops into the flames.

The scent of burning meat filled the air. She hoped to finish
before any bears or wolves arrived.

She retrieved the blue textbook, turning to the marked page.
Squinting at the diagram, then the sky, she oriented herself,
zeroing in on Orion's Belt. A couple of moon widths to the east,
she located Alpha Monocerotis.

Of course, that wasn't what the Picts called the star two
millennia ago when they ruled what today is Scotland. No
one knew their name for it. Almost all their knowledge had
been lost. One scrap that survived: their high priestesses wor-
shipped this star for luck.

No bars on her phone. Not a problem. The student pulled
the folded printout from her pocket, silently rehearsing the
spell. There wasn't a person alive who could reconstruct the
enchantment the way the Picts originally spoke it. Her new
friends on the dark web assured her that Modern English
would work fine, as long as it rhymed.

The past few weeks, she experimented with charms and
simple conjuring. Enough to prove to herself that magic was
real, and she possessed the power to wield it.

The phone beeped. *Now.*

She stood before the fire, hand raised to the sky, pointing at
the faint red star.

The paper rippled in the wind. She focused on the magic, emptying her mind of all other thoughts.

As she recited the words, all feeling receded, as if her consciousness left her physical form behind, merging with the fire, the star, the spell.

Goddesses of the Night, hear my plea
Bring Success and Prosperity
My offering to you, a favored sheep
A promise to you, I will always keep
To my endeavors great and small
I call upon you, one and all
With a whisper soft and a heart so true
I conjure Fortune to come anew
Bring me riches, bring me fame
And banish all my doubts and shame
I summon the forces of Star and Sky
To grant me Destiny that cannot die
By my will and desire so strong
This Magic now shall not go wrong
Bringing Luck to my life at last
So mote it be, this Spell is cast.

She became aware: clothes sticking to her sweat-drenched body, mouth dry, hair plastered to her head, heart pounding. She stumbled to the boulder, resting, regaining her strength.

An owl screeched in the darkness. Good sign? Owls were supposed to be magical. Or was that some Harry Potter nonsense?

The owl quieted. No crickets at this altitude. No sound but the wind and faint jet engines as red-and-green navigation lights hurried across the sky.

The student didn't look or feel different. No supernatural power coursing through her veins. No enhanced perceptions allowing her to observe a secret world. No ethereal light enveloping her.

How anticlimactic. What do you expect for $9.99 a pound?

No way to know if she cast the spell correctly.

No way to test if the magic was working.

No way to tell if this ceremony was a big waste of time.

Not waiting for any predators that caught the scent of the sacrifice, she doused the flames with three bottles of water. Buried the ashes with her collapsible shovel.

Only you can prevent forest fires.

She scoured the area, gathering any trash.

Leave no trace.

She slipped the pack on her back and began the four-mile hike to the trailhead. She stifled a yawn. At least it was downhill.

Thirty minutes on the trail and her mind was numb. Legs on auto. Step, step, step. Leaves crunching in her feet. Another three miles to go. All she wanted was to get back to her dorm, make a cup of hot cocoa, and crawl into bed.

Gack! A spider web across the trail on her face, in her mouth. She spit and raised a hand as the toe of her hiking boot caught a root. She pitched forward, losing her balance, falling toward the sharp rocks on this section of the trail. Arms flailing, she couldn't stop herself. In the darkness, her hand grabbed a branch, wrenching her shoulder, but arresting her fall.

The student righted herself, let out a deep breath, her palm scraped and scratched. Need to be careful. Could have broken a leg or worse. Been stranded with no way to call for help. And no one knew she was up here. Pretty lucky.

A smile spread across her face.

Pretty lucky.

"It works!" she shouted into the night.

***

SUPERSTITION (Book One of The Secrets of Van Buren University) by James Blakey and published by City Owl Press available as an eBook or paperback from your favorite book retailer.

Made in the USA
Columbia, SC
25 February 2025

54410408R00162